Dark Crossfire

Books by Stephen L. Thompson

The Crossfire Series

Colorado Crossfire
International Crossfire
Israeli Crossfire
Believer's Crossfire
Spirit Crossfire
Faith Crossfire
Chinese Crossfire
Texas Crossfire
Dark Crossfire
Island Crossfire
Jagged Crossfire
Violent Crossfire
Russian Crossfire
Nuclear Crossfire
End Times Crossfire
Revelation Crossfire
Gates of Hell Crossfire
Assassin's Crossfire
Albatross Crossfire
Global Crossfire
Far East Crossfire

The SFO Series

Station Force One - Creation

Dark Crossfire

Combating an Ancient Evil

Stephen L. Thompson

Dark Crossfire

The Crossfire Team is appointed by God to battle both the natural and the spiritual in the human realm. Pursuing the cause of millions of deaths pits the team in a running battle against the demon "Vorbleg" and his earthly representative Hermann Lutz. The team loses a member and plays out the role defined by God in the Mexican desert.

- Stephen L. Thompson

Dark Crossfire

Published by
Stephen L. Thompson
Facebook.com/CrossfireNovelSeries

ISBN- 978-1-943879-05-2

Electronically Published in the United States of America

Foreword

To my Christian readers –

The Crossfire series of action/adventure stories include depictions of violence which are unusual in Christian literature. It would be nice if there were no conflict or violence in our world. But we live in a time when evil is increasing instead of diminishing, when some men seem to be controlled by selfishness, madness, or evil forces. When the enemies of decent mankind are bent on subjugation of other men and women, righteous men and women must stand against evil. Please remember that the yoke of oppression is not lifted by prayer alone. God is our shepherd and we are his sheep. As long as there are wolves about, God will use some of us as sheep dogs to defend the rest of us. These stories are about people like that and the forces they fight against. The stories describe violence because it occurs in the real world and it is active in the lives of all people whether they recognize it or not.

To my non-Christian readers –

The Crossfire series include depictions of spiritual warfare and spiritual activity with which the non-Christian may not be familiar. These stories describe the realms and activities of both God and Satan because they are real and active in the lives of all people whether they recognize it or not.

Steve Thompson

CHAPTER ONE

At the quiet hour of three o'clock in the morning the private hanger at Denver International Airport or DIA was bathed in the light of a full moon. Everything was stark white or pitch black. The soft sounds of the airport hardly invaded the silence of the early morning hour. Jack Malone walked out of the hanger into the cold December pre-dawn hours and his breath formed a cloud as he exhaled.

Violence struck suddenly out of the dark in the form of two men who operated as a well-coordinated team. The first man ran from Jack's right and pulled a short sword from a hidden sheath under his coat. He planted his feet and swung a fast two-handed horizontal cut at Jack's neck. The other man ran in quickly from Jack's left and displayed a short sword or large knife. He lunged with the knife at Jack's torso from his left side. A normal person could easily fall prey to this double attack. By focusing on one attacker they would be taken unawares by the second.

But, tonight their prey was not a normal person. Jack Malone not only had years of martial arts training and taught it, he also had been in almost constant combat for the last two years. He had detected the combined attack as it began. Rather than try to figure out what to do, he relaxed and let his training take over.

His left hand deflected the wrist of the hand holding the knife blade thrust at his side by the attacker to his left. At the same time he leaned to the left and let the higher horizontal cut whiz past over his right shoulder. He drilled a full-power side kick to chest of the attacker on the right which knocked him backwards hard enough he lost his balance and fell down.

At the same time as he kicked the man on his right, Jack drove a full-power, right-hand knuckle strike to the other attacker's throat. He had been able to break two-by-four boards with his knuckle strike for years and the effect on the man's throat was far more drastic. The man's larynx was crushed and suddenly he had no way to get air into his lungs.

By then the first attacker had regained his feet and raised his sword in a two handed high guard position in preparation for slicing and dicing Jack.

With a thunderous slap of sound, a .45-calibre bullet slammed into the man's hands and the sword hilt. The bloody sword flew out of the man's hands to clatter to the tarmac in front of the hanger. The man tried to stem the blood flow in each hand by grasping it in his other hand. Mark Connelly aimed the pistol at the man's forehead and told him to get on his knees.

The man desperately tried to draw a second knife but his hands were too mangled to accomplish the task. Mark shook his head and walked over to the man and struck him with the butt end of his gun in the side of the head. The man collapsed to the ground unconscious. At the same time, his partner quit kicking as he suffocated.

A six-foot tall, athletic blonde with an excellent female form stepped out of the hanger. Laura Malone had her pistol out and walked over to her husband Jack. "What was that about?"

Jack stared down at the unconscious man from his six-foot, four-inch height and shook his head. Jack's face was handsome with blonde hair and blue-green eyes. His physique was muscular with solid muscle masses under taut skin. His skill in martial arts was the best in the team and his combat skills were becoming professional. He looked at his wife. "I don't have a clue. What do you think Mark?"

Mark Connelly was muscular and what was known as "buff" by the current generation. Mark stood six foot, two inches tall with a full head of black hair and a ruggedly handsome face. The former U.S. Navy SEAL's combat skills were the best of the team and he usually was in the lead in firefights. He finished checking the man for anything that would identify him, expecting nothing and finding none. He looked up at Jack, "My guess is that this a back-up plan from our old enemy, Hermann Lutz. Put in place just in case their Phoenix plan didn't succeed."

Mark's wife, Sarah, also had her pistol out. Slightly shorter than Laura, she was a dark-haired version of her best friend. As a recently retired top field agent for the Mossad she was as deadly as her husband and almost as knowledgeable in combat skills. Her background as a spy continued to be a big asset to the team. She didn't look at the men on the ground or even the other members of the team. She kept her head turning, constantly scanning the area around them for new threats.

Sarah said, "I have a bad feeling. Let's move back into the hanger. I wouldn't trust those vehicles since they were here, unattended, while these guys were here before us." Mark agreed and they pulled the unconscious man and his dead partner back into the hanger and closed the large door which they had opened ten minutes ago to admit their corporate jet.

Sarah saw a glint within the darkness of the unlit hanger and yelled, "Get down, now!" Everyone dropped to the floor of the hanger as several dozen silenced rounds flew overhead through the place they had been standing. Unfortunately for the shooter a silencer removes the noise but doesn't completely hide the muzzle flash. Four .45-calibre pistols fired almost simultaneously and the man standing by the wall of the hanger aiming a rifle was slammed back into the metal wall of the hanger and slid down the wall leaving a bloody trail.

Sarah was angry enough for everyone. "What in the hell is the security team doing these days? Letting anyone with a gun or a knife in here?"

Mark put a calming hand on his wife's arm. "My guess is that they were taken out before we got here. Let's get some more help." He flipped open his cell phone to call the police when new shots rang out and bullets struck the concrete of the hanger floor near and even between the team members and caromed off into the walls. There were at least two shooters this time and there was no cover available for the team. Sarah grabbed the body of the dead attacker and held it up in front of her with her left hand while she aimed her pistol with her right. Two more rounds struck the already dead man and she replied with four rounds. This time the shooter was careful to stay behind cover and wasn't hit. The knife man Mark had knocked out came to and sat up. Four rounds from the shooters by the wall knocked him back down deader than dirt.

The other team members attempted to move towards any type of cover they could find. The two shooters were ranging their shots trying to hit any of them when a new player joined the battle. Su Li, the team's pilot leaned out of the aircraft doorway and fired a M-249 at the shooters. The Asian woman had loaded the squad automatic weapon with one of the chain-link, two-hundred round box magazines which allowed her to fire it at its full seven-hundred, fifty round-per-minute capacity. The unrelenting fire power was too much for the two shooters and they both bolted from their positions and died trying to flee. Su Li kept the smoking rifle moving from side to side as she looked for new targets.

Mark completed his call to the police and then he called the security branch at Denver International Airport. In a few minutes several security cars arrived and the officers started a search for any other possible attackers.

As Laura got off the floor and stood near the aircraft, She recalled how they came to this point. They had been returning from a battle with the Soldiers of Zultan in Phoenix with a new threat on their minds. After Su Li landed them at DIA, she had taxied to the hanger and opened the door with a remote control. The team had disembarked and was headed for their vehicles when the first attack occurred.

Sighing, she wondered if this would be her life until she died or Yahshua came back. This was not a glamorous or chic lifestyle. It was exciting but it could be very tiring and didn't leave much time for a break. Maybe she'd have to ask Jack if they could take some time off to relax. She was going to ask sometime soon too.

CHAPTER TWO

The day after the attack at the airport, Jack went to his plant to make sure everything could stand another absence by the President and to catch up on his backlog of paperwork. He knew his Crossfire activities kept him busy and this allowed his corporate duties to pile up. He was delighted by the progress that Technical Alternatives had made in his absences. All the programs were ahead of schedule and very successful.

To Jack this was further evidence that it was the grace of Yahveh that was giving him and his company such success, not his talents. In fact, during his time with Bob Wexler, his partner who was running the company in his absence, he had been asked for new projects since the Research and Development department had just about completed all proposed projects and were mainly working on finding ways to upgrade existing projects such as the Wrecon weather system or the latest version of the NovaStar Home Defense Systems. He had several ideas for new projects himself and he would call his father and uncle and see if they needed R and D on anything.

After handling all the paperwork and generating a few dozen memos and emails he felt things were ready for his departure. First though, he wanted to check with God to make sure that he was doing things properly. He started praying and the weight of the communion pressed down on him pleasantly. An hour later he was still sitting at his desk, in his office, deeply in prayer.

As he had relaxed, he considered how he could use his good fortune to help the needy and the people that were striving to be good Christians but failing financially. He had prayed that the Spirit of Yahveh would allow him to put his good fortune to work for others rather than himself. He was already giving out the LifeCape free to all needy people. The food program for the homeless was doing so well that they had opened up two more in Denver and there were other groups using the same techniques in over a hundred U.S. and foreign cities to help the dispossessed.

Following a leading from God, he decided to fund a new program that would give all kids a chance at a good life. First he called Laura and asked her what she thought. She was happy he found a way to obey God and help kids at the same time. She gave her blessing to the project. The money didn't really mean a thing to either of them anymore. She had laughed and asked him when she would have time to spend it, enjoy what she bought, or even need anything the way things were going with Yahveh's plans for the Crossfire Team.

Jack detected a note of sourness in her comments and made a note to see what was eating her when he got home.

Jack then called seven people and set up a think tank starting in twenty days. He would pay each of the people for six months of their efforts out of his own pocket. He wanted them to start with the objective of providing a self-paced education center that would give children of all ages a free opportunity to excel. The guiding principles for this new school were to accurately determine the potential for each child and develop their minds along those lines. Rather than put all the square and round pegs into eight-sided holes, they would attempt to put each child in the right path for their own life. If the right methods could be developed, they could pre-determine a child's potential for college, trades, or other possible careers. This determination would be rechecked each year of development so that changes or mis-determinations could be re-evaluated.

Jack and TA would foot the bills including lunches, supplies, teacher's salaries, and transportation. He suggested a year-round operation with the different educational levels starting on different months so that the classes overlapped throughout the year. But the children would only be going for nine months a year. If the people in the think tank could distill and optimize the education process so that it was not only fun and challenging then it would again become interesting to the students rather than a required grind.

He tasked them to develop psychological and ability tests for the children at all grades K through 12 and offer them a curriculum with goals that matched their capabilities and their desires. It would be interesting to see the results in ten and twenty years. Since this school would not be funded out of public funds there would be no way the liberal extremists could demand that they keep Yahveh or Yahshua out of the school. Morals and principles would be taught along with the arts and sciences.

As far as the funds needed to staff and run the school Jack would start it off out of his own money. God had shown him that the more he gave to the works of God and the "least of His brethren" the more he would be given to use. He had been surprised on finding his net worth had climbed to over seven hundred million dollars in stock and options in the company. Since he had instituted an aggressive profit-sharing program he knew that everyone that worked there was worth at least two to three million dollars. His unexpected wealth gave him the money to kick-start the think tank and fund the first year of the school. After it was a success he would ask Yahveh how to continue the venture.

He called in two attorneys that he trusted. They were an oddity in the legal world. They were all Christians who kept their values and dealt fairly with everyone. He explained what he was doing for the school and gave them control of two hundred million dollars to oversee the project. He had the funds transferred to an account the attorneys could draw from and would allow for strict accounting by his accountants.

After they left, he sat back and relaxed. He noticed that it was already dark outside and that the second shift was in high gear. He was about to shut down the office and head back to the fortress when he felt a heavy burden laid on his spirit. He had learned that was a clear signal from Yahveh for him to seek the Lord in prayer.

As he felt the weight of the Spirit and he dropped deeper into communion with God, he asked what the Father wanted him to pray. He felt a concept come into his mind that was beyond his capability to understand. It was so deep into physics that he couldn't grasp the concepts or even the terms.

He prayed for wisdom as the Bible told him to do it. James 1:5-7 said, *If you need wisdom—if you want to know what Yahveh wants you to do—ask him, and he will gladly tell you. He will not resent your asking. But when you ask him, be sure that you really expect him to answer, for a doubtful mind is as unsettled as a wave of the sea that is driven and tossed by the wind. People like that should not expect to receive anything from the Father.*

Jack reconsidered the concepts that he had gotten. Now they made sense but he was still uncertain as to the use or meaning of their application. He began to write them down and draw sketches to illustrate them.

Three hours later he sat back and reviewed his notes and drawings. Suddenly he knew what they were for and he was shocked. He carefully went through the information again and reached the same conclusion. He started to pray again and he saw the face of one of the physicists that had been working on the LifeCape project. The man was a theorist and brilliant in his field. Jack tried to remember his name. The whole LifeCape concept had been created on the molecular level. Seven molecular scientists had been hired on contract to handle the related physics. A unique laboratory had been built on the TA property to house the project and included two nuclear tunneling microscopes and associated video gear. That gear was still there. The LifeCape design concept had required a new way of looking at molecular bonding, construction, and nanoelectronic transfer devices. This new concept was pretty much up the same alley but much deeper.

The phone rang and he answered it seeing on the caller ID that it was Laura. She asked him if he was planning to come home eventually. He knew then that there was an attitude in the air. He explained that he had been given a burden by God and was working it out. He apologized for not being there for her. She softened somewhat and her voice regained much of its natural pleasantness and softness. She told him, "Jack, we need to get a break for a few days. I'd like it to be just you and me if that is possible."

Jack thought about it and agreed that he would make it possible.

Jack then called Bob Wexler at home and Bob told him that the scientist's name was Dr. Byron Clashire. Bob was also able to give Jack the man's home phone number in California. When Bob asked why he needed the man, Jack told him that he was working on a new project concept and wanted to consult the scientist.

When Dr. Clashire answered the phone, Jack identified himself and asked the man if he was available. It turned out that his last contract had just finished successfully and he was looking for a new challenge. Jack thought for a few seconds and asked, "Doctor, would you be willing to hire on full time here at my company and head up a five-year project that would give you that challenge?"

Dr. Clashire asked, "What terms would I be working under?"

Jack said, "We will pay you a minimal salary of say, two hundred thousand dollars annually but will give you twenty thousand shares of TA which is trading at fifty dollars a share at present. That's a million dollars up front. If this project has the potential I think it does, TA shares will probably shoot up to somewhere around two hundred and fifty dollars a share before splitting four for one, maybe twice. You will be independently wealthy either way. We also offer really good benefits."

Dr. Clashire coughed and said, "Put that in writing and I'll sign it tomorrow when I start to work. Can we discuss it then?"

Jack laughed, "See you tomorrow."

When Jack arrived at the Fortress he noted that everyone was already in bed. Checking his watch he saw that it was after two in the morning. Probably a good reason they'd all gone to sleep.

He took a quick shower and slid into bed next to Laura. He put his arms around her and held her as she slept. She rolled over and snuggled into his embrace. The thought crossed Jack's mind that he loved her more than anything on the earth. He was startled when he heard her mumble, "You'd bettered."

At eight o'clock he was back at the office. Bob escorted the scientist into Jack's office. Jack told him to take off his suit coat and relax. They completed the paperwork and gave the signed copies to Jack's Assistant for filing and notary. Jack called the stock company that he and Bob had signed on with when Bob took the company public earlier in the year.

Jack had them assign twenty thousand shares of stock to Dr. Clashire and had them fax him a copy of the transfer. Jack checked it and handed it to the doctor. "Here's your million dollars. It'll be yours if you decide you can do the project. If you do accept, I'll expect you to drive this project from day one to completion."

Byron smiled, "I'll do what I can. Tell me what the project is and if you can, tell me the source of the invention, for example, who generated the initial concept.

Jack nodded, "The concept is similar to the LifeCape project but at a much more fundamental level. It is a generated field that absorbs incoming energy and converts it."

The scientist tipped his head to one side. "Doesn't sound too complicated, a silicon solar cell does that."

Jack smiled, "This is a little more complicated. This field will take the energy of an explosion and absorb it and convert it to useful energy."

Byron was intrigued, "How big of an explosion?"

Jack shrugged, "I don't know for sure. But, if my calculations are correct it could stand up to a hydrogen bomb and handle it with ease."

The doctor thought for a few minutes, "A generated field? Is this some kind of science fiction like the energy fields around a space ship that take hits from energy weapons and keep the ship safe." His tone was concerned for Jack's basis of information rather than skeptical.

Jack gestured, "Theoretically I suppose it could do that. But, the one I want to develop will shield a single person."

Dr. Clashire frowned, "How do we power it and how does it work?"

Jack took out his drawings and notes. "I'll let you work through these later, but in summary, the field is generated by a device worn on the body that creates an altered type of atomic structure as a field surrounding the person. This structure is refreshed once every ten picoseconds and has the unique property of regeneration."

Jack showed the doctor several drawings and explained them to him. Then he looked through his notes. "When energy is applied to the field from the outside, the valence electrons begin to absorb the energy. Conventional atomic structures jump the valence electrons up to new energy levels as the input increases. This continues until they disintegrate and destroy the molecular structures they make up. This new structure absorbs energy up to the change level and then collapses into a more compact structure and dissipates the additional energy by creating a new atom in the space vacated by the original atomic structure. Since all the atoms in that area of the field are affected at the same time, the covalent bonds are also recreated."

Jack pointed to another drawing," As the energy continues to mount; the process is repeated as many times as necessary between refreshes from the field generator. I estimate that the sequence could be repeated several thousand times between the refreshes at ten picosecond intervals. The structure of the field simply becomes thousands of times more dense and impenetrable. When the refresh takes place, any additional energy is converted into gravitational waves by magnetic alteration. The gravitational wave anchors the field in relation to the earth, resisting any movement due to the force of the incoming energy. The cycle repeats itself until all the energy is dissipated."

The doctor wanted to argue or dismiss some of the theory but he couldn't find anything wrong with what his new boss had just suggested. He would have to research this a lot. "What powers the field?"

Jack pointed at a whole section of his drawing of the field generator. "Electro-Magnetic-Gravitational energy. EMG."

Byron frowned, "EMG? How can you harness it?"

Jack pointed at the drawing, "Remember how the field dissipates the unwanted energy? Just reverse the process and use the denser field collapse to power the generator. It should work without having to be attacked first. The gravity field interacts with the atomic structure to provide sufficient power to generate the field."

Byron sat back and thought for about ten minutes. He went over every conceivable objection and possibility of impossibility. Coming up blank without his having time to research it he smiled. "If this is correct, and right now I can't see why it wouldn't work, you will have created the most effective protection solution ever made. But more than that, you will have created the ultimate source of energy that would replace gasoline engines, batteries, wind power, solar energy, and any other form. The effects on the world's economic and political structure that this thing would cause would be almost beyond comprehension. Its simplicity is wonderful. It's so simple that it makes one think that it wouldn't work, but, it should." He looked at Jack with a small amount of concern. "If one glimpse of this should get out before we can perfect it, there will be five million people trying to get it, kill us to keep it from ever happening, or to use it to control the world. I wouldn't even trust our government. Actually, I don't know that I could trust you or me to have this kind of power."

Jack nodded, "That's why we need to keep it between ourselves and my partner. The only other people who will know about it will be my team and perhaps one other person, all of who I will stake my life on. I expect you will be circumspect in hiring help or ordering material and things like that?"

Byron nodded. "I most certainly will. In fact I will come up with a parallel phony project and we will keep this quiet. You know, you misinterpreted the effect this device will have on our stock. You can't estimate the amount of sheer desire to own this process. It will make everyone here so rich that money won't mean anything, again, ever."

Jack shook his head. "The production output of this "field" will be kept limited to a very, very few groups. I doubt that the world at large will know anything about it for years to come. These few groups will drive the stock up."

Dr. Clashire smiled. "I may be your newest employee but I am definitely vested in the stock department so let me be the first to repeat that a protective field is only one use for this process. It can have applications in transportation, medicine, astrophysics, flight, energy, and sports. In fact, this will change the world as we know it. Consider the geo-political implications in just replacing the need for oil. Whoa! If we are careful to keep the process secret and make it so it can't be reverse-engineered, we could rival the largest companies in the world for products and profits."

Jack smiled, "We will keep the process secret and proceed slowly on other uses. If we can help people we will but we won't let the cat out of the bag. Byron, can I count on you to head this whole thing up and to keep it safe from misuse? Is that an acceptable responsibility?"

Byron nodded. "I think I have just found my life's work. You can depend on me, but, I also need checks and balances and I will rely on you and Bob to do that. Now, where did this marvelous concept come from? I don't think that you are deep enough in the physics of the thing to understand what you have so I don't think you thought it up."

Jack smiled, "You're right, I didn't think it up. God gave it to me in one complete package."

Byron wasn't sure if Jack was kidding or not. "Really? You got this directly from God? I'm supposed to believe that the Creator just gave this to you?"

Jack nodded, "Believe it. If you don't believe me, just ask Him yourself. God himself is in charge of this project and will protect it. I don't have to tell you that He's a jealous God."

The scientist began to see that God could very well be real. This was a new concept for him. But it was enough for the Spirit of God to work within his spirit.

Doctor Clashire stood up and extended his hand to Jack. "Thank you for this opportunity and everything else. I need to start to design the lab." He stopped and thought for a minute. "No, I need to start designing the tools we will need to make the tools we will use to make the laboratory so that we can investigate this concept. And we will need to come up with an acceptable alternative project as a cover."

Jack nodded, "Okay, I will assign my best security manager to keep you up to date on how to maintain your privacy and secrecy. He used to report to Mark Connelly. He's very security minded. You'll like him, his name is Will Carol. He doesn't need to know what you're doing but how you want to protect it. After that he will see that you are safe. Once you have your tools and your lab figured out, let me know and I will have a secure building built and outfitted for you. I know some really good architects and design engineers."

Jack was quiet for a few seconds and then he looked the Doctor in the eyes. "I meant it when I said that God will keep this from getting out. Learn to listen to Him and follow His leading. It will save you a great deal of time and probably a great deal of pain. He is behind this and wants it to become a reality, but, it will be for His uses, not ones we think it should be used for. Do you think you can kneel before him in true humility and do his work?"

Dr. Clashire felt the wind blowing over the bottomless chasm that Jack had seen before, as he looked into his soul. He also felt the presence of what he thought might be God nearby. He took a deep breath and said, "Yes, I can, and, I most likely will agree. But first I need to think long and hard about all of this, especially the part a God would play in my life. This is your God and while I've heard a lot of pros and cons I am not prejudiced against the concept of a supreme being. Is that alright with you?"

Jack grinned, "That will be fine Byron. Like I said, This is God's project and I think you two will get along very well, you both think in big concepts."

CHAPTER THREE

Turning all of the corporate projects, including the new one, over to Bob Wexler, Jack headed back to his alternate life with the Crossfire Team. He arrived home close to five o'clock on December 6th after fighting the traffic and the weather. Snow had fallen for almost nine hours and the homeward bound traffic was snarled up and in some cases almost frantic. Jack was glad he was driving the new Cadillac Escalade with four-wheel drive. He was also very glad to pass the signs warning others to go no further. After crossing three sets of tire-shredding grills, the road turned to the right and then arced back around a curve to the left. At this point, signs were no longer needed as the road ended in a twenty foot gap that was thirty feet deep and as wide as the road. Across the gap was a granite cliff with a massive gate set flush into the cliff. Several TV cameras were visible as well as a variety of ominous closed ports that concealed weapons.

Jack operated the remote control. He waited several seconds until the gate had swung outward and up from the bottom and inward and down at the top. The entire assembly then moved outward and descended into the gap to form a bridge across the open span. The bars of the gate were twenty-four inch square beams with six-inch thick walls. This would allow the heaviest truck or tank to cross it but, when it was up, it would also resist all but the heaviest of military ordinance attempting to breach it.

As Jack drove across the bridge/gate in the driving snow, a series of lights came on in the tunnel behind the gate. With the snow behind him he drove through marble walls which rose twenty-five feet to the arched ceiling in the thirty-foot wide tunnel. The tunnel made a gradual turn to the left and then another turn to the right before resuming a straight path for two hundred yards. This prevented any direct fire from one end of the tunnel to the other. At the other end of the tunnel was another bridge/gate combination that was already in the lowered position.

Jack drove past the second gate and turned left into the large enclosed parking area. Upon exiting the SUV Jack sensed warm but fresh, flowing air smelling of mountain greenery

The familiar, well-lit entrance stood at the end of the parking area. As he approached it the NovaStar sign lit up requesting identification. Jack identified himself. The sign went out and a satin-chrome finished set of elevator doors opened and Jack got on the elevator. The satin-chrome finish hid the inch-thick armor plating behind it.

The living room was a circular-shaped open area of over two thousand square feet of floor space. The entire far side of the circle from the elevator was floor-to-ceiling windows. The ceiling was twenty feet above the carpeted floor. The ceiling was matte-finished, polished stone in a light brownish-white color which added to spectacular view of the valley below the dwelling and the mountains on the other side of the valley. Again the air smelled fresh and mountain clean. Jack was aware that the huge panoramic view of the outside world was actually piped in from over a quarter mile away and represented by the "View Port" system. He knew that on the actual granite wall overlooking the valley there were twelve, 10" ports that acted as lenses for the system. The protection scheme was good enough to be undetectable. If you stood at the window and looked down, you'd believe you could see almost straight down into the valley.

Since TA had started marketing the View Port windowing systems the demand had been fantastic. This demand had doubled their corporate stock price within three months. The military and the security sectors were the leading buyers of the technology but the private sector was growing quickly.

Comfortable furniture and dramatic art was placed strategically around the room. The lighting was subtle with recessed lamps providing back lighting and tasteful use of light panels throughout the room. A large rock fireplace and chimney graced the right wall and a large display television screen was prominent on the left. The colors and scents and accents were done with class and it was obvious that the same interior designer that had finished the first two NovaStar-equipped homes had also done this one.

Jack walked over to the door leading to the War Room and opened it. Seven members of the team were at their consoles working on building a case on Hermann Lutz and his demon Vorbleg. Jack walked over to Laura and kissed her on the cheek. She smiled and continued talking to the Chaplain of a U.S. Air Force base in Germany. "Thank you Major. I appreciate your help. Let me know if anything new pops up. Goodbye."

She took off her headset and stood up to stretch. Jack took her in his arms and hugged her. "Hey good looking, what's cooking?"

Laura looked at him with wide eyes, "I thought you were bringing home dinner." Then she laughed at the lost expression on his face.

She took him off to a quiet corner and told him that she was sorry for being so grumpy the previous evening. "I had a long talk with God this morning after you left and I'm much better now."

She assumed a serious face and told him that while he was off playing CEO they had all been hard at work tracking down their nemesis, Hermann Lutz.

Jack looked over at Mark and asked, "Any headway so far?"

Mark walked up to them and smiled, "Oh yeah, courtesy of my wife's ex-employer. I guess they went all out in memory of Joey Goldberg. I'll let Sarah give you the highlights." He gestured behind him with his thumb at Sarah.

Sarah sat back with a grim look on her face. "It seems that the information has always been available but no one thought to put it together as being a single individual before Joey stumbled onto Lutz after he thought he'd removed him from the scene in Germany two years ago."

She held up the data and summarized it. "Hermann Lutz was born to an impoverished family in the Rhur Valley in the year 1878. He worked in a mine when he was old enough to hold a shovel. His father died in a cave-in when Hermann was eighteen. He then became the bread-winner for a family of six. A late night fire destroyed the house he lived in and the rest of his family less than a year later."

She continued, "Alone, with no education and with no one to sponsor him, he was destined to die poor and forgotten. Then, miraculously, he was granted admission to a German military academy. There is no record of who paid for his time there but he had a good mind and a sense for the correct military response for any given situation. He rose through the cadet ranks until he was the student commander of the academy when he graduated. Knowing talent when they saw it, the army sent him to their equivalent to today's OCS. Again, he excelled and left the school as a Captain in the German army. In 1905 he ended his enlistment and retired from the military."

She looked at Jack, "This is where things get weird. He reappears in 1912 as a military attaché for the German high command. Our analysis now indicates it was his plan that inflamed the First World War. He had the note sent that was received in Zagreb at a Cafe called "Zlatna Moruna in late April, 1914. That set up the assassination of Archduke Ferdinand. After that, everywhere there was strife or tension, Lutz seems to have had a hand in it somehow. At the end of World War I, Lutz was 40 years old. He then disappeared for eighteen years. The next record of his activities was a special advisor to Hiendrich Himmler, the man in charge of eliminating the Jews from Poland and Germany."

Sarah decided a bit of history was in order. "While no specific order from Hitler authorizing the mass killing of Jews has been found, the evidence suggests that sometime in the fall of 1941, Himmler and Hitler agreed in principle on mass murder by gassing. The Wannsee conference, held near Berlin in January of 1942, was attended by fifteen senior officials, led by Reinhard Heydrich and Adolf Eichmann. The records of this meeting provide the best evidence of the central planning of the Holocaust. Between 1942 and 1944 the SS, assisted by collaborationist governments and recruits from occupied countries, systematically killed approximately 3.5 million more Jews in six camps in Poland; Auschwitz-Birkenau, Belzec, Chelmno, Majdanek, Sobibor and Treblinka and one in what is now present-day Belarus, called Maly Trostenets. Other Jews were killed less systematically elsewhere, or died of starvation and disease while working as slave laborers. The Holocaust, or we call it, Shoah, was Himmler's final solution to the "Jewish Problem". From what our investigators are now discovering, it was probably Lutz's idea which Himmler adopted as his own."

Looking at Mark she continued, "It wasn't just the Jews you know. Other ethnic groups and social categories were also subject to persecution and in some cases extermination. Thousands of German socialists, communists and other opponents of the regime died in concentration camps, as did a large but unknown number of homosexual men. The Gypsies were regarded as an inferior race and were also shot or sent to death camps. About three million Soviet prisoners of war also died in camps or as slave laborers. All the occupied countries suffered terrible privations and mass executions: up to three million, non-Jewish, Polish civilians died during the occupation."

Sarah tapped the papers in front of her. "As I said before, there is no known document in which Hitler explicitly ordered the Holocaust, although there is documentation that he approved of the Einsatzgrupen, where Jews throughout Russia were stripped naked and shot in front of ditches. Most historians believe he not only knew of the Holocaust and the gas chambers but ordered Himmler to carry it out. Certainly it was entirely consistent with his lifelong beliefs and his growing interest in the occult."

Mark asked, "Did Lutz take any part or any credit for the Holocaust?"

Sarah shook her head, "Lutz never seeks the limelight. He stays back, in the shadows where he can move others to do what he wants done. Anyway, in the closing days of World War II, when Hitler and his girlfriend were committing suicide in Hitler's Berlin Bunker, Lutz slipped off to South America with many of the SS. He was caught in a photo, disembarking from a steamship in Columbia in late 1945. At this point he still looks to be about 40 years old."

Looking at the data she continued. "It now seems that he has been traveling all over the world to accomplish his master's will to destroy the Jewish nation. Now that the possibility has been raised, investigators have been combing their files and they have turned up records and clues to his appearance in the Middle East in every conflict that Israel has had since its inception. They have concrete evidence that he was involved in the planning for the attack that resulted in the 1948 Seven Day war with Egypt. He appeared in two photographs in Syria just before they declared that they were going to wipe Israel off the map, leading to the Six Day war with most of the Arab nations aligned against Israel."

Sarah shook her head, "All at once, now that the concept has been accepted, there is data showing connections between Lutz and all of the rogue Arab nations. He has been photographed working or meeting with every known radical Arab terrorist group right up to Al Qaeda. He never acts overtly but always in the background, as an advisor or ally."

Sarah took on the look of veiled angry fire that only indicated the amount of passion that was behind it. "I find it significant that he was involved in or at least in the vicinity of at least four of the combats that we have taken part in over the last two years. He is mentioned in some of the papers you got out of Don Miland's manor south of Denver. He was a major supporter and confidant to the Believer's Church Prophets in their effort to blackmail the world. He was an advisor to the Arab Neo-Idealist League group that created that air-borne poison that would kill all non-Arab children. He was, it turns out a major decision-maker in the ASF in the poisoning of Israel and the United States. He has been in Zyngola more than two dozen times recently. His contact in the Zultarian Religion in Zyngola? Abdullah Hami. This guy, it turns out, looks to be a key to many of the problems we as a team have been facing."

Jack nodded, "That makes sense. If he is the wholly controlled agent of a major, ancient demon he would be at all the places that generate hate and death. Especially, death to Israelis. It also makes sense that he would want control of the crucifixion nail."

Mark added, "Now all we have to do is to find him, kill him, and exorcise his demon."

Laura said "This is going to take a lot of prayer. I think it is time we asked God as a team what we need to do to accomplish his will in this matter."

CHAPTER FOUR

The assembled team included Jack and Laura, Mark and Sarah, Su Li, Gary Eisenthal, and Sensei Grady. The experiences they had gone through over the last two years left no wiggle-room for denying the reality of Yahveh, Yahshua Messiah, or Yahveh's Holy Spirit. Each of the team had fallen into a loving relationship with the true God of the Universe. It was because of this relationship, the team was comfortable in seeking Yahveh's Will.

Later that night as Jack prayed alone in his room, a glow appeared before him even though his eyes were closed. A powerful entity with piercing eyes floating in the glow before him. It resolved itself into the angel Caleb. Caleb spoke, "Greetings from Yahveh on high. Your request for wisdom concerning the demon Vorbleg is wisdom itself. He hasn't existed for all these years as an enemy of Yahveh by accident. He is well protected and extremely dangerous to those who seek to destroy him. The Most High has decided that he has become too vain and prideful of his horrific deeds, so he shall be destroyed. Yahveh has decided that your team will be His agents on Earth to achieve this destruction, if you can.

Understand that you are not the first person nor is the Crossfire Team the first group commissioned to eliminate Vorbleg and his agent Lutz. You will all have to stand without sin against the demon and without weakness against the human. Now hear the word of the Lord. "*For though you walk in the flesh, you shall not war according to the flesh. For the weapons of your warfare are not carnal but mighty in Yahveh for pulling down strongholds, casting down arguments and every high thing that exalts itself against the knowledge of Yahveh, bringing every thought into captivity to the obedience of Messiah, and being ready to punish all disobedience when your obedience is fulfilled.*"

The angel seemed to gather power and he held out his hand towards Jack. Jack felt a sensation of that power in his right hand. Looking at his hand he saw a silver lance or spear. It was about five feet long and had a head that looked like diamond, tapering to a point that radiated sharpness with a gleam. The lance faded out of sight.

Caleb spoke again. "Jack, this weapon has the unique mission to destroy Vorbleg. He doesn't have to be in your dimension for it to work. But, you must make sure it is Vorbleg and be sure your throw hits him truly. He has no armor that can prevent this spear from penetrating to his black heart. You will know when to use it. Pray for the strength to destroy the demon when you want to use it. Remember, Yahveh Almighty is with you, always."

With that the angel disappeared and the glow faded out of his vision. Jack opened his eyes and sat in the chair in his bedroom. He thought over everything he had just learned. Chuckling to himself he realized he was definitely going to be the "point" man on this conflict.

Going back to the War Room he sat down at his console and asked the Holy Spirit on what he should tell the others. He realized that he didn't need to mention the spear but should tell the others what he had learned from God about their mission.

After mentioning everything but the spear, Jack asked for comments or insights.

Sarah nodded her head slowly. "I agree with the mission and the word from God. I'm a little amazed but I too heard from Yahveh. Rose appeared to me and told me that we needed to start our search with the Neo-Nazi movement in Berlin. This will be Vorbleg's next main effort through Lutz."

Mark asked Jack, "How do you think we should handle the ability of Satan and his minions to track us and to interfere with us, pray for coverage like we've done before?"

Jack nodded, "Yeah, but I think we also need to seek God on other things that need to be done. One of the things I'm learning is that we empower heaven to act by prayer. Gary, would you get with Minister Throman and see if we can have twenty-four hour intercessory prayer for us while we're on the actual attack phases of this mission? I believe the additional prayer coverage will be critical when we confront Vorbleg and his troops."

Laura asked Jack, "Do you believe that we will succeed where others have failed?"

Jack thought about that for a few seconds. "Well, I'm not sure that matters." In answer to the surprised looks he got, he continued. "The Lord of the universe has commanded us to confront and destroy this demon and his earthly agent. Whether we do it or die trying, it will be the best thing we could do. Yahveh rewards obedience more than sacrifice and we will be doing His will. I do believe we have a superior group and have been blessed by immense favor from Yahveh because we willingly do His Will as He asks. So, yes, I think we will win, but, as I said, that's not really important. The important thing is that we do the best we can and we do it in Yahveh's name and to His glory."

CHAPTER FIVE

Mark used his laptop to access his terrorist data base and reviewed the information on the Neo-Nazi movement. He summarized it for the others. "The former East Germany as a whole accounted for roughly 45 percent of right-wing acts of violence nationwide, though only 20 percent of the population lives there."

"A wave of neo-Nazi attacks, mainly against asylum seekers, followed German unification in 1990. After a brief respite in the middle of the decade, many observers fear a new escalation of right-wing violence, especially in eastern Germany, where the unemployment rate is higher than 20 percent, twice as high as in the western states."

"Yet, the dismal economic situation is only one reason for the high incidence of right-wing activity in the former Communist east. The East German regime propagated social conformism and repressed institutions that fostered a civil society. The few foreigners in East Germany were isolated from the main population. And while West Germany openly confronted the Nazi past, Communist rulers in East Berlin inflated themselves as inheritors of the "anti-fascist resistance."

"Mark stopped to take a drink of coffee. Then he continued to read from the data base. "After unification, the combination of these factors with the new political, social, and economic realities led to widespread disorientation in eastern Germany, and more recently, disillusionment.

"The people in the east live in a value system that is very vulnerable to right-wing extremism because it connects with their previous experiences," says Bernd Wagner of the Center for Democratic Culture in Berlin. Herr Wagner is a former East German policeman who has been monitoring neo-Nazi activity, Herr. Wagner says right-wing, xenophobic thinking in the eastern states has taken on the insidious form of "cultural subversion," burrowing into daily life and taking on the attributes of normalcy."

"While violent teenage skinheads make up a small but visible minority, Wagner says they have a lot of support among the population, where neo-Nazi thinking is "an omnipresent frame of mind." In an opinion poll published recently in Der Spiegel magazine, 55 percent of eastern German respondents agree that foreigners in the country live at the expense of Germans, while 38 percent think like that in the west."

"Almost half of the eastern German respondents believe foreigners take away jobs, and twice as many in the east as in the west think "a dictatorship could solve current problems better than a democracy." Nevertheless, it is highly unlikely that a far right party will muster enough votes to enter parliament in next September's federal elections. In contrast to right-wing extremists in France or Austria, German Neo-Nazis lack a charismatic leader to make their cause popular".

"Wagner says the fact that because right-wing extremists in Germany do not have a political voice is the reason they take their activities to the streets. In Knigs Wusterhausen, officers in the MEGA squad remark that the town is unusually quiet. In expectation that neo-Nazi skinheads would try to disrupt a local antiracism day, uniformed police patrol the main streets. Critics and officers alike agree that the MEGA force can fight only the symptoms, not the roots, of the prevalent neo-Nazi subculture in the region. "

Mark sat back and thought for a minute. "It seems that the German society, especially in the east, would not support any action of ours against the Neo-Nazis. We need to work our operation so that the public is not involved or is unaware of our activities."

Sarah commented "A lot of the criminal element in Germany is into brag and strut to show their importance. I'm sure if we were in the right area we would get enough information on the streets to locate Lutz. But, it is a double edged sword. Contacting those type of people could get word to Lutz that we are there looking for him. Also, if he is bound by a powerful demon, what will we do when we find him?"

CHAPTER SIX

Mark considered the situation. If they couldn't go to the criminals to find Lutz because of possible exposure, then they could go to the police.

Considering the help they had been given in the past by their friend in the FBI office in Denver, Mark called and talked to Senior Agent Gary Rhodes. After he hung up he told the others that he had gotten a contact name in the German Tactical Police in Berlin. The man spoke English because he had trained in the U.S. for two years.

Looking at the map, Mark figured the eight-hour time difference meant that it would be after five p.m. in Germany. But, since it was a cell-phone number Mark tried it on the assumption that the officer would have it with him at all times.

On the second ring the phone was answered, "Kaufmann, Ja?"

Mark replied, "Herr Kaufmann, I understand that you speak English, is that correct?"

The man on the other end said, somewhat impatiently, "Yes, yes I speak English, what it is you need?"

"My name is Mark Connelly and I got your name from the Senior Agent in Charge of the Denver, Colorado FBI office in the United States. He suggested that I call you concerning some information on the Neo-Nazi situation in Berlin."

Herr Kaufmann asked, "You're not a reporter or something like that are you?"

Mark laughed, "No sir, I'm a member of a counter-terrorism team here in the United States called the Crossfire Team."

There was a moment of silence and then the German said, "Yes, yes, I have heard of your team and its operations. Especially the one in Dallas earlier this month. That one was very impressive. How can I be of service to you?"

Mark thought for a second, "We are attempting to track a terrorist who is reportedly now working behind the scenes with the Berlin arm of the Neo-Nazis. We don't want to come into your territory and start investigating without your permission and, to be honest; we could use your help."

Herr Kaufmann asked Mark to wait one. In the background Mark heard him talking to someone else in German. He heard the terms, "Kreuz Feuer Arbeitsgruppe" which he figured meant "Crossfire Team". Herr Kaufmann came back on the line and told Mark that he would see that they got permission and the help of his unit. He asked when they would be there."

Mark looked at the clock and said, "It's fifteen hundred hours here on Tuesday. We'll be there in the airport at fourteen hundred hours tomorrow."

Herr Kaufmann said, "Excellent, I will meet you when you disembark from your aircraft. I assume you'll be traveling by private jet?"

Mark agreed and gave him the tail number from their Citation X aircraft.

As Mark hung up the phone, Su Li stood up to leave, saying, "Well I'd bettered get a preflight started. We'll do New York, Paris, Berlin. That okay with you?"

Seeing Mark nod she gave everyone a big smile and left. Laura commented, "I wonder if she'll ever get married. Her real love is to fly."

True to his word, Conrad Kaufmann was waiting for them in Berlin, at two p.m. as the team disembarked from their aircraft in a private hanger. Kaufmann was a tall, good-looking young man with light blonde hair combed neatly back and a small moustache. He was wearing the official Tactical Police uniform as were the two men with him. They greeted the team members politely and professionally. Conrad indicated the van behind him and suggested that they travel to his headquarters to discuss a strategy and goals.

The team got their baggage, some of which was heavy and clanked. Loading everything into back of the dark blue van, they pulled out of the hanger and headed for the headquarters in Kreuzberg near downtown Berlin.

The team gazed out at modern Berlin as they rode. After a short time the driver spoke to Conrad in German. He interpreted for the Americans. "Apparently we have picked up some followers. Since there are three of them I would also guess that they will be foolish enough to challenge us." He reached down to a box on the floor and opened it to reveal four sub-machine guns. He handed one to each of his men and took one himself. Looking at the team he said with a smile, "If you have illegally brought weapons into Germany this would be a good time to declare them and have them handy."

Su Li turned in her seat and lifted one of the weapons bags over the seat and handed it to Mark. She got the second one and gave it to Jack. As the bags were opened and the collection of weapons and explosives became evident, Conrad's estimation of the team's capabilities and Su Li's strength went up. Not wasting any time, the team stripped off their jackets and strapped on Kevlar body armor. They then proceed to hang various grenades, knives, handguns, and ammo on their harnesses and belts.

Each person checked their XM8 Carbines and the XM320 40mm grenade launchers mounted below the barrel. Rounds were quickly snapped into the chambers with only the safeties preventing them from being fired. It took less than three minutes for all five members of the team to be fully combat ready. Conrad noted the casual professionalism each member displayed and their advanced weapons. Weapons with which they seemed very familiar. His estimation of their combat capabilities went up again.

The third member of the German team had been talking on the radio, arranging for assistance and backup while the team had been arming themselves. He had just finished and turned to tell Conrad something when the enemy decided to make its move.

The three powerful Mercedes cars surged past the other traffic and closed in on the van. One pulled along the left side while a second one attempted to do the same on the right side. Power windows were rolling down and the barrels of automatic weapons were being poked out in anticipation of bracketing the van.

Conrad pushed the buttons on the console and the windows in the van slid quickly down into the panels below them. He trained his H & K submachine gun out the window at car on the left side of the van. He triggered off ten rounds which caromed off of the armor plating and bullet-proof glass of the sedan. One of the rifles in the car answered back and rounds flew through the windows and tore holes through the roof of the van. All of the other traffic braked suddenly to avoid the battle.

The officer driving the van lost the battle to keep the car on the right from pulling up along side. More rifles were being poked out the windows of this car.

Mark grabbed the grip and trigger for the 40mm grenade launcher fixed under his rifle. Smiling at Jack he nodded. They leaned out windows on either side of the van and triggered the mini-bombs. With only six feet separating the vehicles on either side it was impossible to miss. The car on the right took Jack's 40mm grenade in the driver's window and the explosion gutted the vehicle's passenger compartment and ended the occupant's desire to kill people. Fire and smoke exploded out of broken windows and the remaining windows turned black on the inside from the flame and smoke. The car swung to the right and slammed into the guard rail. Flipping up into the air and smashing down on its roof it was quickly lost behind the speeding van.

Mark's grenade went low and exploded under the rear end of the car on the left of the van. The explosion flipped the car into the air and it smashed down nose first onto the cement. Since it was still traveling seventy five miles an hour when it hit the ground it fell over onto its roof. The roof flattened and the car continued to cartwheel end-over-end and to crush together as it smashed over and over again.

Two men arose out of the sunroof of the third vehicle, which was trailing the van. They opened fire at the back of the van. The rear window in the van shattered into a thousand pieces. The seat back on the rear seat of the van was armored for just such an occurrence. Popping back up after the hailstorm of glass passed, Su Li, Sarah, and Laura simultaneously fired their 40mm grenades at the car. The triple impact shattered the car completely. The passenger compartment split open and spilled bodies across the concrete as the flaming wreck slowed to a halt.

The van driver slowed the van to a halt. All eight occupants of the van got out and walked slowly back to the fiercely burning wreckage to see if there were any survivors. There were none.

A noise of a high-revving engine and more shooting alerted everyone to the approach of a fourth enemy vehicle. The three German officers opened fire on the new arrival. The five members of the Crossfire Team joined them in the assault on the car with their XM8 Carbines. Over ninety rounds punched into and through the sedan and the people shooting at them from the windows. Not being armored, this vehicle had hung back from the initial assault. The tires blew out, the windows shattered, and the gas tank exploded from sparks off the concrete. The now-unpiloted, burning, rolling wreck flew by the team and crashed into the guardrail on the left side of the freeway where it came to a halt. Looking back for the last two miles, Conrad noted that the highway looked like a war zone with burning cars and bodies everywhere. Not wanting to be a part of the festivities, the other traffic had come to a complete standstill further back behind the first enemy car.

Conrad slapped Mark on the shoulder and said, "You live up to your reputation. I'm proud to be working with you guys. Wow! This is going to send a message to the Neo Nazis." He looked at Laura as she reloaded the grenade launcher under her rifle. He asked her, "Do you always come prepared with grenades?"

Laura smiled coyly at him as she put a new magazine into the well of her rifle. "Only if we don't need the heavier stuff." That made Conrad's eyebrows go up a notch. Rapidly approaching sirens announced the arrival of reinforcements which were too late for the fire fight but would be helpful for wrapping it up and controlling the public.

CHAPTER SEVEN

The German Tactical Police forces were very efficient. In less than an hour they had measured, photographed, bagged, and removed all the people and all the vehicles that had been destroyed. Each member of the team, as well as Conrad and his two men, had been individually debriefed as to the entire sequence of events.

Finally, the eight of them were released to go to Conrad's headquarters. Jack and Laura were given a Spartan room for their use, as were Mark and Sarah. Su Li got to bunk with one of the female officers. Mark and Jack decided to have a strategy meeting with Conrad. Su Li was weary after flying most of the time and then going through the stress of combat. She opted out to take a nap. Sarah wanted to review the information that Conrad's group had on the people that had attacked them.

Laura decided to clean their weapons while she had the time. She put a work towel down on a small table in their room and one-by-one, dismantled the XM8/XM320 rifle/grenade launcher combinations. Using a set of patches and rags soaked in powder solvent she carefully cleaned and inspected the parts of each weapon, especially the inside of the barrel.

Dressed in combat camouflage, rip-stop nylon trousers, black combat boots, and a soft, gray short-sleeve pullover, the blonde-haired woman exhibited a contrast of mature beauty and solid professionalism.

Outside the window the cobalt-blue sky with soft breezes blowing and a bird singing seemed at odds with her comfort in accomplishing her military task amid the smell of cordite and solvent. As she continued to clean and oil the mechanisms of the rifles, her mind brought up memories of the relaxed, refined lifestyle that, as a woman of wealth, she had been enjoying just a couple of years before.

A vivid memory picture of the room where she and Jack had vacationed at Sun Valley, Idaho filled her mind. The Lodge had provided them with a wonderful week-long break from their businesses. They had been pampered with every desire fulfilled quickly by a professional and eager hotel staff. With no real agenda, they had slept late each day in a luxurious room, and had magnificent meals in the restaurant or in their room.

Every detail and furnishing in the hotel was top-of-the-line, first-class material with gold accents and polished hardwoods. The decor was comfortable and pleasing to the senses.

She thought of the sumptuous, deep-pile carpeting, down-filled, satin-sheeted, comfortable bed, the wall-mounted, fifty-four inch, plasma wide-screen, color HDTV televisions. The huge hydro jet tub and bathroom dressing areas. The separate, enclosed toilet area and the walk-through shower with three rain heads. The marble tile and walls in the bathroom suite contrasted well with the tasteful wall-papering of the sitting and sleeping rooms. The rooms were provided with subtle indirect lighting that lit everything without glare.

She compared those memories with her present accommodations. Officer Haufmann had provided them with a single, small room with linoleum flooring, two cots with thin mattresses and springs rather than a mattress and box-spring arrangement. The beds had soft gray blankets with a military insignia on them. There were two metal straight-backed office chairs, a small dresser and clothes closet for their hanging clothes. Connected to the room was a small bathroom with a sink, toilet, and shower. There weren't even curtains on the high window in the end of the room.

Having completed Jack's rifle, she finished oiling the barrel of her rifle, swabbed it out, and then wiped it down with a clean cloth. When she had done the same with the receiver group, she reassembled the rifle, loading a thirty-round magazine of 6.8 caliber bullets into the magazine well, and a high-explosive .40mm grenade into the grenade launcher. She finished wiping down the outside of the weapon with a light coat of gun oil and wiped it off. She checked the action and pulled back on the charging handle and released it. This chambered the first round. She made sure the safety was on and placed the rifle against the wall next to Jack's rifle. She cleaned her hands with a waterless hand cleaner and applied some lotion to her hands to keep the chemicals from drying out her skin.

Stretching with her hands above her, she felt the firmness and the strength of her body that this lifestyle promoted. Thinking about the contrast between the Lodge and the room she was in, she realized how useless, selfish, and empty her earlier life had been. Even though it didn't seem that way then. Except for catering to their senses and hobnobbing with others whose lives were equally meaningless, they had accomplished almost nothing.

She was sure the same people would say that her present life was uncultured, unsophisticated, and not very chic. Very boring compared to partying all night, golf or shopping in the daytime, and completely satisfying every craving.

Until Yahveh had taken hold of her life one night in a church in Denver, she would have agreed with them. But after God had touched her soul with his love and His sacrifice for her, everything else became second place to loving and serving Him. She knew that if their sophisticated friends understood Yahveh and the truth of their total dependence on God for their daily existence, they too would learn of a love so great that they would gladly use their wealth and talents in His service. They would attempt to return as much of the love that they had already been given as possible.

She knew it would be an uphill battle for many of them. She had talked to them about God, only to be rebuffed or put down. The culture of the "ME" generation would not stand for the concept of existing to serve others rather than themselves. They were so afraid that they would lose something or not get something that many would not entertain any mention of God. Little did they guess that there was more beauty and joy in serving God and in doing something with eternal consequences, than there would ever be in just satiating themselves.

Laura knew that everyone had times when they considered their lives and realized that all the money, power, drugs, alcohol, and expensive toys did not satisfy them. The only thing that an excess of those things gave a person was a desire for more and more. She knew also that one day, she, and everyone else, would stand alone in front of a loving, but just, Yahshua and have to give an accounting of what they had done with what they had been given.

While the team's lives were about as far from pampered and trendy as could be, they were doing Yahveh's expressed will. She knew that when that day came for her, she would be proud to stand before her Savior. Her life in the last two years may have only had brief moments of luxury and earthly enjoyment, separated by long periods of boredom, searing, traumatic, periods of combat, violent attempts on their lives, and confrontation with the evil that man could become and the evil he did to others.

But, the Crossfire Team stood as a small part of Yahveh's army against the enemy and his efforts to destroy mankind or pull them away from Him. The sacrifice of being a warrior for Yahveh brought incomparable satisfaction and joy to her life. As she sat there she felt the peace and contentment flow through her as the anointing of the Father told her that God was in agreement concerning her obedience and sacrifice. Nothing she had ever felt could compare to this. The satisfaction and pleasure vibrated all the way to every part of her soul and spirit with the knowledge that what she was doing had eternal consequences and therefore was really worth something.

She straightened up the desk and put the cleaning materials back in their packages. She took a quick shower and dressed in a clean set of camouflage clothing. She examined her reflection in the small mirror. She was pleased with the image she saw. She was just finishing combing out her hair when Jack came in from his meeting.

He sat his laptop computer on the table. He sat on the edge of the table and his gray-green eyes focused on Laura. "Do you have any idea how incredibly beautiful and sexy you look right now?"

That was something that Laura needed to hear right then. Smiling back she stared at her handsome husband and said, "No, tell me."

CHAPTER EIGHT

Four miles away from the headquarters building, Officer Haufmann, Mark, and Sarah were sitting in the back of a non-descript German Police undercover van. They were listening to a conversation going on in a second-floor room of an inexpensive hotel. The people in the room had been under surveillance for some time as suspects in terrorist activities. The laser microphone was fixed on the window pane and brought the talk in the room into the van as if they were present in the room themselves.

For all the inflammatory and terroristic rhetoric they had already recorded, the police could have arrested everyone in the room, but, they were concentrating on getting a lead on Hermann Lutz.

Even farther away from the police headquarters, Hermann Lutz questioned his associate with his usual thoroughness and impatience. "Karl, where is this team of Americans now?"

Actually shaking in his shoes, Karl attempted to please the unseen menace he felt all the way to his bones. "At the last report, Sir, they are scattered throughout Berlin. The Malones are with the Tactical Squad in their headquarters. The Connelly's left with Herr Kaufmann but the trackers have lost them for the moment. Ms. Li, the Asian pilot is in downtown. What she's looking for is unknown at present."

Obviously Lutz wasn't pleased with the report. "Bumbling idiots! How do you manage to lose track of forty percent of your assignment?" Without waiting for an answer that he didn't care about anyway, he continued, "What about the ambush you recommended K-group to undertake? Did it result in death or injury for any of the Americans?"

Karl knew that this was quickly becoming a series of unacceptable reports which did not bode well for his immediate future. But, he also knew that lying to Lutz was an even worse proposition. Other people, both men and women, had tried to fool Lutz and make themselves look good. They had died, quickly and horribly.

Therefore, Karl answered carefully. "The men of K-group did not follow my orders or my directions. They presumed to think they were so good; they didn't need any of my planning to take the Americans. Due to that stupidity, they were all killed during the assault on the highway. Do you want to see the assault, I have it on tape."

Lutz considered eliminating Karl, but wasn't sure there was anyone else who was as competent as him. The demon told him that Karl was telling him the truth.

"Actually", Lutz thought, "That took a great deal of courage on Karl's part."

So, he would try again to use this tool, however dull it was. "All right Karl; I want you to concentrate on finding and immediately eliminating the Connellys. Forget the pilot; she's nothing without the others."

Visibly relived, Karl said, "Yes Sir, right away." Returning to his control center he thought he knew the perfect group to use. He picked up the phone and called the Bortz brothers. They were crazy, but were just about what he needed today.

In the van, Kaufmann saw a light blinking. "Our suspects have an incoming phone call."

Hans Bortz answered the phone on the second ring. "Ja, Hans here." Officer Kaufmann translated the German for Mark and Sarah. Actually, Mark knew enough German to get by and Sarah was quite competent in the language. They just didn't think it was something that they needed to reveal to anyone at the time.

Hans' voice came over the wire tap as clearly as it did in the phone in Han's hand. "Hans, I want you to find the Connellys. You need to do it now! It is unacceptable that they have dropped out of sight, you understand?"

Hans answered, "Okay Karl, I understand, where do you want me to report when I find them?"

Karl's answer caused all three members in the van to look at each other. "You may kill them at once along with anyone that is with them."

Hans asked Karl, "Karl, is this one of your decisions, or his? Our last orders were not to kill them but just report where they were."

Karl laughed a small, bitter laugh. "Hans, Hans, you should know by now that he is in complete control. I am not so stupid to change his orders. He wants the Connellys eliminated now. Call me on your cell phone once you've located them. Oh, also pull the two men following the Chinese pilot; she doesn't matter to Herr Lutz. You can use them in your effort. Do not fail me on this. If you do, I will let you explain to Herr Lutz why the Connellys aren't dead. He may just take you and your brother as sacrifices instead!"

The occupants of the van heard Hans break the connection and start repeating the orders. The people in the room left and the connection went silent. Kaufmann checked his equipment as they watched the Bortz brothers and two other men leave the shabby hotel building.

The officer shook his head. "I'm sorry but this "Karl" person used too many cut outs and redirects for me to trace his number or whereabouts."

Sarah said, "Shall we ask the Bortz brothers where Karl is?"

Kaufmann thought about it and said, "No. It wouldn't help to interrogate them. They've always been just hired help and I doubt that they are told anything. That is another reason for the cut outs and redirects. Karl doesn't want the hired help to know where he is any more than he wants us to know."

Mark said, "Can you give them a juicy but empty lead so that they will report it to Karl?"

Haufmann thought about that for a few minutes. Then he said, "When?"

Mark looked at his watch. It was ten a.m. local time in Berlin. So, it was two a.m. in Washington. He thought, "Good enough, these guys are twenty-four/seven anyway." He punched in a complex series of numbers on his cell phone.

The phone on the other end rang once and a man answered, "NSA, Evans."

Mark said, "Mr. Evans, this is Mark Connelly, I have a priority Ultra Red request."

Evans replied, "Wait one." Then he came back with, "General Connelly, your voiceprint has been verified and we have approval to act on your Ultra Red request. Please go ahead Sir."

Mark thought, "Okay, I'm a General again. The rank has had to be reinstated because the NSA wouldn't be that far behind the suspension of our ranks by ex-Senator Lorch's demands." He said, "I am going to give you a cell phone number in Berlin. In the next hour this cell phone will be used to call a particular party. The party in question uses multiple cut outs and redirects to remain anonymous. I need a number and location on the called party."

Evans agreed to the action and told Mark he would let them know as soon as the connection was traced.

Mark looked at the others and said, "Now we wait. Do you think that the Bortz brothers will track us to this van across the street from their nest?"

Conrad Kaufmann laughed, "No, They've proven to us many times, they're not that capable."

CHAPTER NINE

Conrad drove the van slowly along the narrow street. They had been following the Bortz brothers for almost forty minutes now. A new member joined the terrorists and talked earnestly with Hans Bortz. Hans was gleeful and pulled out his cell phone. He hit a preset and after a short wait he was talking to Karl. The occupants of the van hadn't been able to tap into that conversation. A minute after he began to talk, Mark's cell phone beeped.

Mark took the information and gave it to Conrad. Conrad called in the address and location to his headquarters and then slowly pulled away from the curb and left the Bortz brothers to their scheming.

Twenty minutes later they left the city proper and headed into the countryside. Ten minutes later another van pulled in behind theirs and followed them. Conrad assured the Connellys that this was part of his back up.

Eventually they reached a break in the trees on the road and pulled off into an overlook. Handing Sarah the binoculars, Conrad pointed out a medium-sized castle across the valley from where they sat. "That's the location your NSA gave us. If that is Lutz's hideout then he picked a good one. There is no cover on any approach and he seems to still have a working moat and drawbridge. We could try a helicopter but my information is that this group has a supply of American "Stinger" missiles so we probably don't want to use that approach. I'm having the place surrounded but my men have to stay at least a full half-mile away from the castle so that they won't be observed. Do you have any ideas?"

Mark had been thinking about that. "If that is the location the NSA gave us then that is where the phone call from Hans ended up. We still don't have sufficient cause to storm the place but we do have a suspicion that a terrorist is hiding out there. Do your laws allow us to infiltrate the place or do we have to knock on the castle gate and ask to see the man?"

Conrad looked particularly distressed. "You are right in saying that we don't have enough probable cause to attack the castle. Some of Germany's most influential people live in these types of dwellings. We could start a really ugly scandal if we hit the wrong place."

Mark looked out at the darkening sky. "I've got an idea. Do you have access to any air assets other than a helicopter?"

On Conrad's nod, Mark outlined his plan. Conrad got on the radio and two hours later when full darkness had fallen, all five members of the team and Conrad were standing in the body of an ancient American C4 cargo plane as it made its way across the countryside outside of Berlin.

Sarah was checking Laura and Su Li's equipment and quietly encouraging them. "The first night jump I made was when I was nineteen years old. It was supposed to be a practice jump. But, in the middle of my flight and jump training there was a sudden incursion into Israel by forces of the Allied Arab Republic. They were attacking the kibbutzs and killing Israelis. At that moment we were the only assets the Mossad had in the area. So, instead of my instructor showing me how to jump, we both jumped as combatants. The urgency of the situation put the details of the jump into perspective. This is a simple search and define mission and the jump will be simple and quiet. I've shown you the necessary movements and procedures. So just follow my lead and we'll be safely on the ground in just a few minutes. The static line will open your chute for you and then all you have to do is steer it and just before you land, flare the chute as I told you. Are you both okay with this? If you're not, then don't make this jump. We'll find time to do some real training later."

Both Laura and Su Li were nervous but felt that they could handle the jump. The team and Conrad were going to use black parasail parachutes. This would give them the ability to land inside the castle where they wanted to without alarm, hopefully.

Laura prayed with Su Li for wisdom and protection during their jump. Afterward it was time to wait. This was always the hardest time, just before doing something dangerous like jumping out of a perfectly good airplane.

Laura glanced out the open doorway to the dark ground far below them. She admitted that it scared her to consider stepping off into the dark and falling towards the earth. But she sought the Lord and His peace and she felt relieved of the fear and stress. Either way it would be over quickly. She'd either be on the ground with her husband and her friends, or she'd be with God. It was a win-win situation.

Conrad had everyone stand up and get in a short file with Mark standing in the doorway. He had a small light on his helmet for the others to queue up on after their chutes opened. Su Li followed Mark with Laura, Sarah, Jack, and finally, Conrad. This way the trained and experienced jumpers would be in front and behind the first-timers.

Jack was concerned that he would remember to do everything in the proper order. This was normal for him. He needed to do a thing once or twice before he got comfortable in doing it.

The red light next to the door went out and the green light came on. Mark used his hands on the doorframe to push himself out and into the slipstream of the aircraft. As he fell away, each person took his place and jumped into the darkness.

Laura knew that Yahveh was in charge and had his hand on her but when she stepped out of the airplane and started to fall it seemed that her stomach rose up into her throat. The buffeting of the slipstream was harsh but it was gone quickly. Then the cable snapped tight and her chute opened with a snap. She reached for and found the handles that controlled the parasail operation. Then she looked for the light on Mark's helmet. She couldn't find it! She looked again and finally spotted it much farther to the left and higher than she expected. Pulling on the left handle moved her in the proper direction. Soon she was nearer to the light and slightly above it. As they dropped closer to the castle the lights gave her light-enhancing goggles some help in orienting herself to the others which she could finally see clearly. Sarah gave her a thumbs-up sign. They were dropping faster than she expected but by pulling down on both handles her fall slowed somewhat. In almost no time they were coming down inside the castle walls and headed for a grassy knoll.

Trying to remember everything Sarah had told her, Laura pulled down on the handles just before landing. This increased the lift of the parasail parachute and brought her downward momentum to a halt two feet above the ground. She dropped the two feet and flexed her knees to absorb the shock of landing. Using the heel of her left hand she released the harness and the chute floated to the ground behind her. She held her XM8 Carbine in her right hand as she dropped to one knee to cover the others. It had all happened so fast but in hindsight it was a real rush. She knew she'd want to do it again.

The team came together with Conrad and then split up, proceeding to their first objectives. For Conrad this was the power house for the castle. It included incoming power lines and a back-up generator. Conrad put three C-4 charges in place to eliminate the power if they needed to do that. He had a radio detonator in a pocket on his combat suit. He really hoped that the American NSA hadn't messed up on whose place this was.

Mark and Jack went to the main building which was the residence for the walled structure. They had seen no guards and no alarm had been sounded that they had heard. Mark looked at Jack as Conrad hurried up and joined them. "Do you think this place is innocent?"

Jack considered the idea. "Possibly, but then they could just be playing it low-key so as not to arouse suspicions or they could be counting on the demon to warn them. Let's find out which one is right. He turned the knob on the door and it opened without a noise. Mark thought, "Why do I feel like the fly sneaking into the spider's house?"

The three women had slipped over to what looked like a single-story barracks. Sarah peeked into the first window and ducked down quickly. "Oy Vey!" she said. Keying her combat microphone she sent a message to all of the raiders. "This is a trap! There are thirty troops in the barracks, fully armed and just waiting for a signal. Beware!"

Still outside the residence building, Mark immediately fell back to the wall next to the door as Jack let go of the handle and did the same on the other side of the door. Conrad backpedaled quickly and dropped down between two large trucks. Suddenly all the lights on the outside of the castle lit up, catching the raiders in the glare. Conrad triggered the radio remote control and everything went dark again. The darkness was relieved somewhat by the exploding power house. The ball of flames roared into the sky and the shock wave knocked over everything that was loose. Parts of the power house rained down everywhere.

The guards came out of two doors in the barracks and ran into hell itself. The three women laid down a withering sheet of rifle fire and added three .40mm grenades into the doorways. Twenty-three of the thirty guards died in the first minute of battle. Four of the other seven were wounded, two critically. The remaining three guards emptied their rifles out the doors but had no firm targets to shoot at so they hit nothing. Two more grenades silenced the remaining guards. Leaving Su Li to prevent any surprises, Laura and Sarah ran to the main house to support the men.

CHAPTER TEN

The lost of power and communications with the majority of the mercenary soldiers was bad enough. But, the fact that the raiders hadn't entered the death trap that Lutz had designed for them threw Karl into a panic. These people weren't being cooperative and it was his neck on the line!

He told the ten men in the building to charge the raiders and kill them. The mercenary leader told him to let them do the fighting. He assigned four of the men to harass the people outside until they got mad enough to charge into the building. Then the automatic weapons would finish them off in no time.

The four men ran to the windows overlooking the courtyard and carefully opened them, two on either side of the entrance and a floor above the raiders. The four men stepped to the open windows and raked the courtyard with automatic weapons fire. Then they dodged back to avoid the expected return fire. When nothing happened they peeked out the windows at the courtyard. Other than some of their comrades lying on the ground near the barracks they couldn't locate anyone. One of them ran back to tell their leader and Karl. Running into the room he said, "There's no sign of..." He stopped talking when he realized that Karl and the lieutenant were not responding but just standing there. He furrowed his brow and was about to comment when a rifle barrel poked him in the back of the neck. A commanding German voice told him to drop his weapons and put his hands on top of his head. Seeing agreement with that in his leader's eyes, he did as he was told. He was then searched, all his weapons were removed, and he was pushed over to join his comrades sitting on the floor behind Karl.

The other three soldiers were led in at gun point and joined the seven already there. The soldier got his first look at the enemy at that time. Half of them were women! But they were very professional and obviously competent.

Mark took Karl over to a chair and had him sit down. "Karl, do you speak English?" At Karl's nod of agreement, Mark continued, "Where is Hermann Lutz?"

Karl knew that his life was over no matter what happened now. Lutz would kill him for the failure of the trap if these people didn't kill him first. He realized that he could buy some time for his life by answering them. "He left earlier this afternoon when he told me that you were going to attack us from the air. I don't know where he went."

While they were talking, Laura felt a stirring in her spirit and not a good one. She was praying and asking the Father for an explanation when three demons materialized in the room from three different directions. These were the meanest-looking, nastiest, foulest demons she had ever seen. They had large, wicked-looking, black swords which they proceeded to use with grim efficiency. The demon that appeared closest to the prisoners began to hack them to death with great glee. The mercenaries were scrambling to get away and the ones that didn't make it were screaming horribly.

The demon that appeared in the physical dimension near Mark took a swing at him. Mark ducked and backed up so that the blade missed him but it caught Karl in the torso and severed his upper body from his lower. His muted cry of "Why?" was savagely cut off.

The third demon came out near Sarah and Su Li. Before he could attack them, Laura's armor and sword flared into bright light. The demon turned and took two giant strides towards Laura and swung his heavy black blade at her. Laura blocked his swing with her blade. Even though the demon outweighed her by two hundred pounds and his sword was twice as heavy as hers, his blade was stopped and broken in half when it met the gleaming blade handled by Laura. Too late he let out a squeal and attempted to stop his forward momentum. Laura quickly swung a reverse cross body stroke that cut the demon in half.

As that evil one vaporized into red greasy smoke, Laura turned and ran at the demon killing the prisoners. He was enjoying his job against the helpless and unarmed prisoners so much he didn't notice her approach.

45

Mercenary Bob Murtenson had backed up as far as he could against the wall. The monster that was killing his friends was scaring him to death. It didn't care if they could defend themselves or not. It just killed them one by one. Now it was Bob's turn. His heart quailed in his chest as the demon brought the sword back in preparation for the killing stroke. Oddly, even with his life about to end, Bob noticed a golden glow growing quickly behind the demon and suddenly there was a flash of pure white light and the demon's head flew from his shoulders. The horrible creature then seemed to vaporize into steam or smoke and Bob saw the most beautiful sight he'd ever seen. A fantastically beautiful woman in shining golden armor stood behind where the demon had been. It had been the glow from her armor and sword that Bob had seen coming up behind the demon. It may have been the sudden relief of not dying horribly or the fact she was the one who saved him, or it could have been the look of pure, righteous violent anger on her face, but he knew he would dedicate the rest of his life to her. He instantly fell madly in love with the vision in gold that had rescued him. She accelerated away from him with her sword flashing in a gleaming circle of pure white in her hand. He didn't know that she was wearing the wrath of Yahveh as her expression.

Jack emptied thirty rounds from his XM8 into the third demon who stalking Mark. The demon ignored Jack and didn't even seem to even notice the bullets. But when Laura came rushing towards him, he faced her with some trepidation. He had just realized that she had defeated both of his companions and he could see Yahshua in her eyes and he could feel the wrath of Yahveh pouring like fire off of her sword. He turned to flee into the spiritual dimension but he was confronted by two angels with their flashing swords blocking his way. Trapped, he turned to face the woman and realized that by turning away he had made a fatal error. She was already swinging her sword and he couldn't even get his blade around to block the strike. In the end it wouldn't have mattered because her sword flashed with the power of Yahveh and cut both him and his sword in half.

With the demise of the last demon Laura's armor and sword faded from sight. For the first time after fighting with her armor she didn't stagger or collapse. Her anger at the slaughter of unarmed men by the monsters hadn't dissipated. She could have bored holes in steel with her look. Jack wisely took one look at her face and decided that it would be best to let her relax for a little bit before drawing her attention. It reminded him a lot of the imperious look she'd had in Israel when she commanded him to pray for David Zahavy.

Closing her eyes, Laura prayed her thanks to a gracious Yahveh. Slowly the anger died out and compassion replaced it. She walked back to the six remaining prisoners and helped them to cover up their dead comrades. She saw Conrad sitting in the corner of the room with a mixture of anger and sadness on his face.

Jack walked over and took the six men to another part of the room where they couldn't see the bodies and had them sit in chairs and sofas instead of the floor. He could tell that they were cowed by the attack and they now knew the truth. Lutz sent those demons to kill everyone, including his own men. They weren't going to be any trouble for the team in the near future. Still, he had Sarah keep an eye on them just in case there was a die-hard fanatic in the group.

Laura stood there praying that Yahveh would look with mercy on the souls of the men represented by the covered bodies. She was playing the scene of the slaughter over in her mind. It was grievous and painful, but there was something important in the event that she was missing. Jack came up and put his arms around her. She folded into his embrace and laid her head on him. He kissed her forehead and said, "You saved the day my love. If you hadn't stopped them, everyone in here would be dead now."

For Laura it was a special moment that she would always remember. There was the rancid odor of evaporated demons, the coppery smell of blood, the foul smell of emptied bowels and all of it tinged with the smell of cordite from the firing. Both she and jack were dressed in complete battle dress, their harnesses rubbing together, and metal clanking against metal, grenades bouncing off of each other. Jack was holding his rifle in his right hand while he hugged her with his left. There was the smell of sweat on their clothes and the musky smell of humanity too. But even with ten other people moving around Laura felt closer to her husband than almost anytime in her life. She thought, "Ohh, how I love him Father!"

Laura nodded her head against his chest feeling her love for him as a physical ache. Sighing she said, "I know. That's why Yahveh gave me the ability and that armor. But, there is something odd here and it's bothering me. I can't quite put my finger on it yet."

CHAPTER ELEVEN

Mark, Conrad, and Sarah questioned the mercenaries about the activities at the castle and about Hermann Lutz. They weren't very much help. These had been the lower level troops. The leader of the group had been killed by the demon and even though demoralized, these men reacted to military protocol and understood that they were facing many years in a German prison if they didn't cooperate, and probably some time even if they did cooperate.

Laura stayed away from the questioning while she sought the direction of Yahveh's Spirit about the problem she was having with the attack of the demons. That demons could come into the physical realm and do damage was a given. That Lutz would kill his own men was predictable. Then an idea, which wasn't hers, came to her. It was the timing of the various attacks and defenses. Lutz knew when they were going to attack, how they were going to attack, and most important, that they would be victorious over Karl and the mercenaries. He had to have prepared the demons for the ultimate attack before the team even arrived at the castle! That was what had been bothering her.

She called the team together and explained what she felt the Lord had just revealed to her. It caused everyone to stop and think about the situation. Mark nodded and asked Laura, "Do you think it was his demon that told him about what was going to happen? I thought that Satan and his demons couldn't foresee the future."

Jack said, "They don't have Yahveh's ability to see the future, but they have watched mankind for thousands of years and can extrapolate a possible future very easily."

Laura shook her head, "No, I don't think that's what went on here. I think it was a human agency that advised Lutz of our plans. I think we have a mole somewhere." She looked at Conrad, "It's obviously not us and it's equally obvious that it's not you. Who else knew what we were doing tonight?"

Conrad Haufmann thought about that for a few minutes. "No more than six people and the aircraft crew. That makes it nine altogether outside of this group unless Lutz has found a way to monitor our conversations."

Mark smiled, "That is up my alley. I'll let you know in the next twenty-four hours if we have been bugged by a technical means."

Conrad added, "Yet, we still are behind Lutz and don't know where he is."

Jack smiled, "Don't worry; he'll make himself known pretty quickly."

Laura looked at her husband curiously, "What makes you say that?"

Jack looked at each of the others as he spoke. "We've obviously threatened him and I would suspect that with the elimination of the demons he probably now considers us his most important threat. He has to get rid of us quickly because we are definitely fouling up his plans for his latest move in the extermination of the Jewish race."

Mark agreed that the German would try to attack them again as soon as he could and if there was a source of information concerning them coming from inside Germany, then they needed to identify it and use it to their advantage.

Conrad suggested that they tell a different plan to groups of three that could possibly be a mole and see which information that Lutz acquired. If they could pare it down to three people then they could pretty well guess who was involved.

Mark said, "It's easier than that. I would rule out the plane crew because they had no clue as to where we were going until we were almost there. No time for planning to ambush us. Who are the other six people?"

Conrad said, "My superior, his superior and his aide, and the three man team that prepared our equipment."

Mark thought for a second, "Did you even tell the supply people where we were going?"

Conrad considered that. "No, you're right. I never told them about the castle I just spelled out the type of operation. But, couldn't Lutz have inferred that it was his castle that we were preparing to attack?"

Sarah nodded, "He could have, very easily. I think we need to test both groups, your superiors and the supply team."

Having agreed on a plan to smoke out any possible leaks Mark asked, "Okay, now what do we do with these guys? If you arrest them then the whole story has to come out about the demons and Lutz. I'm not sure that would be a good thing at this time."

Conrad looked at the dejected men. "That leaves us three possibilities. One, we could just kill them. Two, we could incarcerate them for the duration until we get Lutz. Or, three, we could deport them, essentially letting them go because of what they've been through."

The team voted on deportation from Germany and Sarah added that customs be given their pictures to prevent their return to Germany.

Conrad called for backup and the team stood down until they could resolve the occupation of the castle and the deportation of the mercenaries.

CHAPTER TWELVE

Hermann Lutz was not pleased. He made that point very clear to the demon he had made an arrangement with almost a century ago. "This is unacceptable! I expected the mercenaries to fail against this team, but you assured me that the demonic crew you sent would be more than sufficient to eliminate them. They not only failed miserably but have shown the Crossfire Team and Conrad Haufmann our alliance. What can we do now?"

The demon, Vorbleg, tolerated the tirade of the miserable human agent as he had done for decades. Vorbleg detested this frail form of damage to the human race. His history was much more violent. He knew that In Teutonic mythology, Nicor were malignant water monsters that drowned people. "Actually", Vorbleg thought, "We did a lot more than that." But his master had ordered him to stay in the background and to use this agent. As a demon he could preserve Lutz for hundreds of years and direct him in an effort to derail Yahveh's plan for His chosen people. They had almost achieved their goal in the middle of the last century but eventually failed again. Now, several recent efforts had been ruined by this accursed team of warriors that Yahveh had fielded against him and his efforts.

Vorbleg decided that they would have to attend to the elimination of this group before anything else could be set up. He spoke to the human, Lutz, and outlined a diabolical plan to ensnare and destroy the team and their allies.

Lutz listened in appreciation of the thoroughness of the concept. It could work, especially if there were egos in the Crossfire Team that he could manipulate. There was a definite possibility that they could destroy all of them this time. He actually laughed out loud. This caused several of his minions to glance at him in concern. Lutz never laughed.

Lutz made three phone calls and left for some personal supervision of this effort. Nothing was to be left to chance this time. This was overkill with a major emphasis on the "over" part. He liked it.

Twenty miles away, Jack and Laura had finally gotten everything cleaned up, oiled, and managed to get a shower for each of them. They fell into the army bunks so tired that they didn't even feel the thin mattresses or the wire springs below them. They were both asleep in less than a minute.

Laura prayed as she fell asleep that Yahveh would talk to them both this morning as they slept. She wanted Him to tell them what was on His heart as far as the Lutz situation went. She felt the peace and joy that she always felt when Yahveh's Spirit was communing with her spirit.

As she fell into the deepness of REM sleep, a glow began to make itself visible in her mind's eye. The glow increased until she saw the angel Rose floating in front of her. There were no words at first, just a detailed examination of Laura by the angel. Laura was sure that the angel was looking at things unknown to her as a human being.

Rose spoke to her in a dreamlike voice. It wasn't the dominant voice but the quiet voice of fellowship. "Laura, times are desperate and you need to manage the team so that you can destroy Hermann Lutz and his people. The team is losing focus because of the presence of the German policeman. Conrad is directing the team's efforts in a futile effort to find Lutz, rather than listening to the team as he should. Remember that you are the leader in spiritual matters and don't take sass from the others when you know what to do, do it. If the others can't keep up, that is their problem."

The angel moved to one side of Laura's vision. "You have been extending yourself greatly in the last several encounters and you have not been getting the credit you should. You need to demand more say in what the team is going to do or you will be used and forgotten. Remember; demand your rightful place as the leader of the team. It is you, not the weaker men that should be running the operation."

The angel faded from view and Laura continued to sleep.

Jack had a similar visit from Caleb with about the same message. He too fell deeper into sleep.

About five a.m. local time, Laura woke up and looked around the Spartan room. For some reason she was extremely dissatisfied with the accommodations. She knew that they weren't good enough for her. She looked over at her husband sleeping near her. "He shouldn't be sleeping when I can't" she thought. Reaching over she poked him until he woke up groggy. "What's the matter?" Jack asked her in the dim light.

Laura said, "I'm really upset by a bunch of things and you just lay there and sleep. I don't like this meager room, I don't like Conrad, and I don't . . ."

Laura had been listening to herself. "I think something is terribly wrong."

Jack had been thinking along the same lines. "This isn't like you, honey. What's going on?"

Laura thought about her emotions and her feelings. Was she right or was she wrong? If Rose told her . . ."Ahh", she said, "I think I had a visit last night from an imposter. I'm going to pray about this."

She got out of the bunk and on her knees on the cold tile floor. She started praying that Yahveh would grant her wisdom about this event. Then she just started praising the Father and letting her love for Him become the loudest thing in her mind.

After a while she felt the peace again and an alien thought came to her. She turned it over in her mind and decided that she needed to act on it at once. She thanked God for his guidance and got up. She told Jack, "Get the Connellys and Su Li. Also wake Conrad and bring them all to the conference room. She started changing into street clothing.

Jack dressed quickly and went to get the others. Ten minutes later they were gathered in the conference room. Laura looked at them and said, "The devil can disguise himself as an angel of light to fool humans. I believe that he did that last night. I can't remember all of it, but I woke up completely dissatisfied with our efforts, Conrad, our room, and just about anything else. I realized that I had been dreaming of Rose the angel. She told me stuff about how I wasn't being treated properly for my stature. This was a direct play to my ego to make me disrupt the team. Did any of you suddenly wake up unhappy with our mission besides me?"

There were five other heads nodding to that one. Jack said, "I'll call Gary."

CHAPTER THIRTEEN

Gary Eisenthal was doing his best to ignore two girls who had decided to either seduce him or drive him crazy, or both. They were sitting in the airport lounge seats directly across from him. They were both in their late teenage years and had, apparently, recently discovered that they could manipulate men with their bodies. They were both in short skirts and tight blouses and both had been given ample charms by Yahveh.

Gary wasn't interested and had tried to indicate that by studiously ignoring them. He wasn't a father as yet, but he would do whatever he could to educate any daughter Yahveh was gracious to give him about the dangers of using sex to get attention. These two young ladies didn't have a clue as to what would happen if they tried this on the wrong man or men in the wrong place.

All his ignoring them did was to challenge them to outdo each other and see which one could make him interested or embarrassed. He would of liked to have gotten up and moved to another seat but there were none. The place was packed with humanity waiting on different flights.

Gary had tried to just close his eyes and put his head back but the man behind him kept bouncing back in his seat and jarring his head. Pressure was building on him to do something. He had just about decided to get up and go over to the girls and take them up on their implied offer. He hoped that would embarrass them, but then, you never knew with this new generation. They might take him up on any offer he made and then he'd have to back out of it. About that time his cell phone started to ring.

Grateful for the distraction, Gary answered his phone. He had been waiting to hear Jack Malone's voice for a while. The Father had been giving him ample notice that he would be joining the Crossfire Team again soon.

Jack asked him where he was. Gary told him that he was in Paris on his way to Berlin. He got up, much to the girl's disappointment, and went to the ticket desk. He was able to check on his departure time.

Three hours after placing the call, Jack opened the door to their room saw the thin man standing there. Gary had a fading hairline of light brown hair and a moustache of the same color. You wouldn't notice the rest of the man because he was so average. A person would have to look closely to see that the one feature that really stood out were his eyes. He had an incredible flame of intelligence and intense passion that would have looked fanatical on a less self-affecting person. Gary had helped them greatly in their walk with God on several of their missions over the last two years.

Gary Eisenthal's mission in life was to use the power God had given him to free people from demonic possession. Through the Lord's power and His guidance and assistance Gary delivered them from bondage to walk freely with the Father. As he obeyed Yahveh and walked in faith he had been blessed with spiritual sight or discerning of spirits.

Gary took a look in the spiritual at Jack. "I see that you've picked up an unwelcome guest. We should definitely get rid of him."

Jack smiled at his friend and stuck his hand out, "Well, hello to you too."

Gary came in, shook Jack's hand, and greeted Laura. Settling down they discussed what they suspected was happening. Gary listened to them with his ears and to Yahveh's Spirit with his mind. After they were finished, he nodded. "Okay, let's take Laura first."

Gary already knew the demon's name was Besemael because Yahveh's Spirit had revealed it to him. Yahveh had also revealed that this was a lying spirit and an anti-Christ spirit."

Gary said, "In the name and the blood of the Lord Yahshua Messiah, who came in the flesh, I accuse you of trespassing on Yahshua. He told Saul of Tarsus, who was persecuting the members of the "Way" that he was persecuting Him. Laura belongs to Yahshua so you are trespassing against the Father and the Son. I ask God to command you to leave this woman and go directly to the abyss, in the name of Yahshua. You are permanently bound there until Yahshua judges you at the last day."

Besemael could not argue with the name of Yahshua and was gone.

Gary inquired of Yahveh's Spirit to see if there were more problems that needed attending to at this time. He got a negative reply.

He did the same thing with Jack. After he had finished, Jack asked Gary to stay with them for the duration of their conflict with Lutz.

Gary said, "Not only can I stay, I doubt that you can get rid of me now that I see the possibilities of what is happening here."

The other four members were cleaned of their riders as easily as the Malones. As Christians the demons couldn't possess them but could oppress them through the doorway of pride their ego had opened. Then the group sat down to try to understand what happened and to determine what they could do to prevent this type attack in the future.

Gary looked at the six people and gave them a synopsis of what had just been done. "From what I understand in the spirit, an ancient and powerful demon set himself to disrupt your team by pretending to be an angel of Yahveh and to sow dissent in each of you. It would seem that to make sure that you stayed angry, selfish, and irritated with the other people of the team he fixed demons to each of you to oppress you."

Mark asked, "What do you mean, "It would seem?"

Gary nodded in agreement with Mark's question. "You are dealing with a much higher level demonic host than any you have probably run into before. This demon has probably been around since Satan was thrown out of heaven. He has watched mankind for thousands of years and anything he does has many levels of clever deceit and misdirection in them. This action is a case in point. He deliberately ham-handed the angel imitation to make sure that you would realize that something was wrong and seek to get it made right. Next, you have to understand that he was willing to sacrifice Besemael and the others to gain something more important. What we need to do is ask of the Father what the devil is going on, so to speak."

As a group they praised God and sought his wisdom concerning the enemy action against them. Because they humbled themselves and sought His guidance, God favored them.

Gary understood quickly what was going on but he felt his role was to train the others to hear Yahveh rather than rely on him or any other human source. So he kept his counsel until, one-by-one the others came to the correct understanding of what God was telling them. It only took twenty minutes and that was a huge improvement over the last time he had watched them struggle to know the Lord's instruction and leading.

Jack looked at Laura and asked her, "If I'm understanding this correctly, this demon "Vorbleg" is attempting to make us over-confident and prideful. Enough that we will walk into a trap Lutz has ready for us right now. Is that what you understand?"

Laura nodded, "I have the same concept with the addition that "Vorbleg" is clever enough to know that we will figure this out, either on our own or with Yahveh's help. His misdirection is now at the second level. His true aim is still to eliminate us as an enemy to Lutz' operations, but he is very shrewd and calculating."

Mark said, "Not only that, but he has a pretty good idea of where we are weak and he will move to exploit those weaknesses."

Sarah laughed, "Duh! I felt the Father was telling me that this Vorbleg has dealt with groups like us before and one of them involved our friend here." She looked at Conrad. "Care to give us some background on your previous encounters with Vorbleg?"

Conrad made a rue face. "Guys, you are so far ahead of me on this thing, I'm not sure of whether I'm coming or going. You are all telling me that you're hearing from Yahveh the Elohim that created the universe? Personally? Each one of you? I'm not sure enough of my understanding of religion to know if that is possible or not."

Jack smiled, "Fair enough Conrad. We'll not try to convince you that Yahveh wants to help you and is just waiting for you to take the first step in His direction. What we will do is ask you to keep an open mind about what we're talking about and what you run into when you're with us."

Conrad could agree with that as he thought back to the demonic attack at the castle and Laura's display of armor and Holy Anger.

Su Li laughed a loud and joyful laugh. She settled down enough to speak, "Conrad, I was an atheist when I met these guys. It only took one demon that stepped into our world to shake me out of my ego trip. I was thinking I was in charge of my life. Up until that time I just couldn't see how Yahveh fit into my neat little worldview. Well, let me tell you that you are now on the fast track to spiritual awakening. You just watched Laura match swords with three very mean and ugly demons."

Su Li smiled to take the sting out of her words. "The way this is shaping up you're going see much more spiritual conflict in the next few days. You really ought to consider choosing the right side while you can. I know, I had to make that same choice several months ago and I wouldn't be here if I hadn't chosen correctly. Just think about it." She grinned and started to quietly laugh again at Conrad's naiveté which was so much like her own not too long ago.

CHAPTER FOURTEEN

Conrad thought about what he had just been through and what he knew he'd seen, even though it couldn't be real. At least, it shouldn't be real. He thought, "Ohh, this was going to be a painful reorientation." He looked at Sarah, "I did not know that a "demon" was involved when I ran as a part of an operation against Hermann Lutz six months ago."

He took a deep breath. The reason he was hesitating was because now he could understand what had happened then. It had never made sense before. "Let me tell you what happened." The memories rose up, fresh as brand new. All his friends and associates suckered into a trap and violently butchered without a chance. He would have been with them except for a fortuitous event.

Conrad looked up and started telling them of the operation from hell. He'd named it that but had never realized that he was simply being accurate, it had been from hell.

-----------------------******-----------------------

"We fielded a team of twenty men from our department." He went back in his memory and it was just as if he was there again. "We were the elite, the best of the best. We had been selected to work as a special strike team that focused on the biggest operations in the drug trade."

He took a drink of water and continued, "We had many successes. We had not had a loss of life nor a botched raid or even a faulty investigation. As a team we had become the shining light in the war on drugs in Germany. Well, the officials and the public took note of our operations, but, so did the kingpins of the drug operations. Just like now, we had become the primary focus of people who wanted us out of the way."

Conrad shook his head in regret. "But, we thought that we were special and unbeatable." He sat up and thought about that for a few seconds. "Very much like I was feeling this morning before Gary "delivered" me." He became very animated, smacking one fist into the other. "I'll bet the farm that this Lutz demon pumped up our pride so that we became careless!"

Sitting back down the German policeman continued the story. "We had been investigating a group of Neo-Nazis that had gotten rich by selling drugs wholesale to dealers. We didn't even stop to wonder how we had gotten the Intel about this group and the "big" drop they were going to get that Saturday night. Like normal we set up all the backup groups and evacuated the area of non-combatants before the raid. We planned to catch them with the goods." He expressed his bitterness by his facial expressions. "We were so gullible. Anyway, as we prepared to penetrate the outer fence, I stepped on a spike that slid inside my boot and poked me in the calf hard enough that my boot was filling with blood. The Captain looked at it and sent me back to a medic to have it cleaned up. I told him I would be only a minute and I'd be back for the raid."

The young man sat there somewhat dejected by the memories. "The medic took my boot off and cleaned up the wound. He said it was going to need stitches and that my police work was finished for the whole weekend. I complained and objected and demanded to be allowed to go back to my unit. It didn't matter what I said. As the medic sewed my leg up I heard the sound of gunfire. The raid had gone ahead on schedule. Then, there were the most chilling screams I'd ever heard. Worse yet, I recognized some of the people screaming. That was my unit! My friends were screaming and dying!. The medic ran out to help and I grabbed a bandage and wrapped my leg and put my boot on over it. It hurt like hell but I didn't really notice it."

Tears formed in his eyes as he continued to relate the events of that fatal night. "I grabbed my rifle and hobbled as quickly as I could to the warehouse. There were Klieg lights everywhere and policemen searching for the drug runners and Neo-Nazis. I wandered through the scene in shock and horror. All nineteen of the best-of-the-best were lying on the floor of the warehouse. Every one of them was dead with looks of horror on their faces. No one could understand what had happened. All the rounds fired had been from their guns. But, the men had been ripped in half, hacked to death. I knew every one of them. It must have been too much for my mind because I woke up three days later in a military hospital." He wiped the tears from his eyes. "The government buried the news of the deaths and there never was an explanation of what had happened to them.

----------------------******----------------------

Now, I know what happened." He got up and walked over to Laura. He bent over and took her hands in his. Looking deeply into her eyes he bared his soul and his heart. "Frau Malone, I am deeply in your debt. I have no words to express my gratitude to you for destroying those nightmares last night. I feel in my heart that it was those same demons that killed my friends, slaughtered them without mercy. You have redeemed them and made their killers pay the price. I thank you from the bottom of my heart and shall remember your efforts for the rest of my life." He clicked his heels together and bowed deeply to her.

Laura nodded her head in acceptance of his gratitude. She sent a prayer to Yahveh that the Holy Spirit would give this man a revelation of the truth about the Messiah so he would be in peace and his spirit would be saved.

CHAPTER FIFTEEN

Mark knew what it was like to lose comrades in arms and he felt sympathy for Conrad. "I'm very sorry that happened to your friends."

Conrad nodded in thanks for the unspoken understanding from Mark. "At least those demons have been destroyed." He evidenced a sense of relief.

Laura looked sadly at the policeman. "Conrad, Yahveh allowed us to deal with those three demons. They probably were the ones that killed your team, but, you need to understand that there are millions of other demons still available out there. Many of them are far worse than the ones you've seen. The only protection any of us have against their tricks or violence is a loving God who is our protection." Conrad accepted the news of the never ending war with stoicism. "I'll have to think about that. Later, I'd also like to talk alone with Su Li if I could."

Gary Eisenthal said, "Conrad, if I understood your story correctly, you feel, with what you now know that perhaps your troop was pushed to pride, to a feeling of being invincible?" When Conrad nodded, Gary went on. "So this Vorbleg/Lutz entity got them feeling cocky and then fed them false information that led them into a trap where the demons killed them, right?"

Again Conrad nodded. Gary thought about that for a second. "Okay then, I would assume that a smart demon wouldn't try the exact same thing twice in a row. Also, we're sure that Vorbleg is attempting to throw us another curve by clumsily attempting to cause dissension in the team. This was an activity which he wanted us to catch on to, as we did. I'm going to pray about this but I assume that he wants us to think we've got him figured out and then he will throw us a sudden, severe curve. This will be designed to make us react suddenly, and possibly foolishly, allowing him to trap us and eliminate us. We need to dictate this operation rather than trying to dance to whatever tune he wants to give us. Mark, you know the drill, "pre-emptive strike".

Mark nodded his agreement with the spiritual guru of their group. "I think we'll short-circuit his plans when we can determine his base of operation and strike it while he's still trying to set us up."

Everyone except Conrad knew exactly what Mark was leading up to with that comment.

Laura spoke up. "Conrad. I believe that the Creator of the Universe plans to use you in His war with Satan. That, I believe, is why you were spared when your team was destroyed. You need to pray to God and see what plans He has for you."

Conrad stood there stunned at the revelation of his injury that prevented him from being part of the assault that night.

Laura looked around and said, "Let's all pray that Rose or Caleb will show us the way.

Sarah got a DVD player and put on a praise and worship disc. As the beautiful music filled the conference room each person sought God. Singing and praising God was exactly what they needed to do at that time because God inhabits the praises of His people. As the worship deepened it filled Sarah with so much love for the Father she got up and started to dance in time to the praise music. God's Spirit moved her to express her love for Yahshua and the Father and she started singing in Hebrew. Even though only Mark knew Hebrew like Sarah, the spirit moved them to join her. Soon the entire team was dancing and praising God in a wonderful harmony. Only Conrad still sat in his chair, moved more than he had ever been by church services as he watched these hardened soldiers in such joyful worship.

This expression of love rose up before the Father as beautiful incense and he was pleased, not only in the praise and worship in the language of His chosen people, but the fact that the team had willingly turned to him rather than rely on their own skills or pride to combat Vorbleg. He dispatched angels to encourage and guide the efforts of this small group of believing warriors.

As they sang and danced before God, a bright glow at the end of the conference room threw dark shadows of the people against the walls.

Jack looked and saw Caleb and three other angels dancing and singing with them. The song took on a heavenly richness and became a glorious sound. The dancing and singing reached a crescendo and gently settled into a silence with the team standing and facing the four angels. The singing and enthusiasm had empowered the angels and the glory of God that shone around them was so bright the lights in the ceiling looked dim in comparison. The beautiful glow spread throughout the room.

Caleb greeted the team, "Take off your boots for the place where you stand is Holy to the Most High." Everyone became barefoot in a hurry. Caleb intoned, "The Lord is pleased with you and your devotion. He has sent us to give you insight and guidance as you asked." His voice was soft but it was commanding and one could hear tones and harmonics that aren't present in normal human speech.

Gary Eisenthal was thrilled beyond words. He just stared wide-eyed at Yahveh's messengers in awe and respect. Laura glanced at Gary and decided it was up to her to place their needs in front of Yahveh. She stepped forward and said, "Praise and worship to Yahveh and Yahshua. We, as fellow workers in the service of Yahveh, salute Yahveh's warriors. We earnestly ask for Yahveh's guidance and His protection in the battle with the evil one's emissary, Vorbleg."

Caleb and the other angels were pleased by Laura's words. Caleb smiled and raised his arms. "All praise and glory to the Lord Yahshua and to the Most High Yahveh. As to Vorbleg, you must be ever on guard against this twisted, fallen angel. He is a foe of great age and slyness and is totally evil. Your victory over him will take all of your courage and strength. He will avoid capture, destruction, or confinement until your abilities match his. Each one of you will be forced to choose between life and death in your combat with him."

Caleb and the other angels spread out their arms in an all-encompassing gesture and power flowed from them into the people in the room. At the touch of the supernatural power Conrad fainted. The rest felt a great joy and sharpening of their senses. Then there was a sweet agony throughout their bodies that bordered on pain. This lasted for what seemed days until it was replaced by an awesome feeling of peace and strength.

Laura got a word of knowledge from the Father that explained the pain. The energy released by His messengers had not only added to their capabilities and empowered them to confront Vorbleg but had also burned out any sin weaknesses they had that Vorbleg could access and affect them.

Caleb looked at the small group and marveled. He had addressed thousands before but had never seen a group so totally devoted to Yahveh at any expense as these people. The humbling thing was that none of them had to be here for this battle. They weren't forced by circumstance to fight, they each choose to be obedient to Yahveh's call and put their very lives on the line. This amazed the angels. "You have been given special new capabilities by the almighty to combat this new evil that has been generated during the last days. This power will allow you to meet Vorbleg's thrusts and defeat them during battle. Remember! *The Lord has given you authority to trample on snakes and scorpions and to overcome all the power of the enemy; nothing will harm you. However, do not rejoice that the spirits submit to you, but rejoice that your names are written in the Lamb's Book of Life.*"

Jack asked Caleb, "How shall we proceed?"

Caleb seemed to look at something far away and then said, "You have a two-fold mission this time. One is still the original requirement to destroy Vorbleg and his agent. A new development has arisen. An agent of the evil one has just acquired twenty packages of death from one of the new republics. These in themselves are not dangerous but they will lead to a much worse evil in recompense. The groups you are involved with are the go-betweens for these transactions but the power that wants them is far from here. Remember the reason you came to this country. That is your answer to both of these dangers. May the peace of Yahveh be ever with you."

The angels faded away and the room seemed to almost darken into night until everyone's eyes adjusted to the lesser light of the overheads.

CHAPTER SIXTEEN

Su Li and Gary helped a groggy Conrad up into a seat. He was obviously befuddled and at a loss for the moment. Mark looked at Jack as they sat down. "And why did we come here?"

Jack thought for a few seconds. "Because we were told that Hermann Lutz was here and working with the Neo-Nazis."

Mark smiled, "If that was guidance it was pretty meager."

Laura laughed, "What did you want Caleb to do? Pull out a map of Berlin and point at it and say, "Lutz is here?" That wouldn't be any good in the next twenty minutes. What Yahveh has given us is a dynamic moving target that will be as true tomorrow as it is today. Lutz is definitely on the move but if he's with a particular Neo-Nazi group then we can track him and throw him off his time table for killing us and whatever this new thing is."

Jack looked at Mark and an understanding passed between them unspoken. Jack knew that they had to handle the Lutz problem before they tackled the new "packages of death" scenario.

Conrad cleared his throat and got everyone's attention. He asked if he could talk to Jack and Laura alone for a little while. The others took a break and went to find some food for everyone.

When they were alone, Conrad shook his head and smiled at the couple. "You know something? I've seen just about every side of mankind for the last ten years. Especially the dark, slimy, evil side represented by greed and lust. But then, these are the people and organizations that we investigate, hunt down, and jail. I had reached the point of believing that this caliber of people represented the world and that people like myself are a small minority and fighting almost alone against the rest of the vile world."

Laura was listening to Conrad's words and to the urging of God's Spirit at the same time. "What changed that?"

Conrad sat back and closed his eyes. In his mind's eye he recalled the incredibly powerful presence that had touched him when the angels opened their arms. He had felt more power than there was in the sun but it was a power of love. Such love transcended all things in life and reduced the evil he had known to its proper perspective, it was simply a harmful nuisance that was being tolerated for the time being as Yahveh was preparing His people to rule with him.

In that instant, Conrad Haufmann had been in the presence of Yahshua the Messiah, the first born Son of the living Father of the universe. Even though he felt inferior and worthless as he expected he would, he unexpectedly felt complete love and total acceptance, toleration and forgiveness. It was an entire system of order and strength based on an overwhelming love of God for the people of earth. That instant had changed him physically as well as spiritually. The creeping invasion of evil power that had been eating at him had been totally banished from his life. It couldn't exist in the tremendously honest light flowing from the love of Yahshua and Yahveh. Conrad knew he would never forget the one word that he heard from Yahshua while he felt a joy and excitement about being alive that he hadn't known since he was a child. The word was "Come".

He opened much wiser eyes and asked the Malones, "How can I respond to Yahshua's invitation to "Come"?"

Jack smiled, "It's quite simple really. Yahshua stands at the door knocking. To those who willingly open the door He will come in and have fellowship with them."

Laura and Jack explained the need for Conrad to be right in his heart concerning a commitment to Yahshua. He easily assured them that there was nothing else in the world that mattered. They led him in the sinner's prayer and he opened the door to his heart for the love of Yahshua.

Conrad knew the second that he had willingly accepted the Father through the Son that they were one in spirit. His joy was complete and the tears of happiness flowed for all three of them. Another warrior had joined the Kingdom of Yahveh to gladly do Yahveh's work. Laura prayed a prayer of protection for Conrad and Jack told Conrad they would help him get baptized in the name of Yahshua. Conrad assured them that was his next order of business right after getting the information they needed to find Lutz.

Jack opened the door and called the others into the conference room. It was obvious that a smiling Conrad had joined them in the love of the Father. Su Li pointed her finger at him and said, "See, See! I told you that you can't stay around these people for more than one or two demon or angel demonstrations before you realize that you need Yahveh." Everyone laughed with her on that one.

Conrad also agreed with the slim Asian woman. "I had no idea how right you were. Anyway, let me call two of my people here. They are specialists on the Neo-Nazis and if there is any one who'll know what group that Lutz is operating with, it will be these guys."

Conrad had been accurate in his evaluation of the two men. They had their fingers on the pulse of the Neo-Nazi movements in Germany. They quickly eliminated all but two groups, both of which operated out of Berlin. Their estimation was that Lutz was using or cooperating with both groups.

Mark looked at the profiles of the individuals and the organizations and quickly saw the signs of Lutz' organizational skill. These two groups were compartmentalized and efficient in their efforts. They weren't the type to burn a Jewish temple or to scream in the streets about Aryan purity. They had marketing capabilities, lawyers, and moved in the higher strata of German politics. No rabble here, just smooth, slick leaders with followers that were fanatical to the cause. It reminded Mark of the Third Reich. This made sense, because of their devotion to the same evil deity that had directed Hitler and his minions.

Mark and Sarah discussed tactics with Conrad and his two investigators. Then they called the rest of the Crossfire Team together. Mark outlined their next moves. "We need to isolate Lutz' location and try to eliminate him. He is the one unifying force for these two groups and the money and power behind them. We feel that if we go outside the present conflict we can drop off his radar and come at him from an unexpected direction."

Sarah jumped into the discussion. "But, we know how smart he really is, and we need to move up to his level of cleverness if we are going to outsmart him. We have no doubt that he will have anticipated our change of tactics. So, we are going to do something that is so totally out of character that he would never expect us to do it."

Gary Eisenthal thought to himself, "Oh boy! This should be interesting."

CHAPTER SEVENTEEN

Three hours later Conrad Haufmann smiled a small smile to himself as he walked into the operations room for his Tactical Police unit and looked around. He knew what the Crossfire Team was doing and Lutz had no idea of what was going to descend on his little operation. Spotting the communications specialist, he walked over to him and handed him a message to be sent in a cryptographic form.

The man took the message and entered it into the Crypto machine. The computer performed nine different alterations to the message so that it would be indecipherable to anyone without the same algorithms on their computer. He sent the message immediately.

The signals man at Lutz' new headquarters intercepted the message and ran it through his computer which had exactly the same algorithms as the Tactical Police computer. The algorithms had been provided by an associate within the police last week. He took the decoded message to Herr Lutz and left immediately.

Lutz read the message twice and sat back in communion with his friend. The demon Vorbleg spoke to Lutz' mind. "You convinced them that they couldn't compete with you. They ran home with their tails between their legs."

Lutz picked up the telephone and punched in a number. He let it ring three times and hung up. Several minutes later his phone rang. He answered and heard, "Ja Mein Herr".

Lutz asked the only important question. "Did the Crossfire team leave Germany?"

"JA, Mein Herr, they left two hours ago and flew from the airport for the United States. Herr Haufmann is back with his unit again."

Lutz said, "Good" and hung up. Dismissing the American team he focused on how he could now begin the operation he had been contemplating for quite a while. This would involve alienating the nation of Germany from the nation of Israel as the first step of igniting a real war between the two countries.

The man who had just hung up from talking to Lutz found himself staring down the barrel of an automatic pistol as two other officers frisked him and removed his weapons. He wanted to argue and deny but Conrad Haufmann walked up to him and switched on a micro recorder. He heard his conversation with Lutz clearly. He looked for mercy from his previous friends and brother officers. He couldn't see any. They led him away to a lock up and eventually he died of cancer in prison where he had been given a life sentence without parole for his part in the slaughter of Conrad's old strike team.

Conrad worked with the electronics genius of their department. After two more hours they had a large selection of words and sentences for their previous friend. Conrad redialed the number and Lutz came on immediately. The specialist touched his controls and the newly departed ex-officer spoke. "Conrad and his new team will be at the Jewish Cemetery near the Brandenburg Gate at eleven o'clock tonight. They are hunting Neo-Nazis. There will be eight of them in a black van." The specialist hung up which is what the mole would have done.

Lutz sat back and thought about this opportunity. Vorbleg was not inclined to have more of his kind killed. But, with the American woman and her sword gone it would be as before. Lutz spoke to the air but knew the demon heard every word. "This would be a very good demoralizing demonstration of our power. If we could eliminate Haufmann on the same day we drove the Americans away it would be a coup."

The thought came back to him. "You arranged for the castle defense. You said that it would be easy. We do not like losing. You want this coup, you do it yourself."

Lutz shrugged, "No matter. I will have the Bortz brothers handle it. Not even they can mess this up. The thought was impressed on his mind. "If it were me, I wouldn't bet my existence on those buffoons. See to it yourself!"

Lutz thought about that for a few seconds. He had noticed that he was beginning to tire of the constant put-downs and nagging done by Vorbleg since the current series of failures. He also noticed that he was feeling tired all the time. This would be expected in someone over one hundred years old. Still, he would continue the partnership, for a while longer. Like all humans that engage in commerce with the spiritual plane without Yahveh, Lutz felt he knew more and was truly superior to the demons. Even the dumbest demon laughed behind Lutz's back because they were far more powerful and smarter than Lutz.

Lutz dialed a number and told the man that answered that they were going out tonight at ten p.m. and there would be eight dates they needed to handle. He hung up and got out the 9mm German Luger he had carried since the nineteen forties. Checking the magazine and that there was a round in the chamber he put the gun into its holster under his arm and went back to business. At precisely nine fifty-eight he walked out the door to meet the car.

For some reason he noticed that the evening was beautiful. The temperature was in the low seventies, the breeze was light and out of the west, and the parking lights of the cars seemed almost festive. He realized that it had been far too many years since any of that had any meaning for him. As he walked across the street to the waiting Mercedes he noted that they had brought four cars with six men in each one this time. "Good." He thought to himself.

The cars rolled out and headed for the Brandenburg Gate area. Lutz, sitting in the back of the first car, watched their progress with interest. It was like he had reached some kind of watershed event in his life. His senses knew something and it was letting him experience more than normal. He guessed it was because with the death of Haufmann there would be finality to the war the two of them had waged for the last ten years.

CHAPTER EIGHTEEN

At this time of night the cemetery area was deserted. Homeowners in the area were safely in bed with the doors barred. The narrow streets gleamed with reflected light off of the water from an earlier washing. Hermann Lutz set his trap up carefully, fully aware of the capabilities of the crack anti-terrorist team represented by the Tactical Police. Eight snipers, who would also act as lookouts were already in place. The target for the police was a small band of Neo-Nazis who held monthly meetings in a parking lot next to the cemetery. Lutz was familiar with their routine, and although he had nothing to do with their disorganized group, they would do just fine as bait.

By ten minutes of eleven everyone was nervously waiting when one of the snipers spotted a black van moving towards their position. Lutz waited in his car to watch the action from a safe distance. The lights of the van illuminated the street leading to the parking lot. The strike was set to go when the police exited the van.

The van stopped a half a block from the parking lot where the small band of counter-culture terrorist wannabes were talking each other up. The doors opened on the van and eight members of the Tactical Police got out.

Lutz waited for the attack but it didn't come. He keyed his radio but there was no answer. He didn't understand it. Eight snipers and eighteen men and not a sign of any of them.

Instead of heading for the parking lot, the eight man squad of police turned and walked over to the car that Hermann Lutz was in. Conrad Haufmann tapped on the window next to the older man. Lutz pushed the button and lowered the window. There really was no reason to play a cat-and-mouse game with the policeman. They both knew what was going on. Lutz was furious because he had been outsmarted but he was so tired he didn't really care. "JA, Herr Haufmann, what do you want?"

Conrad smiled, "Herr Lutz, would you please exit the vehicle?"

Lutz opened the door and stepped out. Shutting the door he opened his coat so that Conrad could take his handgun. One of the other police frisked him anyway. Then they handcuffed him and led him to the van. Before he got in, Lutz turned to the officer and asked him what he was being arrested for.

Conrad cited several anti-terrorist laws and a minor infraction of carrying a loaded firearm without a permit within the city limits. Lutz nodded, while at the same time he said to Vorbleg in his mind, "Well, are you going to allow them to question me and hold me?"

Vorbleg's answer was a laugh and one word. "Watch."

There was a baleful yellowish-red glow that appeared next to the van and Vorbleg himself stepped into the physical world. Vorbleg was way past ugly in human terms. He was terribly grotesque in a very evil way. He stood about seven feet tall with very powerful arms and legs and yellowish claws that matched the fangs in his mouth. He moved quickly towards Lutz to remove him from the police custody when he felt a threat. Stopping, he turned to his left and faced the woman from the Crossfire Team with her armor and sword flaming with the power of Yahveh. Without having to check, Vorbleg was certain there would be many angels of Yahveh to prevent his escape back into the spiritual world. So, he had to destroy the woman, rescue his tool, Lutz, and then battle his way out of this world.

Before he could accomplish any of these things he saw a man step up beside the woman and in his right hand was a pearlescent spear with a shining tip. The man threw it right at Vorbleg's chest. Vorbleg was impressed because it was an excellent throw. A large black shield appeared on Vorbleg's left arm. It was solid obsidian stone over one foot thick. He raised the shield just as the spear got to him. To his amazement the spear flashed through the stone shield and into his body. As it pierced his heart, the diamond head of the spear exploded into flames of Yahveh's wrath. The flames consumed the demon totally.

Lutz watched all this with amazement. He realized that there was a small amount of satisfaction in getting to watch the irritating demon die. But the overriding question in his mind was, "What will happen to me now?"

As Vorbleg dissolved in the flames, the demon's protection for Hermann Lutz dissolved with him. Like the portrait of Dorian Gray, all of Hermann Lutz' year's fell on him along with all the infirmities and illnesses he had never received until now. The shock and degradation was too much for his body and he died where he stood as the demon that had controlled him vaporized.

Conrad Haufmann walked over and looked at the dried-out desiccated husk of a body that was all that remained of Hermann Lutz. All he could feel was pity and sadness that the enemy had stolen another human being. He prayed his gratefulness to God for their victory. Then he turned to Jack and Laura Malone and said, "I don't know how to thank you for everything you've done since you've been here. I know I will miss you."

Laura, in her normal clothing, hugged him and told him, "Thank you, for all the help you've been. Maybe this will keep the local rabble from being so well organized, at least for now."

Jack smiled at his new friend and then hugged him. "If you need us, you know how to reach us."

As they left the scene, Jack told Laura, "I think God would be pleased that it worked out the way it did."

Laura nodded and took Jack's hand. "I especially liked the part where we used Lutz's own tactics against him."

Jack thought about the set up. It had been the leading of God that let them know that Lutz and Vorbleg would be there tonight. The rest was easy because they were obedient and willing to pray for guidance and wisdom rather than doing it in their own strength.

The couple walked up the street towards the van where Mark and Sarah were and Laura raised her arms in a victory "V". The other couple celebrated with them. Su Li started the van and headed for the airport.

CHAPTER NINETEEN

Seven hours later Laura, Jack, and Mark were onboard the Citation X as it flew across the Atlantic Ocean discussing the events in Germany with Gary. Sarah was at the controls while Su Li taught her navigation and communications.

Laura was uneasy in her spirit but couldn't identify what the problem was. She hadn't gotten any answer to her prayers concerning the problem either.

Sarah came back from the cockpit and sat down. She had a serious look on her face and everyone stopped talking and paid attention to her. She shook her head and said, "Whatever it is, I didn't do it."

Mark had a quizzical expression on his face. "Didn't do what, spylady?"

Sarah pointed at the cockpit. "We've got some kind of problem with the fuel supply to the engines and we're losing power. We've dropped four thousand feet already and Su Li is worried." Sarah looked at the map she'd brought back with her. "Su Li is trying to raise anybody on the radio but all we get is static, same for the satellite communications link. We're halfway across the Atlantic and there isn't any place to land. We're quickly running out of options."

Laura spoke up. "It's an attack by the enemy. They've interrupted our fuel somehow." Laura continued to pray while the others discussed the few options they had left. She felt the closeness of the God's Spirit and earnestly sought Yahveh for a solution to the problem. All she got back was a feeling of peace and love.

Mark went up to the cockpit and slid into the co-pilot's seat. He glanced over at Su Li and could tell she felt shame about the problem, as if it was her fault. He reached over and patted her on the arm. "Don't fret about this; it has nothing to do with your preflight or your piloting. We've been set up by something they've done to our fuel. Laura saw that much.

Su Li felt relieved that everyone wasn't blaming her for the impending loss of their aircraft. She asked Mark, "What do you think we should do? I'm trying to stretch every mile I can out of our altitude, but to be honest, I don't know why. Even if I can get an extra hundred miles we still don't have anywhere to go. We're still eight hundred miles from the first landing field and we can't get more than two hundred as it is. Plus the fuel system seems to continue to degrade. All communications have failed completely. I can't even advise anyone where we're going down at, let alone get help, to our location."

Mark grinned at her. "Don't go all pessimistic on me now. We're still in the air and even if we end up in the water, remember that I was a Navy SEAL. We can do a lot with what we've got on-board this plane. Just do your best and let me know when we're about five minutes from splash-down, okay?"

Su Li nodded and kept trying to get more lift out of the wings.

Mark came back to find everyone praying. He sat down quietly and joined them. The prayer continued for many long minutes while Mark could feel the plane dropping lower in the air.

Gary sat up suddenly and said, "There's a place to land directly off our right side!"

Laura added, "It's about twenty miles ahead. Tell Su Li that she can land on the beach of the island, but, on the other side from where we are. It's very important that we use the north beach and not the south one, even though it will look like its okay."

Mark got up and stepped into the cockpit and sat down again. This time he strapped in and put on the headset. Speaking on the intercom to Su Li he told her about the island and the north beach. She nodded and began a slow bank to the right which caused the plane to lose more altitude. Mark could see the moon on the water now and was surprised that they were already so low.

Seeing a faint blur on the horizon he pointed it out to Su Li, She turned the aircraft so that it lined up with the blur and put the moonlight behind it from their position. It was a solid object. Su Li still had the plane in its smoothest form, trying to pull every foot she could out of what was not much more than a glide.

She looked over at Mark, "We're going to have only one shot at landing and it has to count. Do you want to help me bring it in?"

Mark was watching the island as it grew in the night. "That's an affirmative, Su Li. You drive and I'll support you."

Su Li showed him the controls he would have to operate for them. Even though it had looked like they would never get there from far away, now the island seemed to be rushing at them. Su Li was good; she waited until the right time to run out the flaps for more lift and to have Mark lower the landing gear. The aircraft begin to drop quickly as it came over the end of the island. Seeing Mark's concerned look at the length of the beach ahead of them she said, "Relax, we're at 30,000 lbs weight and only need 3200 feet to land this plane on concrete. We're going to get some drag out of the sand and that will slow us down to where we only need roughly a half a mile."

She fed more power to the engines which struggled mightily to produce sufficient thrust using the reduced amount of fuel they were getting. It wasn't much of a push but it was enough to get the plane to the end of the white sand beach before the wheels touched down. Su Li flipped up the flaps to eliminate all lift and shut down the engines because there wouldn't be much counter braking available. She threw the circuit breakers to prevent fire in the event of a crash. With Mark's help she kept the Citation X on a more-or-less straight run down the beach. The sand wasn't as much help in braking the plane as she thought so she started using the wheel brakes. They had used up most of the beach by the time she started breathing again.

The plane was still moving when Su Li turned it to the left and away from the water. She didn't know if it was at high tide or low tide and she didn't want the water to come up on the plane later. She managed to get the plane completely reversed on the beach before she ran out of momentum. Running the shutdown checklist with Mark she shut the plane down and then undid her belt and took off her headset.

Mark got up and lifted the smaller woman out of the pilot's seat. He hugged her and told her that was the best dead-stick landing he'd ever seen. They went back into the main cabin where the battery lights were on. She bowed in response to the clapping.

CHAPTER TWENTY

Mark went back to the cockpit and reset the communications breaker. Then he methodically checked every search and rescue frequency and the satellite link. They were all solid static across the bands. Turning the radios off, he thought for a few minutes. He got up and went to a panel above the engineer's station. Reaching in he pulled out the portable emergency radio. He turned it on and keyed the microphone. Releasing the push-to-talk button he listened. He was able to hear some radio traffic but at a great distance. Nothing the portable radio could reach anyway. If an aircraft were to pass directly overhead, then the radio could conceivably reach it.

He walked back out to the others and announced his findings. "Apparently, whoever sabotaged our fuel also set our radios on the fritz too. I think it was done in Germany with some kind of delay built in to catch us over the Atlantic with no hope of rescue. I guess they didn't count on this island or on Su Li's superb skill as a pilot."

Su Li smiled and thought "If they only knew how close it really was." She could imagine a bunch of angels holding up the wings until the plane reached the island.

Mark got a large flashlight out of the supplies closet and strapped on his sidearm. "I'm going out and check the area and the plane."

Jack got up, "I'm going with you." He got another flashlight and his gun.

After putting down the stairs and reaching the sand, Jack looked at Mark, "What are you really looking for?"

Mark started an inspection of the aircraft on the outside, including the wheel wells and the cargo area. "I am beginning to believe that this particular someone who doesn't like us is probably smart enough to have added insurance in the event we didn't all go down to a watery grave." He was looking in the port wheel well as he was talking.

A petite black-haired head popped up next to him and Su Li said, "Then perhaps you should remove that gray box up there by the front panel." She pointed at a box about the size of a desktop computer monitor.

He looked at the Asian pilot and said, "Good call. I would have missed that. I was looking for something much smaller." He reached for the box when Jack's hand stopped his motion.

Jack simply said, "Booby trapped?"

Mark let out a snort of exasperation. "I think I'd better go back in before I kill us all."

Jack laughed, "That's what makes us such a good team. If one of us doesn't think of the right thing, someone else will. How do we approach this thing in the event they put a tamper switch on it?"

Mark looked at the innocuous box and said, "Carefully. Su Li, could you get my backpack for me?"

She held it up, "You mean this one?"

Mark smiled, took it and opened it up. "Yep, this is the one all right." He took a small meter out of it and turned it on. Taking a small probe he carefully ran it around the box. A red mini LED flashed at him. "It's wired all right. Pulling out an inspection mirror, similar to one a dentist would use, he used his flashlight and the mirror and checked around the flat side of the box which was against the bulkhead. There were no wires or contacts visible. He backed away from the device and thought. "Okay, it's apparently held to the bulkhead by a magnet which is inside the box. That means that if we try to remove the box and break the magnetic bond, boom!"

Jack had never played with anything like this before. "What do we do?"

Mark smiled in the dim light, "We get inventive." He rummaged around in his backpack and brought out a small welding torch not much bigger than his hand.

Su Li looked at him, "You aren't planning to cut away the bulkhead are you?"

Mark shook his head, "No. We're going to do something much more direct and dangerous." He fired up the torch and started cutting the back panel off of the box. He made four quick passes because the box was plastic and not metal. The tiny torch cut through it like a hot knife through butter. He turned off the torch while still holding the back panel on the box with his left hand. Getting Su Li to shine the light so that it illuminated the box, Mark inspected inside the cut as best he could with his mirror. Then he carefully withdrew the panel slowly about a half an inch. Checking it again with the mirror he pulled the panel away and dropped it on the beach. Then he took the light and investigated what was inside the box. When he finished that he went a couple of yards away from the wheel well and sat down on the beach, facing the water and the breakers rolling into the shore.

Su Li looked at Jack who shrugged his shoulders. Jack went over and sat down next to Mark. "What did you find?"

Mark was silent for a few seconds. Then he turned to Jack and Su Li, "I found that we are supposed to be dead already and that if Yahveh didn't love us we would be."

Seeing the question on Jack's face he continued. "That is a Russian military bomb setup. It has four triggers and about twenty pounds of Sematex explosive in it. That's why the box is so big. The Russians were never the ones to miniaturize anything. It can be triggered by a button, a radio signal, an altitude setting, or a timer."

Jack sat silently waiting for the rest of the story.

Mark shook his head. "The people that set that up weren't amateurs. They set the altitude switch to detonate the bomb if we descended below one thousand feet. They set the timer to go off about an hour ago. I wouldn't doubt that they have somebody following us and broadcasting the proper signal to blow us up if the other triggers don't do it first."

Jack asked quietly, "Then, why are we still alive?"

Mark laughed grimly, "We shouldn't be. The timer clock has reached zero and the altitude switch closed when we went below one thousand feet. Neither caused the explosion and the only thing that explains that is that Yahveh stopped it. Nothing else figures. I'd bet if we had pulled the box off the bulkhead it wouldn't of gone off then either."He got up and called Su Li. "Listen, I want you to check the rest of the plane for any more surprises while I disarm this one. Jack, I want you to find the manuals on the fuel system and let's start seeing if we can fix that problem. I don't think they tainted the fuel like we thought. It is probably a shut-off switch added to the fuel supply.

Look for a place where both engines would be affected on the flow charts. Tomorrow we will see if we're right."

Within the hour, Mark had the "boom" box off of the plane and disarmed. Su Li had completed her inspection and declared the rest of the plane clean. Jack pointed out three places where both engines could be affected by a fuel shut-off. Mark called it a night and everyone sacked out.

The next morning Jack woke to a banging noise on the top of the Citation X's fuselage. Stepping outside he found Mark and Su Li hard at work covering the aircraft with a tarp and palm fronds. "What are you doing? Don't you want anyone to find us?"

Mark shouted back, "No, I don't want anyone to find us. The only people that will be looking will be the bad guys and we don't want them to find us, now do we?"

Jack had to agree with that.

CHAPTER TWENTY-ONE

After hiding the aircraft from aerial view, they examined the fuel system. It only took them an hour to find and disable the shutoff valve which had been inserted into the engine fuel system. Since the shutoff had replaced a piece of the fuel line, they rigged the deactivated shutoff valve to act as part of the line without impeding it.

They removed some of the camouflage and Su Li was able to restart the engines and test them. They ran up to full power without a hitch. She shut them down and the whole team started looking for whatever disabled the radios. It was Laura who found the small box that sent a jamming signal out to disable the radios. When Su Li asked her how she found it considering that she didn't have any electronics training, Laura said, "I just asked the Holy Spirit where the problem with the radios was and He showed me this little box."

Su Li thought, "Some times you just have to ask the right person the right question. Next time ask the Holy Spirit."

Mark, Sarah, and Su Li walked off the beach from the plane to the end of the sand. It was just over 3300 feet. Su Li said, "With an overall weight of 28,000 pounds we'll need roughly 3600 feet to achieve takeoff. The sand will slow us down somewhat also."

Mark looked down the beautiful shore line and asked the pilot, "How much more thrust do you need to get it airborne in 3000 feet?"

Su Li did the calculation in her head. "About a 1000 pounds more thrust for about ten to twelve seconds. Why? You got something in mind sailor?"

Mark grinned at the reference to his earlier Navy days. "Yep, I certainly do."

He went and took the box of Sematex and a shovel. He walked behind the jet to the end of the beach and set the box on the ground. He spent a few minutes resetting the radio detonator's frequency. When he was satisfied with that, he started building a four-foot sand pile on each side, above, and behind the back of the box. Then he covered the entire assembly with a two-foot thick layer of sand and put a few inches of sand in front of the box. Then he came back to the plane and told Su Li to start up the engines and get ready to take off. When she had finished her preflight checklist, she taxied the plane onto the beach. The engines were high enough and far enough to the sides they didn't blow away Mark's creation. Mark sat in the copilot's seat and everybody strapped in.

Su Li pushed the engines past their maximum rating and released the wheel brakes. The plane quickly picked up speed as it ran down the beach. Mark watched the distance and when the plane was halfway down the beach he pushed the radio detonator button he had been holding.

Three hundred yards behind the speeding plane the four pounds of Sematex exploded and the pressure wave was directed mostly down the beach due to the construction of the sand bunker that Mark had built. When the explosive power of the pressure shock wave hit the plane they had reached three hundred and fifty yards and the pressure wave accelerated the plane so much that Su Li had to pull back on the control yoke and start lifting the plane off of the beach. It was that or bury the nose in the sand which would have been disastrous.

With the additional push from the explosion, the powerful engines on the Citation X lifted the plane away from the beach and into the air with almost three hundred feet of beach left. Su Li trimmed the aircraft and retracted the landing gear. She sought more altitude and the plane responded quickly. Banking around to her left to head for the United States, Su Li gave everyone a good view of Mark's handiwork. Most of the trees had been knocked down within several hundred feet of the huge pit blown in the beach. The water was washing into the crater as they watched.

Su Li smiled at Mark and they slapped hands in a high-five salute. Then she said, "I hope you didn't blacken the back end of the plane with your "booster"."

Mark shrugged, "I don't know if it did or not. You want to step out and check?"

Su Li grinned and said, "Later. Thanks, that was more than enough help to get us off the beach, but weren't you worried about damaging the plane or its flight surfaces in the back?"

Mark frowned, "I wasn't sure if it would do that or not. I was rather hoping that it would expend itself as extra boost rather than damage things. The key was the distance and the speed of the plane away from the blast. The pressure wave would have severely damaged it if it had been sitting still and it wouldn't have provided enough boost if we were too far away. So, I took a calculated guess as to the right time to push the button. If I had to do it again, I'd wait two more seconds."

Su Li stared at her friend like he was from Mars. "I can't believe you took such a risk with all our lives when you weren't sure of the results."

Mark smiled at her. "In my business you learn to rely on calculated guesses. I've had a lot of experience with plastic explosives and this one wasn't that much of a stretch or I wouldn't have done it. It did give us a little more boost than I expected but it certainly was within the parameters I expected."

Su Li nodded in agreement. She had just learned a valuable lesson in how to make what she came to call "a hip shot". She asked Mark, "Do you think we should use the radios now?"

Mark nodded, "Whoever tried to kill us will know they failed pretty soon anyway and we want to advise the FAA of our unscheduled stopover last night. I doubt that your flight plan included an extra twelve hours in flight."

Mark called the international flight controller over the satellite link and told him that they had suffered some mechanical problems that necessitated a layover of twelve hours. He had them re-include the flight into the day's schedule and the fact that they were going to land at Kennedy in New York for an examination of the aircraft for flight worthiness.

Mark went back and explained the arrangements to the others. Jack decided to leave the Citation X at Kennedy for a full maintenance overhaul and inspection. He went to the cockpit and arranged for another aircraft to take them on to Denver. He arranged for a direct, side-by-side transfer of cargo because a lot of their luggage was weapons. Things frowned upon by the airport authorities.

The rest of the trip was fairly uneventful and Su Li was happy because she got to fly a different aircraft as co-pilot and expand her catalog of planes she could pilot. She told Laura later that she had checked out the Citation X's back section and the blast hadn't even peeled any paint off of it. But still, she thought that the back end looked a little fatter than before. The refitters would check that out.

CHAPTER TWENTY-TWO

Early the next morning, Laura rolled out of her comfortable bed and took a shower. Jack was still sleeping and she let him rest. She had an agenda she wanted to follow this morning because something was still not setting right in her spirit.

She dressed in jeans and a sloppy shirt that covered her pistol and got a cup of coffee and a breakfast roll. Then she made her way to the garden/greenhouse part of the fortress. The air of the fortress was cycled through here to provide the plants with carbon dioxide and to draw off the oxygen they produced and use it throughout the complex. In the event of a catastrophic event such as volcanic gases or ashes in the outside air, the fortress could be sealed and could survive on the air produced in this area. The automatic machinery sensed the condition of the plants and provided them with water and fertilizer as they needed it.

Laura liked it because of the peace she felt when she came here to talk to Yahveh. The ozone component of the atmosphere in here was higher and reminded her of the air right after a thunderstorm. So fresh and clean it invigorated one. She sat down in her favorite overstuffed chair in the shade and relaxed. Staring up at the sunlight beaming into the garden she was still amazed that her father-in-law had created the design that allowed it to be here inside a mountain. Her brain told her that there was almost a half-mile of solid granite above her but to her eyes it looked like a normal sky.

She relaxed and sat back in comfort. She started her communion with a song of worship and then shifted into her prayer language, praising the Father and thanking him for all his goodness and mercy. When she felt the closeness of God's Spirit she inquired why she was still feeling wrong when they had done as He had directed them and dispatched the demon Vorbleg and his human agent Hermann Lutz after they had plagued the Jews for over a hundred years.

She felt Yahveh speaking to her in her mind and she humbled herself and listened closely to what the Creator of the universe was telling her. She made herself as much as she could to be a vessel, receiving, not even processing what she was getting. When the Father was finished she prayed her thanks and then started processing what she had heard. She knew it was the Father because everything was crystal clear and she didn't have to make any effort to remember every detail. Her spirit felt the peace of Yahveh as she listened. She was writing it down as she thought through it so that it would remain for review later.

Halfway through she started getting excited and concerned at the same time. She throttled her emotions as best she could until she had it all down and understood what had been revealed to her. Then she jumped up and ran through the fortress to find Jack.

Jack was doing his daily exercises and katas to keep his combat skills as sharp as he could when Laura ran into the gym. She saw him and waved at him. Jack finished his set and took a towel to dry off with as he walked over to her. That she was excited was obvious. He sat down next to her and raised an eyebrow in a silent question of, "What?"

She put her hand on his arm and took a deep breath. "God gave me a revelation a few minutes ago and I know you need to hear this. Even though we dispatched Vorbleg and Lutz in Germany, something wasn't sitting right with my spirit. So this morning I went to the garden to talk to the Father. Only this time, He was talking to me."

This definitely got Jack's attention. Laura continued, "I told Him that things weren't settled for me and asked him to tell me why. Then I just waited. Jack, what he told me is a bit mind-numbing but, here is my analysis of what He said. There are millions of demons and we've been faithful to confront and defeat the ones that Yahveh has brought us to. But we have started to move up the hierarchy of demons. You're aware that Satan patterns his dark kingdom after that of Yahveh's heavenly one. Well, we defeated two levels when we defeated Vorbleg. But the Father wants us to know that up till now the Team has basically been in training. Hold on to your hat for this next one. Yahveh now feels we're ready for the real conflicts out in the world. He is moving us into a direct confrontation with demons that would consider Vorbleg as an insignificant, lowly, bumbling fool. Don't forget that Vorbleg almost arranged the destruction of all European Jews during WWII. If these demons are that much more powerful than Vorbleg how do we handle them?"

Jack thought for a few seconds. "Obviously, we need to pray for guidance on how we combat them, but, remember all demons have an ego and even though it is warped by their "Father" they think of themselves as much greater than any other demons. Yahveh knows their capabilities and wouldn't send us against them if He didn't think we could take them."

Laura realized that Jack was taking the practical approach to the problem and he was probably right about the future challenges. Those facts made her breathe a lot easier.

Jack watched her re-evaluate the situation and commented, "Remember, the Savior gave us power over all the enemy here on Earth, not just the lower levels."

Jack was praying in his mind that God would direct all their activities and especially his. The thought blossomed in his mind and he realized it was important that he speak it out loud. "The main thing we need to remember is that we are doing all of this as Yahveh directs us. As individuals or as a team, we can't take our eyes off of Yahshua or everything we do will fail. Once we start thinking of our talents or technology or the enemy as the important thing, then we've turned to idols and lost our ability to serve God. There is nothing more important than that. Right?"

Feeling the hand of Yahveh in Jack's statement Laura realized she had just allowed herself to become fixated on what the enemy was capable of rather than what Yahveh was capable of. Humbled she guessed that Jack had just gotten a revelation from Yahveh to remind them all of what was really important. "Jack, you are right. I ask the Father for forgiveness and I confess my thoughts as sin. I repent of my sin of being concerned about the enemy and their strength. Yahveh is in control and I agree that we need to seek Him as to what their capabilities are and how we should train to meet those capabilities" Looking at her husband she smiled, "Let's see if Gary or Alan have any ideas about this."

CHAPTER TWENTY-THREE

Jack took a shower and prayed about Laura's message. After he dressed he told the intercom to contact all the members of the Crossfire Team that were in the local area and ask them to attend a short meeting that night in the living room. The main computer sent out a group call in the Denver area to all the various computers, tablets, cell phones, and Smartphones.

At seven p.m. Jack walked into the living room and counted noses. "Let's see, the Connellys are here, Laura and I, my father and uncle, Sensei Grady, the Wus, Minister Froman, the Hargroves, Su Li, Carol Nolan, David Zahavy and Gary Eisenthal. He thought, "Looks like everybody and then some".

Many of these people had been with them since the beginning of their adventures. Mark had joined them in their fight against Don Miland as had Sensei Grady, Steve and Larry Malone, Minister Throman and Charlie and Linda Wu. Carol Nolan had been an undercover agent for the Colorado Bureau of Investigation investigating the Don. Her cover had been blown but she had been rescued by the Crossfire Team in their first-ever assault.

Sarah Connelly had joined the team after her adventures with them in Libya and Israel. Her background as a top field agent for the Israeli Mossad had been a real asset to the team. She had married Mark after their run-in with the Arab Strike Force in Israel. During the Israeli portion of their adventures they had also met Sarah's friend and boss in the Mossad, David Zahavy. After David had been killed saving Sarah and Laura, Yahshua had brought him back to life and he had become a rock-solid, Spirit-filled Christian. He still worked as a field director for the Mossad but had been given authority to work with the Crossfire Team at any time by the directors of the Mossad because of the service the team had done for Israel during the poisoning and other adventures. Gary Eisenthal had also become a valuable member of the team in matters of the spiritual world during their time in Israel and their adventure in China.

Stan and Debbie Hargrove had joined the team when Stan, who had been a Captain on the Salt Lake Police Force, had been directed by the angel Rose to help save Jack from a deranged group of religious zealots from the Believer's Temple. It turned out that Stan's wife, Debbie, was a contract sniper for the CIA, unknown to Stan when he had married her. Su Li was the latest member of the team. They had met her during the Zyngola mission where she was brought onto the team for her piloting skills and her martial arts capabilities.

Jack gratefully acknowledged each one of the team. Then he looked at his Israeli friend and asked, "David, I didn't expect you, or for that matter, I had no clue that either my dad or my uncle would be able to make this meeting."

David was probably the least physically dominating of all the men in the room, except for the elder Malones and the Minister, but his capabilities as a lethal field agent were well documented. As usual, he was impeccably attired. His taste in clothing was excellent and he knew several world-class tailors in Israel. He smiled at Jack. "It seems God scheduled this meeting before you did. I came to Denver to see the latest military version of your "Viewport" in operation."

At Jack's look of mild confusion, Steve Malone answered his son's mental questions. "Larry and I had asked David to observe the trials of a new version of the viewport. With all the events in your life recently, we haven't had time to discuss any of this with you. But, Bob's schedule for construction is set to start in just three months, if it passed the military trials."

David smiled again. "It passed all right. It was so good it passed with a grade of Excellent as it passed every one of the requirements. I'm glad I was here to get an order in for Israel before they're all gobbled up by the U.S. Military. Admiral Sawyer was beside himself trying to get it classified so that I couldn't look at it."

Jack realized that this was another one of the things his recent adventures had kept from him. "David, you're a part of our team. You would have had a shot at it no matter what classification they stuck on it. I'm going to be very interested in hearing about my new project. Okay then, let's get back to the business at hand."

Jack looked at the faith-based part of the organization. "Alan, Gary, do either of you have knowledge or understanding of the hierarchy of demons and the ascending power and capabilities as the rank of the demon increases?"

Gary looked at Alan, "Why don't you take this one?"

Alan smiled because he knew that Gary was probably more knowledgeable about demon capabilities than himself. But he'd give it a go anyway. He stood up and addressed the rest of the team. "I may ramble a bit but stay the course and I hope to cover whatever it is you want to learn. To start with, Satan's days are numbered. Realize that Yahveh, in many places in the bible, makes it plain that He has ultimate control over Satan. Satan's first casting out as described in previous scriptures, wasn't his last.

Revelation Chapter 12 verse 7 says, "And war broke out in heaven (again): Michael and his angels fought with the dragon; and the dragon and his angels fought. Verse 8 adds, "but they did not prevail, nor was a place found for them in heaven any longer". In Verse 9 you hear, "So the great dragon was cast out, that serpent of old, called the Devil and Satan."

"Satan ultimately loses, but his involvement in the affairs of mankind will help to bring mankind to the goal of living forever. You see, the world is a workshop and Yahveh allows all that occurs because man has to be allowed to go his own way and do his own thing, thereby reaping what he sows. There has to be an example of mankind's way without Yahveh, and this world is it!"

The Minister stopped to take a sip of water and then continued. "Demons have strange powers, and the more powerful ones will have spheres of influence. By their nature, demons will form hierarchies of control. This is not to say that they are ordered, but that stronger ones will attempt to rule over weaker ones. Demons are the embodiment of evil as man knows evil."

"Principalities attempt to influence worldly events, large groups, nations and world leaders to do evil and Satan's will.

"Demons are normally disembodied spirits and were thought to be able to operate in the material world only through possession of men and beasts that have bodies for them to utilize. Our experiences have shown that they can assume a material form when so directed by higher demons".

"It is thought by some that the demons are the evil departed spirits of the pre-Adamite civilization. There is no Scripture to prove this. It is only conjecture. It is an interesting idea, however."

The Minister tipped his head in Gary's direction.

The younger man stood up as Alan sat down and picked up the tread of the teaching. "What is the real nature of demons? They are evil, sometimes intelligent, sometimes powerful, and, normally, they are disembodied spirits. This is shown in Revelations Chapter 16, verses 13 through 16. They not angels; nor human; because they possess men and can be cast out and are individuals. They have knowledge, feelings, and fellowship. They have doctrines, wills, and evil powers. They are allotted more power by Satan as their level permits them. Many times they are stronger than demons on lower levels but are still doing the same things the lesser demons do but with a wider effect. This is what I believe the Father meant when He told Laura that we have advanced several levels."

"Demons have their jobs to do. They possess unsaved people and can cause dumbness, deafness, blindness, lunacy and mania, uncleanness, supernatural strength, suicide, lust counterfeit worship, error, sickness and diseases, lying enchantment and witchcraft, false doctrines, and every evil they can possibly do to man."

"They can teach, fight, get mad, sorta tell fortunes. For example they control Ouija boards. They can cause family lines to be subject to the same sins. These are called familiar spirits. They can imitate the departed dead. They can cause ghostly manifestations. They can also cause people to remember 'past lives." Such demons that were familiar with these people of the past have long memories. They can move into our world for the purposes of Satan."

"Some of them are possessed of more than ordinary intelligence. But, for all of them, their rightful place is in the abyss. They have personality, and are Satan's emissaries, and they will attempt to enter into and control both unsaved men and beasts to attempt embodiment. There is a difference between demon possession and demon influence. Perhaps a good illustration of demon influence would be something similar to those old cartoons that showed a little devil sitting on a character's shoulder, whispering into his ear enticing him to do the wrong thing. Obviously, in these last days, Satan is getting anxious and is occasionally expanding their capability to enter the physical realm to attain what he desires."

Gary nodded to himself for a few seconds and then looked up again. "Demons know their fate and those who have power over them. They fear Yahveh, inflict physical maladies, war on the saints of God, and influence men. All unbelievers, without exception, are afflicted or possessed by them. There are demon spirits for every sickness, unholy trait, and doctrinal error known among men. Faith in Yahveh and prayer are our best defense against them. They must be cast out by the power of Yahveh in order for the sufferers to get relief from them. They attempt to influence or direct the activities of the saints of God but cannot possess them since the Saint's spirits belong to the Savior."

"Disease germs, such as cancer, which are closely allied with unclean spirits, are really living forms of corruption that come into the bodies of men and women in order to bring them death." He looked around at everyone. Remember, communication with demon spirits is forbidden in both the Old and New Testaments of the Bible. If they try to get you into a conversation, do not answer anything, cast them out in the name of Yahshua or, ignore them if possible, kill them if necessary, or, as ordered by Heaven."

"To wrap this up, Satan is the god of this world, and has power to influence any aspect of man's doings on this earth through his influence of those who rule on this earth in government or leadership positions, But remember, Satan and his demons are totally subject to Yahveh's purpose. Read Daniel Chapter 2, verse 21 and Luke

Chapter 4, verse 6. Yet most people do not even believe he exists, which is exactly the cover Satan wants to maintain."

Gary looked at Jack, "Does this answer your question?"

Jack thought about it for a few seconds. "Yes and no. It clarifies our understanding about the hierarchy and their areas of control but it doesn't tell us any specifics of what we might be facing at the higher levels."

Laura sat there in thought while everyone contributed what they thought it might mean. She kept praying for an answer they could use to prepare for what was ahead.

CHAPTER TWENTY-FOUR

While everyone was discussing the possibilities of an increased threat load, Jack and Laura walked out of the War Room and wandered across the living room to stare out the viewport wall at the lights of Denver which were being routed to the viewport from a light pipe view from the top of the mountain. It still looked absolutely real and so clear that Jack reached out and brushed his fingers over the surface of the viewport like it was a window.

Laura snuggled into Jack's one-armed embrace and asked, "I'm praying that the Father will clarify this new walk for us. It certainly isn't like Him to leave us in the dark."

Behind them they heard a voice say, "The Lord would never leave you in the dark Laura, *In him is life, and that life is the light of men. The light shines in the darkness, but the darkness has not understood it.*"

They turned around and seated on one of the couches facing them was an old man. Jack smiled; he'd had lunch and an adventure with this "old" man. Jack said, "Hello Caleb."

The angel waved a hand for them to sit across from him. Once they were seated he spoke. "The confusion you and your team are experiencing is because so little truth is known on Earth about your adversary and his troops. Actually, you don't want to delve too deeply into the details about them because that particular curiosity carries a curse of its own. One, double-edged difference with this level is that the levels of demons above the ones you've been training with don't care to open themselves up to possible damage by entering your space. But, since they don't enter the human dimension, they compensate by using many more human agents."

What the Father wants you to know is that your team and efforts have, as your people say, "come up onto their radar" and are now going to draw some concerted attention from the "heavies" in the demonic world. There are no unique or special powers that the upper levels wield other than power in the form of absolute control of more demons and demonized people. Also, they decide where the pressure is applied."

Caleb stretched out his right hand and seemed to concentrate for a few minutes. When he relaxed he seemed very contemplative rather than his usual humorous self. His eyes bored into Jack's and he said, "Jack, you have humbled yourself in the service of the Most High when you have met the temptations man can have presented to him. Your talents could have led to pride of achievement, your money to the sin of greed; your good looks could have easily led to lust. Yet, you've bent your knee and gave it all to Yahveh. Yahveh is pleased with your sacrifice and that of Laura's and the rest of the Crossfire Team. You have truly become warriors for God and because Yahveh is pleased by this, you and your team are going to be given discernment and wisdom sufficient to stand against the enemy. If your people stay diligent and stand against all the lures, temptations, and efforts of the enemy to destroy each and all of you, you will be able to strike blows against Satan's kingdom to the extent that they will flee from you wherever you go."

Caleb held up his forefinger in a warning. "Remember, your battles must stay on the Earth. Do not be drawn into battle against the enemy in the second heaven. You do not have the authority to do anything against the powers and demons located there. Unfortunately, they don't observe those boundaries and will direct actions against you. They are extreme legalists and know that to attack you with their power will result in their instant destruction. But that doesn't mean that they can't plot and direct activities by the powers on Earth. If they become a "nuisance", pray for the Father to rebuke them, but don't attack them directly because then they have the legal right to come against you directly. Let me assure you, you don't want that to happen." His dark eyes conveyed the distinct impression of great pain and loss from having either seen such attacks or from having been the target himself.

Jack asked, "Is our role going to be one of primarily spiritual combat from now on?"

Caleb laughed, "No my dear friend, that will still be our battleground. Your battles will still be in the physical realm but with the enemy increasing his interest in your team and many of your capabilities. The direction of more territorial demons will cause more human agents of the enemy to direct their attacks against you through any means they can in the future." Seeing the distressed look on their faces he sat back and nodded. "But, you have the capability to defeat everything they do. Remember that Yahshua said, *"I have given you authority to trample on snakes and scorpions and to overcome all the power of the enemy, nothing will harm you. However, do not rejoice that the spirits submit to you, but rejoice that your names are written in heaven."*

Laura nodded, "Luke, Chapter 10, verses 18 through 20. I remember them and recite them whenever we go into spiritual battles."

Caleb smiled again, "Go, Go and reassure the troops. Remember, the power of Yahveh is the greatest power of all and He wants you to represent him and that power for His glory."

Jack and Laura got up and started for the War Room. Jack looked back but Caleb had vanished as suddenly as he had appeared.

CHAPTER TWENTY-FIVE

Jack got everyone's attention and passed on what he and Laura had learned from Caleb. As they were processing this interesting bit of news, Minister Throman spoke up. He looked at the whole group and nodded his head. "If it is all right with the team, I would like to introduce you to my associate minister, Tim Carson, next time we get together. I am bringing him up to speed on our affairs and believe he will make a good addition to the team in my place."

For a minute no one said anything and then Laura asked, "Alan? What's going on?"

The older man thought for a minute attempting to seek the Father for the right words. "While I have been praying the last several mornings, the Father has prompted me to find a replacement for myself in the matters of the church and with this group. Tim, who is my assistant minister, also leads the praise and worship at the church and would make a wonderful senior minister for the congregation." He looked through tired blue eyes at the people in the room. "You see, I'm close to eighty-two years old and since I met Jack and Laura my life has accelerated greatly. I've felt more alive than I did for the two decades before I met them, and all of you. My prayer life has become a wonderful time of communion with our Father. My feeling is that he has a duty for me to perform that can't be done here on Earth. Even though the time is short, I believe that there is still time to prepare Tim for his part in the team if you approve."

The thought of losing their friend and fellow warrior saddened the group. He looked around and smiled, "Don't be sorry, this is the best thing I've ever had the chance to be a part of and it has prepared me, in my heart and my walk to do great things for the Father." He got up to leave and stopped. "Don't worry about saying goodbye either. There will be plenty of time for that before I'm promoted."

Alan waved to the group and headed for the elevator.

Laura had been praying and put her hand over Jack's. "He's right; the Father has wonderful things for him to do.

We should celebrate his "promotion" with him before he moves on."

Jack smiled wryly, "That's the most positive spin I've ever heard. I will miss his commentary and his wise counsel. I think that tomorrow you and I should go to Denver and meet his assistant."

Larry Malone coughed to get everyone's attention. "Why don't we summarize what we need to do as a result of this new information from Caleb and call the meeting to a close? I've got a presentation tomorrow that starts at nine a.m. and want to be fresh for it."

Jack agreed and summed up the team's new responsibilities with a final warning about the increase in temptations, lures, and outright attacks. Everyone had a cell phone with group call. If anything out of the ordinary happened, the team would know about it immediately.

Everyone headed for the garage or their rooms talking in small groups until they reached a parting of the ways.

As the living room became silent; Jack thought over everything that had happened since their return from Germany and decided that the team needed to upgrade several things. One thing was their weaponry. What he was contemplating would require both state and federal approvals.

He took out his Pocket PC and started sketching out who to call and what was needed in the way of hardware. Hitting the call button he paged Mark and asked him if they could have a short discussion about this. Mark came back so fast he must have been standing outside the War Room door.

"What's up?" Mark inquired as he dropped into the chair next to Jack.

Jack outlined his concept for more firepower for the team and what he though would be a good replacement for the 9MM and .45-calibre handguns they carried at present. Mark thought about it for a few minutes and then nodded. "I like it but let me research it first, okay?"

Jack nodded and used his cell phone to call Charlie Wu. Charlie answered it on the second ring. "Yes Jack, how can I be of service?"

Jack asked him if he and his wife could come back and talk to him in the War Room for a few minutes.

Charlie chuckled, "Sure, we haven't made it to the garage floor yet. Linda and Su Li are discussing the affairs of the universe, I think."

After walking into the War Room Jack concentrated on what he wanted to tell Charlie and Linda. While he waited for the Chinese couple, Jack used his work station to show a floor plan of the fortress on the large screen on the wall of the War Room.

After Charlie and Linda sat down, Jack stared at them for a minute. Then he said, "You two have become an integral part of the Crossfire Team's operations. We are involving you in many of the steps in each of our latest efforts. How do you feel about this?"

Charlie looked at his wife and then said, "I feel that our time is much better utilized working with the team than any of our other activities." Turning to Linda he raised an eyebrow.

Linda smiled, "I feel that God is leading us to a full-time involvement in the team's activities. At first, I did not want to become a part of anything that is remotely connected to a national government. But God has shown me that His will is more important than my wants. I would enjoy being more involved with the people on the team. I think what I'm saying is, if Yahveh is blessing an arrangement like that, then I must give my blessing also." The beautiful Chinese woman seemed to look inside herself for a few seconds. "And, I do it willingly. What do you have in mind Jack?"

Jack indicated the two floor plans on the monitor. "I had them build three more offices like the one that Mark and Sarah are using and had them sealed until we needed them. I believe that we need one now for your new functions and operations".

Charlie looked both cautious and curious, "What new functions and operations?"

Jack sat back and explained his vision for them. "I believe that we are coming to a point where we need full-time security, counter-terrorism, and investigative research capabilities of a higher level than presently available. I want the two of you to design an all-inclusive communication, research, and defense operation that will use as much of the alphabet organizations files, databases, and satellite capabilities as we are allowed, can borrow, or create our own operations where there are none available. That includes putting up our own secure satellites, with the government's help of course. One of the features I would like to see is the ability for one, or both of you, to be able to provide all functions while you're with us in the field."

Charlie looked at Linda and grinned. Turning back to Jack he said, "This could cost as much as three or four hundred thousand dollars, U.S."

Jack nodded, "I figure more like a billion in the long run. But, the funds are available to buy the best that is being built and stay on top of it by upgrading the software and hardware as it improves. The sales of the Viewports can almost sustain the operation by itself."

Charlie whistled. "Okay, what do you envision a typical usage being?"

Jack thought about that and said, "If we get a phone call, landline or wireless, I would want to be able to determine the origin of the call, who was talking, and their coat size if necessary. If we have to go on a mission, I'd want you to outfit the team going and provide for backup and satellite information, real-time monitoring, and intercommunication between the team members and the fortress without being detected. If a sudden identification is needed on site by photo, fingerprint, or DNA sample, I'd like to have that done very quickly. I'd also want you to provide security for the fortress, any of the team members that don't live here, and an isolated security for communications or any other type of penetration attempted by anyone, including our own government."

Charlie didn't look upset by the requirements. "I can do most of that right now but on a really limited scale. If we can get the equipment I need we can do everything you want and a whole lot more that is just starting to show up in the world of espionage."

Jack grinned and pointed out the other floor plan on the monitor. "Pick your suite out of the five that aren't being used. Also your salaries are standard pay for our group. That's a hundred grand each plus bonuses. Your operations should bring in some sizable bonuses for the team and most likely keep us alive to bank them."

Charlie was having a hard time concentrating on the details of business as he was trying to get his mind around the total concept that Jack was asking for. One thought exploded in his mind and he stared at Jack. "Do you think the Crossfire Team can get the government to allocate us ten CRAY X3A Supercomputers? I mean we are talking over 550 TFLOP operations from each one. Linked we would have one of the most powerful computing systems in the known universe!"

Jack asked what ten supercomputers would cost.

Charlie shrugged, "Fewer than two hundred million with all the bells and whistles. But, and it's a big but, that kind of power would cut an equivalent amount out of the other gear we'd need if we didn't have them. You want real time tracking and observation? Then you're going to need that kind of power crunching data to provide the throughput necessary. Especially if we have several different missions going on at once in different locations, using multiple satellites as bounce points. Oh!, another thing. We are going to need to hire four or five unique individuals to handle the programming, the day-to-day computer and surveillance operations. These people can be geeks but they know their stuff and that's what we're going to require so that we can give you what you're asking for."

Jack looked at them both. "Why don't you guys go look at your suite and decide what you want in the way of furnishings? Tomorrow we can look at the office and decide what you need there, okay?"

CHAPTER TWENTY-SIX

The next morning, Charlie and Jack took a tour of the office and tried to determine what they needed now and in the next few years.

After sketching out what he thought they'd need Charlie shook his head. "I don't see how we can cram all this gear and people into even two of the offices." He threw the pencil onto his drawings and sat back. "Maybe we need to find another facility in which to base this part of the operation."

Jack thought about that and shook his head. "No, we need it to be here where the action is and where the most security is at present. Let me call our architect, Gary Danning, and see what he would recommend."

Later that afternoon, a Navy helicopter got permission to land and ten minutes later Major Danning walked into the War Room and shook hands with Jack. "I'm back a little quicker than I though I'd be. I hear you're outgrowing the little shack already."

Jack laughed and explained their expansion needs. The Major looked at Charlie's drawings and thought for a few minutes. "I'll tell you what. Let's go take a ride on the elevator."

Jack looked at the Major with a quizzical frown on his face. "Is there something you'd care to tell me about that may have been overlooked in your earlier description of the fortress?"

The Major winked conspiratorially and said, "You'll see in just a minute."

The three men got on the elevator at the front room and the Major took out a key from his pocket. Unlocking the panel holding the push buttons for the floors, he swung the panel aside uncovering five additional buttons that did not have cut-outs in the panel. He pushed the lowest one of the new buttons. The elevator went sideward for several seconds and then ascended for ten seconds. When the door opened, Jack was astounded by what he saw.

There was an unfinished space of roughly sixty thousand square feet, lit by several hundred ceiling lights. The flooring was in place and a ceiling was there but at least thirty feet above the floor. Twenty massive structures were spaced evenly around the room keeping the mountain from falling down on them. Jack walked into the area and shook his head. Turning to the Major he said. "Were you going to tell us about this or was this a special surprise?"

The Major smiled, "It was for future expansion. After meeting you and Mark and discussing your needs I was fairly certain that you'd need additional room before long. The other four buttons under the panel will take you to four more floors of approximately the same amount of space. I was able to do this within the cost parameters because of the caverns that were here. All five of these floors were really one cavern. We divided it up into fifths and put floors and ceilings along with power, plumbing, wiring, heating and air conditioning. It was almost as if the mountain had been designed as an accommodation for exactly the type of structure we needed."

"Thank Yahveh" Jack said, "And I mean that. Only He could have seen this and prepared it for us. Was there a reason you didn't tell us about it before?"

Major Danning nodded, "What you didn't know, you couldn't tell anyone else about. These spaces can be approached and entered without knowledge of the other levels. I have a special, software-controlled, panel we can use that will work differently for different people. For example, the people you need to use for this communications center do not need to know about the main floors of the fortress. To them this will be the only place they can get to. I can program your keys to select the floors you want them to go to and only where you want them to go."

Charlie had walked off and surveyed the area. "I'll tell you what gentlemen, this not only is sufficient but will be good enough for growth over the next few years if we have to." He turned to the Major. "Can I get you to help me design the layout of this place?"

Major Danning turned to Jack. "If Mr. Malone, oh! Excuse me, "General" Malone can have me reassigned I think we can mold it into shape in a couple of months."

Since the structure of the room was already built it actually only took forty-eight days to complete the "ComSec" room as it was dubbed by Sarah when she toured it and had a feeling for its applications. The first two weeks were spent in planning the functions, hardware placements, and the necessary staff to run the whole thing.

Jack and Mark were discussing the security of having new people in the mountain and not being able to really determine their true dedication to the cause. Jack shook his head at the concern. "Charlie is only bringing in five people, at least at first. He and Sensei Grady have known these people for several years and have a good idea of their patriotism for the United States and their loyalty to the companies they've worked for before. Remember, we put Charlie in charge of security and I doubt that much will get by him. If it does, Linda will be all over it in a flash. I've watched how they've worked on setting this thing up. There isn't a foot of this mountain, inside or out that isn't visually monitored with the computers doing the majority of the watching. The software they've put together can watch a room full of people and pick out anything out of the ordinary being done. It's amazing."

Mark looked at Jack, "Every foot?"

Jack nodded, "Don't worry; our private areas are off limits even to Charlie. He agreed to that on the contingency that we would take care of any problems in those areas. I want the whole team to be here for the dedication of the ComSec department tomorrow afternoon. It should be an eye-opener even for the most computer sophisticated among us."

CHAPTER TWENTY-SEVEN

The next afternoon the same group that met two months before in the War Room assembled at the outer doors to the ComSec room. Charlie opened the doors from the inside and ushered everyone inside. Linda stood beside him beaming a smile that added to the brightness of the room.

Laura was impressed that Major Danning had been able to transform the cavern look of two months ago into the present, light, even airy space. While the room had lost a third of it's height it seemed to be even higher. The entire roof of the chamber was made up of ViewPorts shaped into a huge glass dome that covered the majority of the floor. The sun was shining and the sky was a beautiful deep blue. If one didn't know any better they would have thought that this room was on top of the mountain because the ViewPorts continued down to the floor at eight locations equally spaced around the room. If you walked over to one of those places you could actually look down the mountain and out over the valleys. The view was so clear and the light breezes coming from the wind generators on either side of these ViewPorts made it seem that you weren't in a room, let alone one in the middle of a granite mountain. It truly seemed as if you were standing on the top of the mountain in an open air structure.

The room had been divided up into four major areas by rows of columns. This didn't distract from the views but gave a definite division between areas. The first area they visited was the satellite control and tactical communications area. Each work area had its own triple set of seventy-two inch wide by forty-eight inch high monitors. There were twelve work areas. At present only two of them were being used. The team watched as Charlie put the operation through its paces. Charlie asked Mark to give him an area of the world. Mark thought for a second and said, "Zoo Park, Moscow, Russia, at the intersection of Volkov Per and Ul Krasnaya. Charlie told Robin Templeton, who was at the console, to bring the location up on the main screen and put the demographics and analysis graphics on sub-screens on the other half of the main screen.

After typing for three or four seconds on her console, a real time satellite picture of the intersection appeared on the left half of the central monitor screen. There was a bewildering array of data being presented to the right of the picture. Charlie pointed out one sub-screen that indicated the number of people within a hundred yards of the intersection. Thirty-two people were listed and scanned for weapons at the same time. The probable path of each person was indicated by the dashed lines in front of their travel and by a solid line behind them. Three people were highlighted as having weapons. All three were Moscow police. The weather, temperature, humidity, and percentage of sunlight were shown in other sub-screens including the direction of the brightest light, the Sun, and the noise level.

Jack asked Charlie if they could actually hear what was going on from their location. Charlie reached over and moved a joystick. A green circle moved across the screen until it stopped at two of the policemen. Touching a button on the console brought a clear rendition of the Russian language being spoken by the police as they surveyed the intersection. Mark listened intently and then shook his head. "Apparently there are poor drivers all over the world."

Robin punched another button and moved the joystick and a blue square surrounded the two policemen. A new sub-screen appeared with a head and face shot of each man, a brief history of his career, his age, years on the force, and his marital status.

Laura smiled and asked, "Okay Charlie, how do you do that from a satellite several miles above the Earth?"

Charlie said, "Remember those CRAY Supercomputers we bought? Well, they can usually see enough of a person's face, unless the satellite is directly above them, to build a composite which the computers compared against the personnel files for the Moscow Police until a match was made. Then the information is displayed. This time it was easy and only took 2.35 seconds to accomplish all of it."

David Zahavy said, "What satellite are you using?"

Charlie looked at the reference data. "One of yours, David. A TESCAR series three to be exact. And to answer your next question, No, we did not ask for permission and it is unlikely that anyone even knows we are doing it."

David looked thoughtful for a while.

Jack asked Charlie, "This is the away team communication and control system. How many operations can you handle at once?"

Charlie shook his head. "Originally I thought we could possibly handle ten separate missions simultaneously. Now I think we could do twice or three times that many. The CRAYs are performing way beyond my expectations."

Larry Malone was eager to see the rest of the facility. Charlie led the way to the next area which was the security area. By the time they had seen what he could do with everything from heat sensors to modified ViewPorts everyone was awed.

The last action area was the communications area which included world-wide communications all the way down to local intercom capabilities. Charlie handed out new satellite cell phones to each one of the team.

"These beauties should keep you in contact no matter where you go. If you'll notice, they're receiving full power signals even here in the middle of the mountain. Nice technology, huh?"

The fourth and last area was the computer area. This was not out in the open area but was reached by two separate, air-tight, sealed door bulkheads. The second one did not open until the first was sealed. Inside the room were the CRAY supercomputers and a host of other work stations. There were three people in the room concentrating on their work. Charlie explained that two were highly-skilled computer programmers and the other one, a bushy-browed middle-aged man who looked like he was completely wired into the computers he had so many connections running between him and his console.

Charlie smiled and said, "Everet Moline is probably one of the world's best computer whizzes. He was the one that accelerated our schedule by creating the unique software we're using. He's so in touch with the way the CRAY supercomputers work that he was able to write thousands of pages of code in days. Get this! Debug didn't find any errors in his codes, not one! That is almost impossible. But it is his brainchild and it gives us a definite edge over any other system out there. This is the leading edge of world-class computer operations. I'll introduce you to him later when he's not working. He would ignore us completely right now."

After they had finished their tour and everyone was headed to the dining room for lunch, Jack and Mark pulled Charlie and Linda aside and spoke quietly to them.

Jack asked, "Do you two feel secure with the personnel you've selected? And, are you taking steps to prevent serious damage if you were wrong about one or more of them?"

Charlie looked at his wife and turned back to Jack and Mark. "We've bet our lives on all four of these people in the past and they've come through. Yes, we feel very secure with them all."

Linda spoke up. "But, as you know our backgrounds, we have taken steps to prevent any malfeasance on their parts. For example, even though Everet is writing the software for the CRAYs, we have a secret program, hardwired into the operation that will let us override any software commands or console inputs. Only Charlie and I know how to activate it and if we have to, we will. I assure you of this."

Charlie looked at Mark, "What is this "mandatory" training session you've set up for later today?"

Mark grinned at the Chinese man. "We're upgrading our personal weaponry and I want everyone to try it out on the range to see if anyone needs extra training."

Charlie shook his head. "I dunno buddy, I'm pretty happy with my Glock."

Mark laughed, "After you see what we've got you'll change your mind. I guarantee it."

CHAPTER TWENTY-EIGHT

When the entire team assembled on the firing range in the lower level of the fortress, Mark explained the need for more firepower and what he had come up with as a solution with a future.

"Jack and I have decided to switch the team's combat weapons from the M-16 Rifle and M-10 Carbine to the new M8 weapons system. You'll remember we used these as XM-8s in Germany earlier this year. But there is a new twist that makes it even more effective for us. Let me explain this weapons system first."

Mark held up the compact version of the weapon. "The Heckler and Koch M8 is a model of efficiency in use: its operation controls are ambidextrous, it has three firing modes; single round, three-round burst, and fully automatic, and can handle a variety of magazines, including a 30 round semi-opaque to allow you to see how many rounds are left in the hard plastic magazine, which can be rapidly reloaded in close combat situations, and a 100-round drum, for sustained fire,."

"Whether the user is a sniper or part of an attack team, the M8 can accommodate all uses. It uses four different interchangeable barrels, a 9" compact, a 12.5" assault, a 20" match grade sharpshooter, or a 20" heavy barrel for sustained high firing applications, each of which can be swapped out in the field in less than 2 minutes. The weapon can also be equipped with a 5-position collapsible stock, a flat butt plate, for an extremely small weapon profile like that one over there." He pointed to a small version on the table. "The M8 can also use an adjustable sniper stock, or a folding stock."

"Forward hand guards incorporate non-slip materials to improve weapon handling and retention. The M8's non-metallic components are manufactured from fiber reinforced plastic polymers which can be molded in numerous colors, and can be removed or replaced by the operator without specialized tools. In other words, whether you're in the jungle or on the sand, the weapon's "skin" can be changed to blend with its surroundings."

There were some appreciative "ohs" and "ahs" from the team at that point.

Mark continued, "The M8 doesn't skimp on optics, either. Its optics/sight package is an "all-in-one" combination: an infrared laser target designator, IR target illuminator and 1x close combat red-dot sight. In addition to incorporating the three sights into one system, the sight is zeroed at the factory and can be removed and reinstalled by the operator without specialized tools, or the loss of zero."

"The M8 is designed as a modular weapon; different barrels and other modules can be swapped quickly depending on our operational requirements. The M8 is also lighter and more reliable than our existing M10 carbine and M16 rifles."

"The M8 Carbine can quickly add on an M320 40mm Grenade Launcher. We all know how handy those things are." There was considerable laughter at that comment.

"Now we come to the compact carbine version of the system. This will replace our handguns in combat situations. You might find you like it so much you'll carry it whenever you'd carry your handgun right now."

"The compact carbine version has a short nine-inch barrel, a butt cap receiver cover, and can be used with a ten-round magazine that doesn't protrude as much as the twenty-five round version. This weapon is designed for personal defense applications and can be carried on a shoulder strap or in a holster."

Mark shrugged, "We've had some jams on the M-16s but only a minimum because we have very short combats. Still, while no gas-operating weapon, including the M8, is immune to the effects of fouling, the M8's system presents a clear advantage over the M-16: The receiver utilizes a six-lug rotating bolt that fully supports the cartridge case and is driven by a "pusher" type gas piston. This piston is unaffected by barrel changes, and is even capable of operating if the weapon's barrel is full of water. Most importantly, it eliminates fouling of the bolt face, which dramatically improves the weapon's overall reliability in a sustained firing situation."

Mark put the rifle down and picked up the compact carbine. "Now for the twist. A major move is in process to replace the 5.56 mm cartridge with the new 6.8 mm. This adds twice the punch while not affecting the shooter significantly. The 6.8 allows a greater accuracy at a greater distance than the .223 or 5.56 mm. I want each one of you to try this weapon on the range. Sarah will show you how to handle it from a concealed carry position.

Sarah walked up wearing a light summery dress with a white jacket. She approached the range and stood there like she was watching a distant object. The range snapped up a target at fifty feet. Almost in a blur, she reached under her jacket on the right side and produced the M8. She fired a tight four round burst that cored the center mass of the target.

Everyone got their turn and a unanimous agreement was voiced for the new hardware. Mark handed a dark gray version of the compact model to each person. Sarah then gave them a cleaning kit, an instruction manual, and two hundred rounds to take with them.

As they got ready to leave, Mark said, "You all turned in impressive scores for the first time with the 6.8 SPC rounds and the compact carbine. I want each of you to practice until you've got a tight group on the targets and can do the walk-through range without a mistake. Try to do this by next week, okay?"

After the last person had left the range Mark said to Sarah, "And that, Ladies and Gentlemen, concludes the festivities for the day."

He couldn't have been more mistaken.

CHAPTER TWENTY-NINE

Mark had just walked out of the shooting range when he got paged to the War Room. Walking in he found Jack, Laura, Sarah, Su Li, and Charlie Wu already there. Looking at Jack he asked, "What's up?"

Jack made a face and answered, "Charlie intercepted some Jefferson County Sheriff communications that seem to indicate the active presence, in our dimension, of a demonic force. Charlie, play that back for Mark."

Mark listened to the recorded communications.

A deputy in the field was reporting to his superior. "Heck, I don't have a clue, sir. Whatever it was stopped a family on I-70 at the Grapevine Road exit. It tore the roof off of their mini-van and took a couple and their two pre-teen children captive. It went to the north of I-70 about a quarter of a mile and went into a small dead-end canyon. Our problem is that we can't get near the canyon. When we try we lose our vision and hearing. Luckily we were able to get the two deputies back and they're all right now. I can't see into the canyon either. It looks so dark in there from here. What are your orders?"

The officer on the other end of the conversation told the deputies to watch the canyon mouth and see if it led anywhere at the other end. He was going to get help.

Charlie shut it off. Mark asked, "How long ago was that recorded?"

Charlie looked at his watch, "Eight minutes or so."

Laura had been praying during the playing of the conversation. "I think God wants us to respond to this situation because of the supernatural aspects of it."

Jack nodded. "Okay, this group is the team except for Charlie. Charlie I need you to contact the Sheriff's office and let them know that we are going to show up at the site to see if we can help. If he has any questions, have him call the FBI office in Denver for confirmation of who we are and why we should be involved."

Charlie stood up. "Okay, but include Linda on the team as security liaison, okay?"

Jack nodded again, "Tell her to suit up and meet us at the heliport in five minutes." He got up and went to the locker room behind the War Room, closely followed by the rest of the team.

Five minutes later they were dressed in gray camouflage uniforms and boots with body armor, helmets, and web belts with a variety of knives and grenades hung on them. Each member had the new M8 rifle with the 40mm grenade launchers and optical sights.

Linda joined them as they climbed on-board the UH-60 Blackhawk helicopter. Su Li had called ahead while she suited up and one of the helicopter techs from the Army was warming up the engines and had started the rotor turning before they got there. Su Li took over the left hand pilot's seat and Linda took the right seat to handle communications.

As the landing pad lifted above the ground level, the setting sun blasted into the helicopter with a vengeance. Undeterred, Su Li lifted the chopper up and interfaced with air traffic controllers and the military at Cheyenne Mountain to advise them of their flight.

Linda patched into the intercom and told the team that Charlie had gotten a green light from the Sheriff's department for their involvement in the incident. It seems that Charlie called them while they were calling the fortress. Their call for help to the FBI had led them to call the Crossfire Team due to the apparent supernatural involvement.

Jack, Mark, Laura, and Sarah were praying for guidance on how to save the family. Jack looked at his wife. "I don't think you're going to need your rifle honey. You might want to have your hands free for this one."

Laura agreed with him and took her web belt and harness off and hung her rifle on a rack behind her seat.

The trip took less than nine minutes and one of the deputies was signaling with a flashlight as to where to put the Blackhawk down. Su Li set it down gently and shut it down. This time she was determined that she was going to be part of the action and not just the bus driver.

As the sun set and darkness covered the countryside, Jack and Mark conferred with the deputies and then walked over to the area that the officers said was the edge of the area of deafness and blindness.

Jack walked ahead several feet and felt the pressure on his sight and hearing but it did not disable him. He waved the rest of the team to his position. One of the deputies attempted to follow but was affected again. Sarah took his hand and led him back to the safe area.

The deputy shook his head, "Why can you walk in there without trouble but I can't?" was his angry question. Sarah didn't want to belittle him or seem superior so she said, "Because God is allowing us to do it, not as a special thing for us, but because we are servants of the Most High and the power that is affecting you is not able to affect us."

She patted him on the hand and turned back to the team which was moving toward the entrance of the canyon.

Mark said, "Light' em up!" and the team activated their M3 Tactical Illuminators and turned the night into day. They advanced quickly and without deception because they were sure that this was going to be a spiritual battle when they got there.

About thirty yards into the canyon they came upon the family laid out on a rock and not moving. Sarah and Linda approached them and touched the mother's hand.

She sat up and cried in terror, "Help us, we need help! I don't know if you can hear me but I can't see or hear anything!"

Mark, Sarah, Su Li, and Linda each took one of the captives and got them to their feet and started walking them back towards the deputies.

Jack and Laura stood between the departing group and the rest of the canyon. Jack's M3 light was the only one shining when a grotesque figure strutted into the light and towards the couple.

Jack shouted at the creature, "Why did you have to attack those people?"

The materially present demon stopped and looked at the two of them. "To get you here, of course. I have been assigned the honor of killing you both."

Jack shook his head. "I don't advise you to attempt that."

The demon laughed a deep laugh, "No, I don't think you would suggest it. But, too bad anyway for you. He suddenly leaped up in the air and came down three feet in front of them. Jack held back the trigger of his M8 and fired ten rounds into the figure, stitching him from crotch to hairline.

The bullets tore great holes through the body and the look of dumbfoundness on the face of the demon was almost comical. He disappeared in a cloud of red smoke.

Jack turned to Laura who had stood there quietly through the whole thing. "Now what was that about?"

Laura said, "I don't think his master told him about the potential for damage when he entered this realm. This was just a test to see how quickly we would jump to their provocation."

Jack looked at her, "You didn't seem to be too jumpy."

Laura laughed, "I wasn't too worried about this one. Notice that my armor didn't appear?"

The rest of the team came back about that time. Mark watched the rest of the red cloud dissipate and said, "Apparently we are too late to see the show?"

Jack reloaded his M8 and shook his head. "No, I think you're just in time for the main event. This bozo was just a preliminary round."

CHAPTER THIRTY

Linda said, "Jack, its Charlie on TAC-1."

Jack keyed his microphone. "Yes Charlie?"

"Jack, the FBI wants to know what's going on. Their agents still can't get into the canyon without losing their sight and hearing."

Mark overheard the conversation, "Charlie, tell the FBI and the Jefferson County Sheriff's office to establish a parameter around this canyon and don't attempt to enter at this time. We believe that there is going to be a major spiritual battle here very quickly. If they've got anyone who is a true believer and is fully submitted to Yahshua or God as they know Him, they can come in here. Otherwise they can serve better out there."

Charlie came back. "Ten-four Mark, I'll tell them. Be advised I can see into the canyon and I think I was able to record Jack's elimination of that demon."

Mark was about to reply when Jack raised his rifle and Laura's armor sprang into full light along with the sword streaming with the glory of Yahveh. It looked like the night sky had opened up and dozens of demons came literally screaming out of a fissure in the fabric of the dimension.

Something new had been added though. Red balls of fire flew out of the rift and whatever they hit they exploded. Jack started targeting the demons and Laura waded into them with her sword flashing back and forth. She beheaded a small demon and used her sword to deflect two of the red balls of fire coming at her. When her sword struck them they died out without exploding.

Mark found that if you shot the red balls before they hit anything they'd blow up then. In between shooting every demon he could, he worked his way back to the red fire balls just exiting the rift and even to ones that hadn't flown out of the rift as yet. He blew up two of them inside far enough that they stopped coming out.

Sarah, Su Li, and Linda were using two round bursts to puncture demons as they exited the rift and the cloud of red smoke was growing quickly. As the last two demons dropped their swords and evaporated, the rift closed.

Laura's armor faded out and it left only the Tactical lights for illumination.

Responding to the urging of the Father's Spirit, Jack said into the sudden quiet, "Reload now! There are more coming. Quick, form a circle with our backs to each other."

They formed the circle and waited. Several minutes went by with nothing and Linda kept talking to Charlie the whole time. Suddenly Laura's armor sprang back into existence and three rifts formed one hundred and twenty degrees apart and equidistant from the team's position.

With a mighty screech, dozens of sword-wielding demons started to flood out of each of the three rifts at the same time.

Mark estimated the odds and wasn't encouraged. There were already almost a hundred demons against their band of six. All of the weapons were firing almost continuously and for a few seconds they were keeping the enemy at bay. All the 40mm grenades were fired and took out quite a few demons. But, more and more demons were coming out of the three rifts every minute and there was a finite limit on the amount of ammunition available to the team. And then there was the stink. The stench accompanying the demons was almost as horrific as their looks. They smelled like meat that has rotted in the heat for several days. The putrefaction would have gagged the team members if any of them had time to notice it.

Laura was slashing and chopping demons left and right but the press was slowly becoming more than she could handle. Everyone was shooting demons at skin-touch range because of the front ones were being shoved ahead by new ones from the rear.

It seemed that the demonic forces were planning to win this one if they had to use all of the demons in hell to do it. It was rapidly becoming hand to claw warfare. Jack had his body armor slashed by both a hand full of claws and a sword at the same time. Something grabbed his leg and he fired downward without looking. The attack on his leg went away. Holding his rifle back so that the demons couldn't grab it, he emptied his magazine at full auto and cleared a large area in front of him. He let the rifle drop on its sling as he drew his Cold Steel Master Tanto and parried a thrust by a demonic blade. Balancing on his left leg, he used his right foot to kick another demon away and he could see Su Li and Linda standing back-to-back with their knives and kicking the smoke out of demons left and right. Mark and Sarah were systematically shooting as many of the enemy as they could, but even with the talents and heroic efforts they were making; the team was being overwhelmed by sheer numbers.

All at once a great light lit up the battle scene and a defiant roar shook everything as three Hellfire missiles flew past the team in different directions and one went into each of the rifts. There were three, literally hellacious explosions which blew demons and parts of demons everywhere. The three concussive waves battered the six team members every which way but the energy stopped suddenly when all three rifts were blown out of the human dimension by the missile explosions.

The bright light was still there and Jack calmed his breathing enough to realize it came from a tactical searchlight on the bottom of an advanced Apache Attack Helicopter hovering directly above them. Seeing that the missile attack had demoralized the demons, he started to charge a group of demons with his knife but they were shredded and blown away by a chain gun from the helicopter. What demons were left in the area quickly disappeared back into their own dimension.

The six members of the team slowly sank to the ground. Mark stared at the smoke coming off of the barrel of his M8 and smiled. "Well." He said to no one in particular, "I think we've proven the capability of the new weapons." He looked at Jack, "You want to run that bit about less demons and more human enemies by me again?"

Jack looked at Linda and she gave him the thumbs up sign. There were cuts, bruises, and burnt flesh among the team but nothing life threatening. Each one of the team was praising God for their survival and the defeat of the demons this time.

More armed men surged into the canyon. FBI, NSA, Sheriff's deputies, and a couple of Colorado Highway Patrolmen. Jack got up and reloaded his M8 with his last magazine. Slinging his rifle he walked over to the approaching men and picked out the lead FBI agent. When they got close to each other they both said, in unison, "We've got to talk."

CHAPTER THIRTY-ONE

The team was being bandaged by two medics from the FBI as the combat Apache helicopter landed eighty feet away from the group. Mark noted that Charlie himself had been manning the chain gun. He was in full combat dress with his rifle hanging by the sling over his shoulder. He looked quite natural armed to the teeth, as he and the pilot were jogging over to the group with a large plastic crate. Stopping near the majority of the team, Charlie opened the case and started handing out new magazines to each of the team members. He also provided new batteries for the tactical lights and the night vision gear. He lifted a laptop computer out of the case and went over to where Jack was talking to Bill Perkins, the senior FBI agent.

Perkins was a no-nonsense agent who had risen rapidly in the agency because he was bright, insightful, and usually right. That he had bitten into something distasteful with this action was obvious from the sour look on his face. He shook his head at Jack and said, "I know your team's reputation and I know you have the backing of dang near everyone in Washington, but I can't believe a pitched battle with demons. You can't convince me of that unless you can produce one for me."

Jack smiled grimly at the young man as a whiff of demonic stink blew by them making them both cover their noses. "You really don't want that to happen."

Charlie read the man's name on his badge hung around his neck. He said, "Excuse me Agent Perkins, but I think I can do almost that for you. If you'll look at this laptop monitor." Charlie typed a sequence on the keyboard and a view of the battle appeared on the monitor as seen from a helicopter viewpoint. Actually it was from a keyhole satellite seventy miles up in space but the optics on those satellites are very, very good. Charlie added, "Like angels, demons apparently do not register on video or cameras because of their spiritual natures. Our computer complex inserts representative computer-generated graphics to represent the actual demons."

As the battle progressed, Jack was amazed at the number of demons flooding in to attack the six of them and the combat going on, even around him. Then the helicopter came into view and fired its missiles. Charlie let the recording run until it showed Agent Perkins coming into the picture himself.

The agent asked Charlie to run it again and several times he had him slow it down so he could observe individual demonic eliminations. Afterward, he sat down on a boulder and shook his head. "What is this world coming to?" he wondered.

Jack soberly said, "The last days before Yahshua returns, that's what it's coming to. Satan senses the approaching doom for himself and his demons and he is pulling out all the stops in a last ditch effort to separate as many people as he can from Yahveh God."

Agent Perkins looked thoughtful for a few seconds. "I remember that scenario from Sunday School when I was seven or eight years old. I never thought I'd actually see it happening. Who is this Yahshua you're talking about? I thought it was Jesus that was coming back."

Jack sat down next to him and put his hand on the older man's arm. "We use the original Hebrew names for what is called God and Jesus. God's real name is Yahveh and the real name for the Messiah is Yahshua. There is no reason to be discouraged. It is part of the plan of Yahveh for mankind. It will be played out regardless of who believes it or not. But, I think we had bettered keep what happened here away from the press and that computer recording should only be seen by those who need to see it, right?"

The agent nodded and said, "I need a copy for my report but I will only show it to the top brass and then it will be sealed up. I can assure you of that. Otherwise, my career at the FBI is over and I will be passing out parking tickets at ball games for a living."

Jack laughed, "Don't worry, if your bosses have any trouble believing you, let us know and we'll see that they are convinced."

Laura came over to the group and suggested that the team get together and see what God wanted them to do now that this battle had been won.

As they were walking away, Perkins walked with them and Jack asked the agent how the family that had been abducted was doing. Perkins smiled, "They are fine now that they're over their terror. They are still unsure of what happened and how. I have two agents debriefing them and then we'll take them home. I'm afraid that their van is a total loss and I'd like to see how they explain that to their insurance company." He waved and walked over to a group of his men.

Jack shook his head, "There is a man who got a really sudden introduction into the supernatural."

Jack looked around and called Charlie. Charlie trotted over to him. Jack told him to make sure that the family involved had sufficient funds to replace their vehicle since the demon only snatched them to get at the Crossfire Team.

Charlie smiled, "I'll handle it." He then walked over and spoke to the FBI agent to get the name and address of the family.

The rest of the team gathered together and prayed for guidance. After a while, Jack surveyed the members and got the distinct impression that the battles were done for the day and they could return to the fortress. Looking at the battered group Jack asked, "What was all this about today? Like Mark said, I thought that we were going to be battling human forces more than demonic ones."

Laura was still quietly listening to the Father. She looked up at Jack. "I believe that this was the first skirmish between us and the new level of demonic enemies we talked about a couple of months ago. I think they thought they could overwhelm us and destroy us by sheer numbers. I agree, I don't understand why they went to such an effort with the interdimensional rifts when they knew we could fight them on the physical plane. It just doesn't seem to make much sense, although they almost were able to destroy us."

Mark added, "And they would have if Linda and Charlie hadn't brought in the Air Calvary when they did. This was an extremely close thing here people. You all fought bravely and effectively but we all were close to being killed. Look at the cuts in your body armor, nicks in your rifles where a sword almost got you. It was only through the grace of God that we survived and I think it was an object lesson and the only one we are going to get. Let's learn from this. We need to expect that the enemy will throw everything he's got at us at any time in either dimension."

Laura nodded, "No only that, but remember that the enemy arranged this little ambush knowing we would respond and how fast. They have obviously been keeping tabs on us and now they think they know how to push our buttons to make us jump. They overestimated the effect of their assault by sheer numbers and underestimated our resolve and combat capabilities. They won't make that mistake again. I believe that God showed me that the next time we go head-to-head with this higher level demon next time it will be against his human agents rather than demonic beings translated into our world."

Jack thought about all this and made an announcement. "Okay people, we need to make some primary plans and some contingency plans. But, until Yahveh tells us to stand down, all members of the Crossfire Team are going on standby combat alert."

Jack looked at Mark. "Buddy, I want you to get with the federal and state governments and get us permission to move around armed to the teeth and see if you can get us a full-time person to interface with at Homeland Security as the umbrella organization over the alphabet groups. The last thing we want to be seen as is a loose cannon rather than a member of the team."

Looking at Sarah Jack asked, "Can you get with David and coordinate with the Mossad as to upgraded combat capabilities we haven't covered? It seems the majority of the challenges we've faced lately have been directed at Israel and its people. Perhaps they will want to work more directly with us if you show them a copy of the battles here. Get with Linda and Charlie and make that happen."

Jack addressed the whole group. "Laura and I will get with Gary and Alan and see if we can seek God for a strategy to prevent the enemy from manipulating us or our actions for their benefit."

Mark got wearily to his feet. "Okay people; let's head back to the chopper."

As they were walking back to their ride home, three things happened simultaneously. Laura's armor and sword appeared, two large demonic hands and arms appeared in mid-air reaching for Jack, and Laura swung her sword cutting both arms off whatever creature they had been attached to. The hands and arms turned to smoke and the opening closed. All of this happened so fast it seemed that Laura had struck before the hands had appeared. Her armor faded away with the vanishing of the threat.

What stuck Jack as awesome was the fact that it all happened so fast no one even broke stride. Laura acted as if it was a natural occurrence and looked at her husband and shrugged the whole thing off.

Laura knew how she was able to do all that without seeming effort. As they had started to walk out of the canyon she had been given a vision of the upcoming attack and her response to it. At the urging of the Father's Spirit she stepped up closer to Jack's right side and held her hands up. When the sword appeared she simply swung it overhand and watched everything happen as it had in the vision. She hoped that this was part of their enhanced discernment.

Mark moved up even with the Malones and asked, "Do we have any idea of how to prevent them from sneaking up on us on their side and just jumping over at us like that when they want to?"

Jack shook his head. "I don't know if we do or we don't. I have the feeling that they're not supposed to be able to do that at all. Obviously they're doing it so there is something operating at a level I don't understand. I'll ask those questions of Gary and Alan tomorrow. We need to pray for protection in the meantime.

As they reached the chopper, Laura said, "You know some of the parameters that they are working under because they had to lure us to the canyon to attack us. Doesn't the supernatural world lie right next to our world at all points? Why didn't they attack us in the fortress like they did once before with the tainted M-16s? Because there must be some constrains on their ability to move into this world. At least, that's what I think."

CHAPTER THIRTY-TWO

The next morning Jack and Laura went to the Christian church off of Arapahoe Road which overlooked the southern part of the Denver metropolis. The church setting was serene and quiet even though there was a junior high school directly across the street from the front of the church. It may have been the presence of the cemetery directly behind the church that kept things quiet.

Jack asked the receptionist if he could talk to Alan Throman. She told him that Alan was at home, not feeling well. Would the assistant Minister Tim Carson be of any help to them? When Jack agreed to meet the assistant Minister she paged him to the office.

Tim came around the corner and entered the office area. He was probably six foot, two inches tall, lean, and young-looking. He wore silver-rimmed sunglasses on top of his head and a friendly look on his face.

Jack introduced himself and Laura to Tim and he suggested they go to his office. Although the office was a lot smaller than Alan's it was clean and neat. Jack told him that they were expecting Gary Eisenthal to join them in a few minutes and that they had some interesting questions concerning demons that they hoped the two of them could answer.

Tim smiled, "Well, I'll do my best to answer them but I may have to defer them to Minister Throman because he is really the expert on things supernatural."

As they talked with Tim they got the sense that his dedicated role in life was to be a representative of the Love of Christ to all. Far too few men were like Tim in their attitude of humbleness and devotion to God. Both Jack and Laura were impressed by his knowledge and his gentle nature.

Gary knocked on the doorframe and came into the room. After the introductions were done and the groundwork laid for the discussions, Gary looked at Tim and smiled. "Minister Carson, I. . ."

Tim held up his hand, "Just call me Tim, please."

Gary nodded, "Okay, Tim. I don't know how much Alan has told you about us, the Crossfire Team I mean. But there could be a bit of shock for someone who hasn't been on this walk. Could you let us know something about your understanding of who we are, and what we do?"

Tim nodded his head with a serious look on his face. "Minister Throman has described some of your exploits and I heard some of the happenings with the nuclear missile attack on Denver that your group stopped. But, I don't have any first-hand experience with your efforts on the part of the Father. I will tell you this, I have spent many hours in prayer about working with your team and I feel truly blessed by God and His encouragement for that participation."

Jack asked him, "How do you stand concerning the entry of demons into our world?"

Tim thought for a few seconds. "First Corinthians eleven talks about Satan masquerading as an angel of light in our world. So, Biblically speaking, the fact that they can move into our dimension and function is factual. I thought that demons were only disembodied spirits. I do believe it can happen, but I, personally, haven't seen such an occurrence as yet."

Jack asked the Minister if he had a DVD player in the church. Tim took them to the sanctuary and turned on the main screen above the altar. Jack gave him the DVD and cautioned him to only let people that needed to see it have any opportunity to see it. Also, remember that the demons are only represented by special effects due to their spiritual nature. This is because they can't be seen by cameras or videos even with their "bodies" because they are still spiritual in nature. Charlie Wu is our computer guru and he has taught his computers how to represent the different types and styles of demons and that is what the DVD shows. I assure you that they are even more repulsive in real life."

Curious now, Tim put the DVD into the player and punched "PLAY". As the battle unfolded from the single demon with Jack and Laura into the mass attacks from the three rifts Tim's mouth dropped open. As the pressure mounted from the attacking hordes, a high-pitched scream of terror rang out in the sanctuary. Two young boys, probably about six or seven years old, who had been hiding in the pews were, headed away from the screen as fast as their little legs would carry them. One of them was giving vent to his fear at full volume.

Tim shut off the player and caught one of the boys while Laura caught the other one. They were both so scared they were shaking. After a few minutes they calmed down and Laura talked to both boys and prayed with them. Then Tim said, "Billy and Bobby Pemmon. How many times has your mother told you not to play hide and seek in the church?"

The bigger of the two children looked at the Minister. "Sorry Minister Carson, we . . . will . . . NEVER. . . EVER...do it again." It was obvious that he meant every word he said. Tim called the receptionist and turned the boys over to her. "Find their mom; she's probably in the book store."

After the kids left with the receptionist, Tim walked the sanctuary and then locked the doors to make sure there would be no other people getting in there. He started the DVD from where it had been stopped and he watched it through the end. Thoughtfully he looked at the three team members and then he smiled. "I am astounded, elated, scared, and excited all at the same time. I think I now know why Yahveh wants me to work with your team." His eyes opened wider, "Didn't they almost get you?"

Laura smiled, "Yes, but the operative word was "almost". They suckered us into a trap that almost worked."

Taking the DVD out of the player and carefully putting it into a holder, Tim held it out to Jack. Jack shook his head, "Hang onto it and when you begin to wonder if it's real, play it while you are alone."

They went back to Tim's office. On the way the receptionist stopped them and told Tim that Alan wanted him to use the senior Minister's study instead of his own.

Alan's office/study was more comfortably furnished and the four of them settled into the couches gladly. Jack gave Tim a really short summary of the "events" that had been encountered by the Crossfire Team in the short time they had been working. Tim sat back astounded. "That was your team in Zyngola when God moved?"

Laura grinned, "Oh Yeah, we were twenty five feet from ground zero when He did move. Very impressive and talk about building your faith."

Jack brought the subject back on line. "Okay, what can you two tell us about this incident in the canyon? How can they do what they did, and why didn't they do it before? Can they do it whenever and wherever they want to or are they constrained in certain ways?"

Tim and Gary looked at each other for a few seconds. As the experienced member of the team, Gary took the lead. "A lot of what we're going to talk about is conjecture. Guesses really, because the Bible doesn't talk about this type of thing and the secular press dismisses it as hallucinations."

Gary sat back and steepled his fingers. "As you know, Satan and his demons have to have permission from Yahveh to do anything to God's people. So, then Yahveh is in charge and there are most likely, strict guidelines as to what they can do and what they can't do. Revelation 9, verses three to twelve describes the tribulation appearance of giant locusts with scorpion-like stingers designed to torment unsaved mankind as a punishment from Yahveh. But they are most likely demons. Satan can appear as an angel of light so it probable that his troops can cross into our world also. Examining your video record of the battle last night, I get the feeling that they had to draw you to that canyon to allow them to operate. Outside the canyon, nothing happened did it?"

Jack shook his head, "No, but remember that the original demon stopped a van a quarter mile away from the canyon and abducted the family that was in the van. He didn't have to operate only in the canyon."

Tim watched the by-play between the team members carefully.

CHAPTER THIRTY-THREE

Gary continued his comments. "I don't believe that God would play with us like the government did with the troops in Viet Nam. You know, our government allowed areas of safe haven for the enemy in which our troops couldn't attack. But with no restriction on the enemy for mounting attacks on our troops from the safe areas. No, I think that there is probably a balance and we need to seek the Father in prayer to put us on the same playing field as the demons and their boss. There is no reason to think that we don't have the right to know the rules as well as the enemy, just because they are on that side of the dimensional line." Gary held out a hand to Tim.

Tim had been listening to Gary and thinking out the probabilities in his own mind at the same time. He stood up and started talking softly. "As I see it, the upper level demon or demons you are now faced with have made your destruction a priority. That would be why they'd sacrifice so many demons in the attempt to kill you in the canyon. Since that didn't work and you will now be ready for such encounters in the future, they will switch tactics.

"They will be forced to change their tactics due to the horrendous failure they just suffered. One thing Satan and his upper echelon don't tolerate is failure on a large scale. The upper level demon that devised that trap will pay for his failure along with any surviving demons that helped him try to pull it off. At least, that's my understanding of their domain. The new power or authority that is given your extermination will try to do it differently I'm sure."

Tim paced as he talked. "They will stir up a hate group or a radical jihadist group to attack you in our dimension. You gave them a bloody nose by repelling their version of "shock and awe". They still won't respect you but they will be wary of your capabilities after this. One thing you can be sure of is that they won't hesitate to attack you again, and soon. Also, they are very liable to take out everyone in a square mile to just get one of you," A sobering expression passed over his face. "Excuse me, to get one of us."

Laura was thinking about how to learn the rules. "I think we need to press into the Father for understanding concerning this form of attack. My armor will respond to an attack by an enemy and that's a good sign but it only comes as the attack is launched, not before."

Jack sat back and studied Tim for a few seconds. "So, Tim, now that you see what we're up against, how do you feel about joining us as needed? We believe that God directs all our steps and last night, after the festivities, my wife and I were praying about asking you to replace Minister Throman as the "battle cleric" for the team. I know that it will definitely interfere with your ministry to this church from time to time. It will probably place you in grave danger frequently, but your walk with the Father will deepen more than you can possibly understand at this time."

Tim smiled, "I was sold on the concept before I met you three. Yes, I'll do what I can to fill Alan's shoes on your team. Let me know, if you can, when you'll need my participation."

Laura laughed, "Oh, you'll know all right. First, one of our team, Charlie Wu, will be stopping by to "gear you up" as they say nowadays. He will also arrange for training in the communications and security side of things. You know, things you didn't get at the Seminary, like combat arms and self-defense. From Jack you'll learn how to handle a sword and some martial arts. Our resident field officer, Mark Connelly will guide you in learning team tactics, massed firepower and inter-team field communications. Mark's wife, Sarah, who is a recently retired Mossad field agent, will work with you on spy craft. And, lastly, I will work with you on what I am going to call Combat Prayer Skills. There may be other twists and turns along the way. Just remember, Yahveh is in charge and Yahshua is our leader in all things."

Tim was excited to get started but in his heart he also wondered just what he'd gotten himself into. Then he remembered that it was Yahveh that got him into this. That made it a lot more tolerable.

After the Malones and Gary left the church they went to a small restaurant at the nearby Southgate shopping mall on South University Boulevard for lunch.

Jack ordered his meal and while they waited he opened the conversation. "I like Tim. I'm a little amazed that such a humble servant of Yahveh would be up for becoming a combat soldier."

Laura shook her head. "Are you really amazed? Remember that God is never wrong in who he picks. I think Tim will blend in nicely with the team and I believe he will bring us a continuation of the Biblical teaching and spiritual leadership we had with Alan."

A spiritual pressure fell on Laura. She nodded, "I think we need to go see Alan."

Jack knew where the elderly Minister lived so, after lunch, he drove over to the small frame house two blocks south of Arapahoe Road. He went up and knocked on the door. A minute later a middle-aged man answered the door and asked what they needed.

Jack introduced the team and told him that they were friends of Alan and if it were possible they would like to see him for a few minutes. The man smiled at them, "Certainly Mr. Malone, Alan said that you'd be by today."

Jack held out his hand, "And you are?"

The man shook Jack's hand, "I'm Phillip Wortuski from the hospice. I'm here to help Minister Throman during his last days."

Hearing a car stop at the curb behind theirs, Jack looked back to see the man they'd just left coming up to the group. Phillip smiled and waved at Tim.

Jack introduced his wife and Gary to Phillip. The four of them walked back to a rear bedroom and saw Alan sitting up in bed reading his Bible.

Jack went over and gently hugged the frail man. "Good Morning Alan, how are you doing?"

Alan smiled a weak smile. "Just peachy, Jack, Hello Tim" He turned back to Jack. "And to what do I owe the honor of this visit?"

Laura hugged him and said, "Phillip told us you knew we'd be here, so maybe you can tell us why."

Alan laughed a little and coughed a little. "Seems that a spirit told me that you were headed over here."

Gary hugged him and asked, "Our spirit or theirs?"

Alan smiled again, "Ours, I hope."

Phillip excused himself and closed the door on the way out. Jack was about to tell the Minister that they had met Tim and were pleased by his love for everyone and his peace in God. But, instead he fell under conviction.

Jack looked at Laura and said, "Let's pray."

Laura sat in the chair next to the bed and Tim, Jack, and Gary got on their knees. Jack felt the conviction deepening on his spirit and started out a very earnest prayer. "Dear heavenly Father, engulf us with your love. Yahshua, cleanse us of all our sins and forgive us those sins. We know that you are calling our friend and fellow saint home to you soon. We just plead for your loving touch, peace, and mercy on him Father. He is a most faithful servant of yours and is eager to join you. While we will miss him for a while, your plan is always the best for us. We just add our prayers to others for Alan and commend him to you in the highest."

The heaviness of the God's Spirit seemed to press down on them all and a lovely new voice was added to the room. "Praise from the Most High and Yahshua Messiah to all of you."

Jack looked up and Rose floated at the end of the bed in her fierce whiteness and soft golden hues. "Yahveh has heard your plea and holds it as honor for you, every one of you. Jack, Laura, Gary Eisenthal, it is good to see you again. You also Tim Carson, welcome." Tim looked absolutely awestruck with Rose.

Minister Throman was happier than he had ever been at that moment. "Thank you beautiful angel. Thank the Lord for sending you to anchor my faith in these last hours."

Rose's countenance softened and was the most beautiful any of them had seen. "Alan, your faith has been a rock that many others have leaned on. Yahveh has watched you and found you to be a faithful servant. You now have a chance to thank the Lord in person. I have been given the honor to bring you home."

The angel held out her hand and a radiant Alan floated up off the bed and reached for her hand. Rose looked at Laura and winked. Then she led the radiant Minister away.

There wasn't a dry eye in the room. Laura prayed, "Thank you Father for allowing us to be here at this time. All praise and honor are yours." While still totally stunned by the appearance of Rose, Tim was praying deeply.

Jack looked at the peaceful body on the bed. "I think that is the most beautiful thing I've ever witnessed. He deserved that and I thank the Father for his timing."

From behind Jack another voice said, "Yahveh's timing is always perfect Jack. You should know that by now."

Jack turned around and Caleb was standing there in his old man outfit, smiling at them all. Then he turned serious. "There was more than one reason that Rose came for the Minister today. The enemy was about to counterfeit an angel and come to him to try to break his spirit by telling him that Yahveh didn't want him and that his place was to be in hell forever. It was your prayer here that empowered Rose to take him sooner than Satan thought possible. You know that prayer empowers Yahveh to use the power of heaven on earth. He set it up that way."

After everyone had said goodbye to the Minister the team moved back into the living room with Caleb.

Jack asked Caleb, "I'm grateful that it worked out this way. I do have a question for you though. Are we under the threat of a sudden invasion from demons anywhere they want to attack us?"

Caleb shook his head, "No, but it is "complicated" to attempt to give you an answer you can understand. There are so many things concerning heaven, hell, angels, and demons that the human mind can't understand. Yahveh made it that way for a reason, which is also very "complicated" in it's own way. Just let me say that it requires an enormous amount of power on the evil side to translate evil spirits, which you call demons, into your world. Such was the amount they expended attacking you in the canyon that all forms of evil on the earth dropped by thirty percent over the next seven hours. To legally, in Heaven's terms, enter the human dimension they have to get Yahveh's approval before they do it. None of these demons were here legally, and, since it was unsuccessful, it won't happen again for quite a while. As your discernment increases you will be able to see the gathering of forces before such an event happens again. Eventually, you can become so attuned to the spiritual plane that you will know days in advance when the enemy is going to attack you."

Laura asked, "How do we increase our discernment?"

Caleb started to fade out, "Study His word, and pray for enlightenment."

Tim was now in a direct state of shock. He looked at Laura. "You did say that my walk with the Father would deepen in ways I couldn't expect. But, to meet two angels in less than an hour after accepting a place on your team is so overwhelming that it is going to take me some serious down time to assimilate the implications and try to understand it all."

Laura smiled at the tall man. "This same need has happened to everyone on the team at one time or another. Call us if you need to talk about it."

Jack sent Phillip back into the back bedroom so that he could tend to the Pastor's remaining requirements.

CHAPTER THIRTY-FOUR

The demonic authority named "Vileness" was finally calm after venting his anger through a long, drawn out destruction of all three of the powers that had cooperated in the fiasco in the canyon in Colorado. He didn't let it bother him that he himself had authorized the attack. But, he had fumed enough! It was time to attend to matters himself rather than allowing weaklings and fools to waste precious power on ridiculous schemes.

He spent time as he considered all that he knew about the Crossfire Team and their battle with his domain. Realizing that they were backed by the hated Yahveh and were very capable of defeating normal demonic attacks, he came to the conclusion that he should employ overwhelming force to destroy them. He called for "Catamitous" a major demon of sly evilness and horrific violence against humans especially those that threatened the demonic realm.

A dark reverse of heaven's Rose, Catamitous, or "Cat" for short had more feminine characteristics than the majority of demons and preferred to work through human women to bring human men to their downfalls. Very intelligent and sly, Cat had risen quickly in the demonic hierarchy due to her evil schemes. She had a taste for the morally corrupt that considered themselves as Satanists. They knew nothing about true evil and only played at it. When their egos made them think they were important to the master, Cat showed them the truth. Vileness thought that she should be more than a match for the team.

While Vileness was contemplating how to counter the Crossfire Team, Cat was actually in the human world living as an image of a young, beautiful girl whose innocence drew the moral equivalent of demons in the human populace. She was sitting on a bus bench near downtown Denver on Colfax Avenue. She was fairly sure that the vulnerable image she was portraying would be irresistible to a certain serial rapist and murderer. Not that rape and murder were bad, but this particular individual had destroyed a minor demon that Cat liked. He had done it quite by accident but he had done it and gloated over his power over the dark side. Cat felt a glow growing inside her as she waited.

Max Broman was so confident of his power over women that he now scoffed at the feeble efforts of the law enforcement community to stop him from having his way with any female he wanted. He never left witnesses behind to implicate him. He really got excited by the absolute fear and terror his victims exhibited as he killed them. He was on such a high from his last two victims that he just had to find one more victim before the week was over. He walked slowly through the darkness on Colfax Avenue as if drawn to the area by what he thought of as fate. He was a powerful, stocky man with receding black hair and a weak chin. Standing almost six-foot, three inches tall, his chest and arms were huge from his daily weight-lifting. He could snap a neck with either hand and had done so not too many nights ago.

He remembered an odd happening several weeks ago when he was stalking a beautiful red-head. As he started to close in on her, this scrawny scarecrow of a guy had suddenly shown up behind the red-head. It really riled Carl that this skinny nothing of a guy was messing up his move. In a fit of irritation he had jumped the guy and snapped his neck so fast the idiot never knew what hit him. The odd thing was that when Carl had finished with him the girl had gotten a ride. He turned around to take out his anger on the guy's body but he was nowhere to be found. Now that was really strange. But Charles' obsession quickly consumed him and by the next evening he forgotten all about the skinny guy that disappeared.

Spotting the really cute blonde chick sitting on the bench across the street he reveled in the thrill of his upcoming conquest. Walking quickly across the street in the darkness he quietly scanned the area. Nobody around and it would be ten more minutes before a bus came along. The cars that passed didn't care about anything but their own needs.

Checking again to make sure there weren't any witnesses, Carl quietly slid up behind the girl on the bench and reached over and covered her mouth with his left hand. He reached under her rising right arm and jerked her backwards over the back of the bench and quickly lifted her off the ground and carried her into a dark alley near the bus bench.

She struggled like they all did, but it was useless against his great strength. His whole body vibrated to the thrill of the event. His mouth was dry with anticipation of her fear. He found a pool of darkness and shoved her up against the dirty wall knocking the air out of her lungs. He then pulled out his large custom knife and showed it to her. He said, "Listen baby, you do what I tell you or I'll cut you really bad." He was grinning in anticipation of her fear.

He was taken off guard when the girl calmly looked at him and told him. "Not tonight Max. You've bitten off a lot more than you can chew this time." Max saw a gut-wrenching evil in her eyes that frightened him so badly he wet himself in fear.

Cat then allowed her normal image to appear.

Max looked death in the face and felt the same fear that he had caused in others. He dropped his knife and stepped backwards. He wanted to run but couldn't get his legs to work. His deep-throated scream sent chills through everyone that heard it.

Cat surged forward and used her razor-sharp nails to rip the frightened human being from the groin to his throat. She didn't eviscerate him but just slashed deep enough to make him fall apart. As she continued to surgically slash him to pieces she made sure that he stayed alive and aware as long as possible. That way his terror fed her nicely. When he finally bled to death still standing, she enveloped his spirit and faded out of the human realm. What was left of his body collapsed limply onto the dirty concrete.

Not much later, she got the message that Vileness was calling her.

Receiving her assignment from Vileness and his encouragement to utterly destroy the Crossfire Team, Cat became excited. This was a major task and if she could accomplish some extraordinary results she would become a power in the demonic realm. She reviewed the information that Vileness had given her on previous attacks and decided that lures and temptations wouldn't work on the team because they had already been tried and they failed, miserably. But, she could see their weaknesses and she devised a grand plan that couldn't fail. Unless, or course, their Yahveh intervened and broke the rules. But He wouldn't do that, He made the rules and He couldn't break His own rules. She decided to hinder Yahveh by His own restrictions and thereby destroy the team. This could get her the attention of the master himself.

CHAPTER THIRTY-FIVE

Mark sat quietly in prayer. He felt he was probably the least prayerful of the original team but he had come to understand the concept of Yahveh's will for his life and the importance of prayer. Like everything he did, he went at it in a focused manner. His head was full of combat tactics and strategies but his heart had fallen in love with Yahshua. In his prayer time Mark had come to express his love for his Savior as unconditional love regardless of what came his way in this life.

Mark knew deep down that Yahshua had his best interest at heart and God's love for him was so far beyond his own that there really wasn't any comparison. He just knew that what Yahshua had done on the cross was worth every ounce of his praise and worship and that engendered a love for the Father that didn't require reciprocity. That really didn't matter because Mark loved God with all his mind, strength, heart, and anything else he could throw into the mix.

Mark was the tactical leader of the Crossfire Team and he knew that the lives of all the members were balanced on what he ordered. He also knew that he didn't want to drag any of them out from beneath Yahveh's protection. So, he prayed whenever he had to make a strategy, decision, or even a guess at what they should do in a given situation. Right now, the team was under attack from Yahveh's enemies and he didn't have a clue as to the battle rules or limitations. He was praying for understanding and knowledge to steer the group around the enemy's traps and attacks.

As he continued to praise Yahveh and Yahshua he felt the heaviness on his spirit that accompanied the increased presence of Yahveh's Spirit. He fell deeper into the communion and realized he was floating in the River of Life. The stream of consciousness where he was one in spirit with Yahveh.

He could have floated there for a long time, but he needed help with the problems and he focused on seeking answers. It seemed like a long time but soon he felt a presence near him and he recognized the angel Caleb. How he "recognized" him he wasn't sure. But he knew that Caleb was there with him. Being cautious as Laura had taught him, he tested the spirit and received confirmation that it was truly Caleb and an angel of Yahveh.

As Mark's vision "cleared" he saw Caleb as a mighty warrior angel rather than an old man. Caleb had a pure white garment that glowed with power and was cinched at the waist by a golden belt. A sword was sheathed to his right side. He looked young and very strong in his build and his health. Mark thought, "Hello Caleb".

Caleb's amazing blue eyes fixed on Mark. "I bring Yahveh's blessings to you Mark Connelly."

Mark started to ask, "I really need help on these . . "

Caleb held up his right hand. "Mark. Yahveh already knows the desires of your heart. He also knows that you seek unselfishly to protect the others. The Lord is permitting me to give you much of the knowledge you seek because the enemy is attempting to use the team's lack of understanding to eliminate you. Worse yet, the enemy you now face actually has the nerve to try to use Yahveh's rules and restrictions against Yahveh Himself. This will not be allowed. But, this knowledge comes at a price and with a condition."

"Only a handful of people on the Earth know about these things. You must be wary that your command of this information does not lead to pride in your knowledge of them. You have had a problem with this in the past. Yahveh believes in you and your love for him and is giving this information to you both as a means of protection and as a test. Do not fail this test. The enemy will become aware that your team knows this unique information as soon as you use it. It will take them little time to discern that it is you who holds it. They will do everything in their power to flatter you, cajole you, and convince you that because of this information, you are more special and more important than others. Remember that Yahveh will never let them tempt you beyond your capacity to resist and He always gives you a way out. Keep your heart and eyes on Yahshua at all times."

Mark understood the problem he'd had with pride and thought that he was past that. Obviously, he may not have truly learned his lesson in this area. He said, "I don't know that I should face this test if the lives of the others rest on my humility."

Caleb smiled at him. "That is exactly why the Most High is giving it to you. He believes in you and so do I. In fact you have a whole rooting section up here that believes in you, Mark. May Yahshua be your guide always."

At that the presence of Caleb diminished and left Mark. He continued to float in the river and noticed that he was drawing strength and clarity of mind the longer he stayed. He was so grateful he started praising Yahveh and felt, more than heard, a great chorus join in with him.

Some indeterminate amount of time later he became aware he was in his room on his knees. He thanked God for the communion and for Caleb. He got up and checked the time. That made him stop and look again. He had only been praying for six minutes but it had seemed like days. It dawned on him that it was perfectly logical because the time with God did not coincide with normal Earthly time. Yahveh had created time for man not Himself or Heaven. This knowledge was precise and completely understandable. Mark shook his head. Obviously that piece of information was part of the knowledge he had been given.

Knowing that this was going to make things even more interesting, he went to find Sarah, Jack, and Laura.

CHAPTER THIRTY-SIX

As Mark walked into the War Room he somehow knew that the new information he had been given would be available on an "as needed" basis. When it was needed he would be able to understand and use the knowledge. It didn't even bother him that he had no idea how much data he had acquired or that he wasn't in control of it. That alone would help keep him humble.

Jack looked up from the world's crime summaries gathered and shifted by Charlie's new computers. The report was still thirty pages long even when sorted for only crimes that might affect them or interest them as a team. "Hey Mark. I thought you were going to take some down time."

Mark smiled as he realized that his time in the river had completely refreshed him. "I did. Can I get a sit-down with Sarah and you two?"

Laura had been talking to the FBI and Sarah had been interfacing with the Mossad on the computer throughout the morning. Jack looked at both of them for approval and said, "Sure thing."

The four of them moved into the living room and got comfortable. Mark thought over what he wanted to tell them and then asked God for the right words. He looked at his wife and his two best friends and said, "Let's pray first. He asked God for understanding and wisdom for all of them as a group. Then he prayed for heavenly protection for this meeting that would block out all enemy eavesdropping or understanding of their action. He sat back. "I just had a marvelous prayer time with God and the angel Caleb." He went on to describe what he had experienced and how he understood the consequences of that meeting.

When Mark was finished, Sarah reached over and hugged him. "I'm so glad He gave you this mission." Mark didn't know if that was a complement or a statement of relief on her part that Yahveh hadn't picked her for the task.

Laura was grinning at him. "Mark that was probably the closest any of us have come to heaven other than my "repair" trip. " She was referring to an earlier event when she had been wounded by a demonic sword and a mighty angel had carried her to heaven and the Savior had healed her and returned her to Earth.

Mark's first thought was, "Yeah, it is special." But, immediately he realized the danger in that thought and he prayed that Yahveh would humble his heart. Then, balanced by the understanding that he was only the messenger and not the message, he suggested they talk about the enemy's ability to attack the team from the demonic realm.

Jack had thought through what Mark had told them and understood that he was attempting to access the new knowledge. "Okay, I am definitely concerned that the enemy has an unfair advantage in that they can pick their points of attack and their own timing so that all we can do is react."

Mark thought about that and nodded. "It does seem that they have the edge there but actually, it is they who are constrained by Yahveh. They can not attack us unless they get Yahveh's permission to do so. A rough analogy would be a contractor having to get the government's permission to build a building. They have to petition Yahveh with the general points of their mission and wait for approval. This information is available to the heavenly host as soon as they request it. By prayer and walking closely with the Father we too can be aware of their plans." Mark was amazed at the information coming out of his mouth but he knew it was the truth.

Laura asked Mark, "What information is available to us through these "general points"? Does that mean we might be aware of an impending attack of a certain type but not where or when?"

Mark answered immediately, "It's complicated because of our limited intelligence. The actual petition covers those details but at a level we here on Earth can't understand."

Seeing their confusion Mark tapped into a new thought. Sitting forward he earnestly said, "Listen, if we could hear it, the petition would be in a language we don't know, involving concepts, actions, and parameters we can't possibly understand. It would be presented in a non-verbal, spiritual communication that takes place at a level so far above us we can't even conceive of it. There are many parts to a petition and each part of the petition involves simultaneous events in many other dimensions which are completely unknown to us at this time. A myriad of unique events in each of these other dimensions have to "gel" and mesh with the action requested in our dimension or the petition is denied. Add the fact that we are time-based beings and the spirits, both angelic and demonic, are not. Then the entire operation of petitioning an attack on us becomes an eight dimensional problem that would make no absolutely no sense in our four dimensional world."

"But, Satan and his demons have to make petition to Yahveh to even open a tiny opening between their evil world and the human plane. That is the only time that Satan can violate God's rules by sending illegal or un-authorized demons into our world. See? He can flood our world with demons; both legal and illegal; but only if the permission has been granted to enter this world at all. Every appearance of any demon, even Satan, from the dawn of time has required God's permission. They require an authorized portal between our worlds that has been approved by God in eight dimensions at a particular period of our time."

Jack asked, "How then did they get demons into that canyon in Colorado before we even were aware they were doing anything?"

Mark grinned, "I don't know, but, I can speculate that the one demon that grabbed the family probably had permission to come into our dimension. Why? Only God knows. But Satan used that one opening to expand it into the three rifts and remember, all those demons were here illegally. We killed them with bullets and grenades until Charlie flattened them with the missiles."

"That explains the difference in the legal and illegal demons. Legal demons have been specifically authorized to cross between dimensions. While they present a physical presence they still maintain their properties. The illegal demon can appear here with a physical body but it doesn't have its normal properties because it wasn't authorized to be here. It is kind of like it snuck in through a legally-open portal but, since that particular demon hasn't been given permission to cross the dimensional barrier he doesn't have any real right or permission to be here."

They can hurl curses, demean people, cause fear and terror that hasn't been authorized and they can physically interface with beings and things in our dimension but, the illegal demon isn't protected by his normal properties and defenses. That is why we can destroy them with bullets and explosions like a normal being in our dimension."

Mark shook his head at the information he was speaking. "A fact we need to understand is that the Father is granting us these additional advantages to destroy the illegal demons because they are defying his laws."

Mark held his hands up in mock frustration. "Compound all of this by the fact that millions of petitions are being processed at the same time and that the rules and requirements are different for each dimension. There are also beings contesting the granting of petitions and there are other beings supporting certain ones and not others. Do you begin to see the problem of our understanding any of this?"

The other three sat back somewhat in shock at the situation. Mark decided to reassure them at this point. "But, we don't have to understand the spiritual world until we are a part of it. We are the children of the Most High Yahveh. Our Savior is our big brother and Yahveh's angels are here to help us. If we, limited as we are, have been chosen by Yahveh to be his warriors, then the help and understanding we need has already been made available. All we have to do is to ask for it through prayer and petition."

Laura thought to herself, "I'm so glad Mark can understand the enormity of this information and that it has humbled him as a result." She remembered Mark not so long ago and knew he would have been completely overcome by pride at having such power.

Mark sobered up and looked closely at each of the other three people to stress the importance of a status of humility about their positions. "From our viewpoint we are all important and vital to the Father's plans to deter this egregious effort by the enemy of all mankind. Nothing could be farther from the truth. We have been granted a great honor to do the very tiny bit of work that He has assigned us. If we failed or wouldn't do our part He would have an alternative plan that would serve His needs. I don't know how to explain it but we have to have pride in our efforts for the Kingdom without becoming proud of our part in the grand scheme of history. Just be grateful, love Yahveh and do your utmost to give back the smallest portion of the love he has shown us in life and through His Son Yahshua.

Jack nodded, "I understand the picture better now and I confess the sin of pride in myself. I was beginning to think we, the team, were so special and important that we could demand special privileges from anyone. Now, thanks to you Mark, I see that trap clearly. I confess my pride as sin and ask God to forgive me for the sin of pride and help me to repent of it." Laura and Sarah agreed with Jack and prayed for forgiveness and cleansing from a God that suddenly seemed a billion times larger, more complicated, and more loving than before.

Mark looked intently at the rest of them. "We need to remember we are simply servants of Yahveh and no more special than any other saint. We are here to do a job and then get on our knees in humbleness to thank Yahveh for the privilege of doing it."

The rest of the team agreed. Laura said, "Then I think we need to seek the Father as to what we should expect next."

CHAPTER THIRTY-SEVEN

The prayers led to more waiting and to more intensive training for all members of the team as they waited. There was a major push against them coming soon and they had to be in the best shape they could be to defeat it.

The following Friday night and Saturday were the Sabbath and they celebrated Shabbat as they had been instructed to by Tim. They rested and invited Tim to the fortress for church services Friday evening. After a time of worship and singing they discussed aspects of their recent missions and then listened to Tim as he taught on what God had given him for that evening. It was appropriate, Ephesians 6, the Armor of God.

Mark fell into a deep communion with the Father. After the service was over he got up and left the group to make a phone call. At five a.m. the next morning he got everyone up to make an announcement. "Okay boys and girls, Yahveh say's the war is on. I know you've all been working hard at training and your rest last night was short, but we need to get airborne as quickly as possible. Our destination is fifty miles south of Ciudad Juarez which is on the Mexican border just south of El Paso, Texas. We will join up with the SOG when we arrive. The devil is calling us out and God is sending us to respond. I'll brief you on the details when we are airborne."

Laura listened to the depth of Mark's instruction he had received from Yahveh and sent a prayer of thankfulness to the Father in the name of Yahshua for the spiritual growth and confidence and felt tears of happiness for Mark. Normally that kind of information would have come through her. But, she felt nothing except extreme happiness for Mark and his new spirituality and understanding.

Laura then looked at Jack, "Isn't that one of the areas that the war with the drug cartels is out of control?"

Jack nodded in response.

Both Laura and Jack felt a burden from God. They went to their suite and continued to pray. They had scarcely started to commune with the Father when Jack watched a vision in which Laura walked forward and met with the angel Rose. Rose was in her fierce white with little of the softening gold to tone down the brilliance. Rose was obviously impatient and not in the mood to chat. "Laura! It is imperative that you and Jack take the Lord's Treasure with you to Mexico. Do not fail in this. It is for the glory of Yahveh and the salvation of many souls!" As Rose faded from view she was already rushing somewhere else.

Because Rose's attitude was at such odds with her normal appearance they prayed and asked the Father if it truly was Rose that they had heard from and that the angel was giving them a message from God. They were assured it was truly was Rose and the message was true. They stopped praying after thanking God for the communion; Jack was already on his feet and headed for the vault room.

Two hours later the Citation X was at 35,000 feet headed south from Denver with six members of the Crossfire Team. Jack and Laura, Mark and Sarah, Sensei Grady, and Tim Carson were passengers and Su Li was piloting the sleek jet. Mark was holding a briefing and Su Li listened in on the intercom.

"When we were praying last night, God's Spirit dropped a vision on me that I will never forget. Apparently one of the terrorist groups, which one I don't know as yet, was attempting to smuggle two ex-Russian suitcase nukes into the U.S. over the Mexican border. They were detected by satellite and the Mexican government sent their troops to seal the border while they hunted these terrorists down. Once the terrorists were isolated away from the border and surrounded, the Mexicans started to close in on them. The information I got from the NSA showed the terrorists rounding up two or three hundred Mexican nationals from a village called El Barreal to use as hostages. They threaten to blow up the entire group if the Mexican authorities attempt to capture or kill them."

Jack shrugged, "Sounds like a job for the Mexican Army or at worst, the U.S. State Department. How did we get involved?"

Mark nodded, "Normally you'd be right, but for two things. First, my vision showed us taking out the terrorists and the people were all right. Then it showed us standing back and demons gloating as the people were slaughtered. Second, the terrorists told the Mexican Authorities that they would only deal with the Crossfire Team from Denver, Colorado. The State Department bounced that ball to the Pentagon and our name was called to "aid" our trading partner and ally. The request came from General Miles himself."

Sarah asked her husband, "Sounds like one of the enemies' efforts to lure us in and destroy us. How many terrorists are there?"

Mark shrugged his shoulders again, "Don't know for sure. Guesses range from fifteen to forty. That's why the SOG was redirected to meet us in El Paso. We're going in, with Mexico's permission, in choppers. The general plan is for Jack to open negotiations with the terrorists to see what they want, specifically what they want with us. In reality, almost everyone expects that it is a trap to be sprung on us. So, I'm planning on using superior force and taking them out. Hopefully without losing any of our people or the Mexican nationals."

Laura added, "If there is a really smart demon behind this, they'll be ready for an end-around since it is the obvious move."

Mark nodded, "I know, but until we get there and assess the situation in person there is nothing else for us to plan with at this point. I'm not getting anything from heaven and as usual, things are like gooey plastic and will change with the situation."

Laura had a concerned look on her face, "Let's pray for protection, wisdom, and guidance. I think we're going to need it."

CHAPTER THIRTY-EIGHT

As the Citation X landed in the intense heat at the El Paso International Airport north of the city and taxied to a large hanger, Su Li could see the huge, gray U.S.A.F. Galaxy C5A with the front open and the Special Operations Group troops exiting the aircraft. She taxied the Citation into the spot the flagman indicated and shut down the engines.

The team met with Colonel Baldwin, the leader of the SOG, and Major Mike White between the planes. After shaking hands all around the Colonel said, "I'm glad that little snafu in Washington got resolved and we can work together again General Connelly."

Mark grinned, "Me too, Paul." He looked over the thirty five members of the SOG standing at attention next to the C5A. "Tell the troops to stand at ease. Have them gather around and I'll address all of you about this mission."

After everyone gathered in the shade of the hanger and the giant aircraft to escape the heat of the Mexican desert, Mark greeted them and explained the situation. He then asked if there were any questions. Two members of the SOG were Kevin and Craig Steele. They had fought along side the team in Israel when the ASF attempted to poison Tel Aviv. They were step-brothers of Jack's and had been there in time to help save their sister, Christi from the terrorists. They watched the other members of the SOG as they coped with the new assignment. There were a few minor questions but the important one was from Captain Timbers. "Sir, how will our snipers and other troops be able to distinguish the terrorists if they've integrated themselves within the company of the Mexican nationals?"

Mark nodded, "Good question Captain. Obviously they will be armed but they might be hiding their weapons. Besides the normal body language clues you've all been trained to look for in hostage situations I would suggest asking God's Spirit to guide your search. We don't know the number of terrorists at this time but hopefully the Mexican military will be able to give us that information when we arrive on site. Okay, get your gear and load up the Chinooks."

Two of the unit's Humvees and most of the heavy equipment had already been loaded in one Chinook while the troops loaded onto two more of the tandem-rotored craft. Already warmed up, the three choppers lifted off of the tarmac and headed south. The MH47s could fly up to 11,100 feet and travelled at roughly 85 miles/hour. The trip only took thirty-five minutes.

As they flew towards the enemy, Laura looked casually around at the troops. She saw confidence, professionalism, and a lot of prayer going on. The drab interior of the chopper was lightened by the desert camouflage of the men and women but the seriousness they showed as they checked their weapons and cross-checked each other's equipment darkened the mood. She moved closer to Jack and found him smiling at her. "What?" She asked him.

He grinned; "I'm trying really hard to see that housewife who told me that she "wasn't brought up to do things like this" on the airfield in Houston a couple of years ago."

Laura thought back to that time when they were chasing Max Lister to the Middle East and remembered her lack of confidence as they were being taken out to the jet fighters. "That was a different me. That was when I thought I was the one that had to do it all. Yahveh has given me the confidence to be the warrior I am today."

Jack had tears in his eyes as he hugged her with his right arm. "I don't have the words to tell you how proud I am of you and the dedication and determination you have to do Yahveh's will. I love you more than life and yet I've had to give you to Yahveh for protection because I know how inadequate I am. But, I will tell you this, I'd rather stand back-to-back with you in battle than anyone else because I know your heart and your ability. I really doubt that any man on this Earth has had a better wife than you. Thank you for loving me."

Laura felt the warm glow inside that Jack's words generated. Smiling she said, "Actually, I need to thank you. I could still be a financial VP in some company fighting over dollars if it hadn't been for meeting you and our finding

Yahveh together." She then leaned up and kissed him tenderly.

They held hands for the next few minutes. Jack saw Mark signal him and he raised Laura's hand and kissed it. Then he got out of his seat and made his way over to Mark. "What's up?"

Mark pointed out of the windshield of the Chinook. "We are overflying the Mexican troops south of the standoff. We'll be landing in a couple of minutes. Let's stick to our basic plan. You, Laura, Tim, and Su Li see if you can arrange some kind of negotiations. Sarah, the Sensei, and I will take the SOG and see if we can positively mark terrorist targets."

Jack nodded and hung on as the chopper started it's descent onto the desert floor.

As the helicopter landed, Mark jumped out of the door and walked over to what was obviously a field headquarters building. A ranking Mexican officer exited the tent flaps and met Mark with a salute and a handshake. "Captain Ramos at your service, General Connelly."

Mark liked the man. He was about five foot eleven inches tall, had a full-head of black hair and a handsome face. He carried himself with ease and radiated professionalism as a career soldier. He knew what he was doing and expected everyone else to do the same. After introducing Jack and Colonel Baldwin, Mark asked, "Captain Ramos, what is the situation with the terrorists and their captives?"

The Captain ushered them into the headquarters tent and over to a table with a map on it. Pointing at a position about two miles north of their present position the Mexican officer tapped it. "This is where the terrorists and the captives are right now." Moving his finger down slightly on the map he tapped it again. "This is where we are with my reinforced company." He indicated an area equally far north of the terrorists and said, "This is where my second company is securing the northern front."

Jack asked, "How do we communicate with the terrorists?"

The Captain looked at a loss. "Communicate with the terrorists? I don't understand what you mean."

Jack looked at Mark and then back to the Captain. "We were told that they wanted to negotiate with our team. How do we negotiate with them?"

Understanding came to the Captain. "Oh, you mean how do we deal with them. I see. We have an enlisted man who came from this village. He has talked to one of his relatives by cell phone. That is how they told us what they wanted."

Jack nodded, "Can I talk to this man and use his phone to talk to the terrorists?"

The Captain beamed, "Of course. Come with me." Jack walked out of the tent behind the Captain and past several dozen troops until they reached a patch of shade under an awning. One of the soldiers came to attention as the Captain spoke to him in Spanish. The man took out a cell phone and punched in a number. He started to talk and then handed the phone to Jack.

Jack heard the man on the other end speaking in Spanish. He handed the phone to Laura. She spoke fluent Spanish and Italian. Jack's other languages were Chinese and Japanese with a general knowledge of Russian.

Laura conversed with the man for a short period and then pressed the "off" button. She handed the phone over to the soldier and walked with Jack away from the awning. She looked around to see who was near and there was no one within ear shot. Looking up at Jack she said, "The Uncle of that soldier gave the phone to one of the terrorists. They asked for two people to meet them half way and open the negotiations. Who do you want to have the honors?"

Jack thought for only a second. "Why don't you and I start the ball rolling? I really doubt that these are serious negotiations because whatever we work out, the Mexican authorities would have to approve. Not too likely. The terrorists know that so this has to be some kind of trap."

Jack keyed the combat microphone on his helmet. "Charlie, Laura and I are supposed to meet two of their people for talks about halfway between where we are now and where the large mass of people two miles north of us is at present. Can you keep an eye on us for possible traps or tricks?"

Charlie's answer was so clear it was hard to realize he was sitting at a console in the fortress in Denver, hundreds of miles away. "You got it chief."

Mark walked up and listened to the recap. "I'll take a couple of my people and back you up. If they don't have anything like Charlie's eye-in-the-sky they won't know we are there." He trotted off to find Craig and Kevin Steele.

Jack looked at Laura, "When did you tell them we'd be there?"

Laura smiled, "In about an hour."

Jack looked out over the hot desert sands north of the encampment. He took a large drink of water. "Let's get going."

CHAPTER THIRTY-NINE

Five minutes after leaving the Mexican encampment you couldn't tell that there was any human life on the planet. Other than scrub brush and sand there wasn't any terrain features. Sand towered above them to the west and again not too far to the east. Their path ahead was fairly flat but still hard going in the sand. Every time you stepped forward you sank into the sand up to your ankles. It didn't take too much walking like that to work up a good sweat.

Jack figured that they were three-fourths of the way to the meeting place when he saw two men walking towards them from the north. At first they were just gray blurs in the blinding sunlight that bore down from above with fierceness and reflected off of the sand with almost the same brilliance. If it hadn't been for their dark sunglasses they would have seen nothing.

The blurs became two men that walked cautiously towards them. When they were about ten feet apart the two groups stopped. Jack decided to take the upper hand in the negotiations by speaking first. "My name is Jack Malone and I am a leader in the Crossfire Team. He indicated Laura, "This is my wife Laura and she is also a member of the team." He then fell silent.

The man on Jack's right held up his hand, "I am JalAi and this is Hassan. We have a list of demands and they are not negotiable!" The man was either a good actor or he was really stressed.

Jack walked another five feet closer so that they didn't have to shout. "What is your list of demands JalAi?"

The man pulled a paper out of his shirt pocket. "One, we demand a helicopter for our people and an equal amount of hostages. Two, we demand free, uncontested passage from Mexico to Iran. After we reach Iran we will release our hostages. Three, we want the sum of ten million dollars; American, delivered to us in small denomination bills. Any deviation from these requests and we will detonate our two nuclear bombs and kill everyone."

Jack nodded, "How many people total will the helicopters need to carry?

JalAi didn't hesitate, "Sixty two."

Jack said, "I will have to discuss these demands with the Mexican authorities. I will call you when I receive their answer." He turned around and started walking back to the south accompanied by Laura.

The two terrorists looked at each other and also turned around and headed back north.

Jack spoke to Charlie Wu. "Well Charlie, anything out of sorts from your view?"

Charlie gave them a negative. "Just two guys and a mile of sand to walk through. I will tell you that there is something odd about eight miles north of your present position but I can't tell what it is yet. I'll let you know when I find out."

Laura asked Charlie, "Charlie, what do you mean, "Odd"?"

Charlie came back, "I'm getting some strange ferromagnetic readings but there is nothing to see there except rock outcroppings and sand. It could just be some concentrations of magnetic rock."

Jack said, "Keep an eye on those readings Charlie. There's nothing normal about this situation." They kept trudging back to the Mexican encampment.

Meeting with the other team members Jack told them. "I don't hold out any hope that we will see a negotiated settlement to this problem. Their demands are a joke. It's as if they've been watching too much American television or movies.

Tim laughed, "Let me see if I have this right. These guys tried to smuggle two nuclear weapons into the U.S. but got caught. Now they want a free ride home and ten million dollars as a consolation prize. No way will our government or the Mexicans agree to those terms."

Mark shook his head, "Those demands are just to fill time, and they don't expect us to accede to their demands. There's something else going on here."

Jack thought for a few minutes. "They were considerate enough to tell us how many of them are there. Mark, can you and the SOG take out all thirty-one of the terrorists without a lot of collateral damage?"

Mark looked at Colonel Baldwin. "I think so. We've got a good handle on the thirty-one people that look to be actual terrorists. There is one we're not sure of because he acts like a bully regardless which side he's on. But, he doesn't have a weapon."

Jack spoke to Charlie. "Make sure to tag the thirty-one suspects and track them for a 2 a.m. strike, okay?"

Charlie came right back. "Roger that. I already have them tagged and located. Check your Combat readouts."

Reaching up to his helmet, Jack lowered his left eye vision screen. He saw a huge map with each of the terrorists marked as a small red dot. Looking up at Mark he said, "Take them out tonight and we'll get the people out of here to safety."

Mark nodded. Turning to the Colonel he said, "Give everyone a target and cross match for secondary targets. We need to be in position at two a.m. without fail."

The Colonel pulled up an assignment list on his tablet and started assigning targets to each of the SOG personnel.

CHAPTER FORTY

Eli Arroyo Lopez stepped closer to his old friend Miguel Quiterez and said quietly "My friend, I don't think these men are interested in us at all. I think that they are only using us as bait."

Miguel frowned and whispered back, "That is not good Eli; everyone knows that bait is expendable."

Eli nodded slightly, "Si."

They had been held for three days with more than two hundred of their friends and neighbors by the thirty or so armed men. There had been little food and less comfort. At least there was plenty of water. Water was very important for them considering that they were being held in the desert miles from their homes, during the summer and without shelter.

Eli thought to himself, "These men are not very smart but they are definitely dangerous. Three of his amigos had been shot for speaking out against their captors. There was no sign of the Federale's or any other group to help the unarmed peasants. The only word they had from the outside was when one of the young men who had escaped the roundup had snuck into their group acting like one of them who had been outside relieving himself. The captors were fooled. Eli was now less worried about what his family was thinking. But, he prayed several times a day for the many captives who were weak and not in good shape. He was only in his sixties and was in good health. He knew he could outlast and out walk these Middle Eastern thugs. This was his country and he knew that counted for something.

None of the women taken were young and so there wasn't that to worry about. Eli mused to himself that there weren't that many young women in his village at any time so it figured that there wouldn't be many among the hostages.

He stared out over the burning desert in the setting sun and wondered what his destiny would be. These Arabs were threatening to kill them all if their demands weren't met, but he had watched them closely and it didn't seem like their demands were important to them. They were arranging something else and whatever it was it didn't seem to include a long future for the hostages. He would have to see if there was an opportunity to overcome these men. He knew that most of the Mexicans in the hostage group were elderly and would not be able to help, but there were some who were brave and strong.

Earlier in the afternoon, two of the thugs left the group and went south for a while. When they returned they had short discussions with the rest of their group. Then the number of men on guard was doubled as darkness fell. That left only twenty of their number to watch the two hundred hostages. Not bad odds, but there was no organization among the hostages and it would take one strike at the same time to overcome the stay-at-home guards.

Eli laid down in his serape and waited to see what the morning would bring.

A mile north of the hostages a company of the Mexican Army was relaxing for the night. Nothing was going to happen until the morning and there was no reason not to sleep. Most of the troops had already bedded down with only the sentries moving about. The five Sergeants and two officers were discussing what action they might be involved in the next day. One of the Sergeants noticed that he couldn't see the sentries to the south and stood up to see better.

A silenced rifle round hit him in the chest, killing him immediately and alerting his companions. As they jumped up or dived for cover they were all killed by silenced rounds. Then a rush of dark figures moved between the sleeping soldiers with silenced pistols and put them to sleep forever. The operation took less than ten minutes to eliminate the entire company of soldiers.

The dark figures checked to ensure they had eliminated everyone and then quick-timed it across the sand to join up with a much larger force waiting for the orders to move south

CHAPTER FORTY-ONE

Charlie's computers, aided by advanced military satellite capabilities were able to map the security arrangements and sentries posted by the terrorists. The entire team, including the members of the SOG were able to move within two hundred feet of their targets without arousing any alarm. The eleven roving sentries were being shadowed by the team members assigned to eliminate them at the right time.

Shift change for the sentries happened every three hours. These guys had been walking their posts since midnight and were tired and ready to give the job to the next man. Hence, they were less observant than a fresh guard would have been.

While it would have been good sense to mix their people in with the Mexicans there was bad blood between the two groups, for good reason, and the terrorists tended to stick together for protection and strength.

As the strike hour neared, Charlie continued to keep a computerized eye on all of the targets and the surrounding area. As he sat there in the comfort of the air-conditioned room of the fortress he felt for the troops in the field. He had done similar duties during his earlier existence as a Chinese agent. He knew the oppressive heat of the daytime had been replaced by the brittle cold of the nighttime desert. But the effort to move silently, to prevent being seen, and to still accomplish a deadly mission was so stressful that not everyone could manage it. In fact there were few that could. Charlie knew that everyone on the team and the SOG had been placed there by Yahveh. They would do a professional job regardless of the stress or the environment.

While not assigned individual targets, Jack, Laura, Mark, Su Li, the Sensei, and Sarah were scattered among the SOG soldiers as command and control and as backup in the event anything went wrong. Laura in particular was praying and seeking the Father as to any spiritual events or attacks that might take place or be a part of the rescue.

Since Tim had the least training or experience he had been left with Captain Ramos as liaison between the Mexican military and the team.

At exactly two a.m. Jack nodded and Mark pushed the button on his battle pack that sent the attack signal. The silent assault was over in less than twenty seconds. Thirty-one terrorists were dead and there still was no outcry or disturbance among the now-freed captives.

Mark quickly located the two briefcase nuclear bombs. Checking them over he brought one over to Jack. "These things were unusable at least ten years ago. There was never a chance they would have gone off. Not only is the circuitry so outdated it doesn't have any microprocessors, there is only a trace of radioactivity where the core should be. Either the guys carrying them were dumber than sticks or they knew they didn't have anything to bargain with at any time."

Jack spoke into his microphone to all the troops. "Gently wake them up and get them quietly together. I don't think this is all the enemy has in store for us and I want to get these people away from this position in the event it is targeted by artillery or mines."

The team had eighteen people that could speak Spanish. These people led their groups and spoke to the natives. The urgency was conveyed to the other captives quietly and quickly. Seeing the bodies of the dead terrorists and the heavily armed troops among them added to the seriousness of the exodus.

Mark, Su Li, the Sensei, and Sarah continued to search behind the troops and the freed people for any stragglers. Jack was bringing up the rear when he spotted Laura standing still looking toward the north. He jogged over to her and stopped. "What's the matter?"

Laura didn't stop looking to the north but answered him quietly. There is a spiritual pressure from the north and it is an evil pressure. I don't know what it is but it isn't good for us or the people we just rescued." She broke off her preoccupation with the northern front and spun around. "We need to get out of here as quickly as possible." They begin to jog to the south behind the rest of the people. Catching up with Mark, Jack asked him, "Can reach Captain

Ramos and see if the Mexican Army help us with the extraction?"

Mark paused, "I don't know. I can't reach Captain Ramos on the radio. The first group should be there about now. By the way, we have roughly 225 people and several that can't walk and are being carried by the others. I've moved the stretcher cases and some of the more elderly to the Humvees and that is speeding up the march."

Jack checked his watch and saw that it was already three-thirty. Just getting the people one mile to the south had taken over an hour. The wind was shifting and starting to blow out of the west. As it picked up speed it also picked up sand and threw it against everyone.

Mark talked on his command radio and signaled Jack. Jack switched on the second channel. "Jack Malone."

Captain Ramos' voice was calm and controlled but it indicated a problem because of the chaos in the background. "General Malone, we have lost contact with our troops to the north. I can't raise anyone and there are at least six radios in the company up there. Also, we are under attack here ourselves by at least an equal number of troops of unknown nature. We have suffered significant losses and . .."There was a shout, the sound of an explosion, and then silence.

Mark had continued to walk with the leading edge of the rescued hostages. He got Jack's attention. "There's a pitched battle going on at the extraction site. Colonel Baldwin has taken the front groups to the east avoiding the battle. The middle group with about a hundred people is following them. Let's leave the SOG to handle this last group and see what we can do to help Tim and Captain Ramos with . . ."

Mark was interrupted by Charlie Wu. "Jack! Mark! You've got a couple of hundred troops coming at you from the north. They've got at least ten main battle tanks and two dozen Bradley-type armed personnel carriers. They're only about three miles away and moving fairly quickly to the south."

Jack was exasperated with the sudden appearance of such a large enemy troop and Charlie's not being able to see them earlier. He coldly asked, "Who are they and where did they come from?"

Charlie shot back, "They apparently were hunkered down about a mile north of you and started moving about the time you were getting the hostages out of the camp. I don't know how they stayed undetectable from the heat, biomass, and night vision satellite detection. But, this has all the markings of a classic trap with demon coverage. I'm trying to get some air assets after the tanks but it looks like they've got Stingers and some AA on the personnel carriers also. The Mexicans have lost four aircraft so far and have had to withdraw to wait for reinforcements. The enemy looks to be a small battalion with all the necessary support. I not only didn't see them but I can't still get any ID as to who they are. I'm sorry I let you down Jack."

Jack realized that they had been outfoxed. "Charlie, I want you to find out how a mechanized battalion could suddenly appear in the middle of the Mexican desert without someone knowing they existed? We're less than a hundred miles from U.S. soil. Find out who they are, if there are more of them, and who owns them!

Laura put her hand on Jack's arm, "I'm not sure, but I think there was a supernatural covering that prevented Charlie's equipment from seeing them. There is an extremely strong demonic presence traveling with the group following us." Su Li nodded in agreement.

Mark called Colonel Baldwin and warned him about the size and apparent professionalism of the pursuit. The Colonel said he would have his forces be on the lookout for an end-around or a blocking force.

As Mark was talking to the Colonel the wind picked up again and started to moan above them. The amount of sand they were being pelted with increased to a constant stinging harassment, blinding them and making it difficult to talk.

Mark called Sarah, the Sensei, Su Li, and Laura to where he and Jack were standing. Jack pulled out a small map and illuminated it with his flashlight. He pointed out the situation. "There is a large mechanized battalion quickly closing in on us from the north and there seems to be a blocking force to the south. The headquarters site is under heavy attack and I've lost contact with Tim and Captain Ramos."

Mark pointed out a flat area to the east. "This is where Colonel Baldwin and our troops are leading the ex-hostages. It looks like a big canyon that narrows to the east right up to a high rock ridge. The rock ridges on the sides have built up large sand dunes in their shelter. According to the map there is a small canyon through the rock ridge ahead of us. That is where the Colonel is making for with the leading group of people. We need to bring up the rear and attempt to keep the enemy away from the people as best we can."

Sarah asked, "How about support from either our Air Force or the Mexican Air Force?"

Su Li pointed up at the unseen sand flying above them. "We're in a sand storm right now and anyway, I doubt that any air assets could get here before the group behind us closes in on us."

Sarah said, "I don't see that our thirty-guns and two Humvees will slow down a battalion very much."

Jack said, "True, of course, then there are the tanks."

Sarah looked at Mark and raised an eyebrow. "Tanks too?"

Mark shrugged, "Only about ten main battle tanks and a couple dozen armed troop carriers."

Laura shook her head, "Well, they asked for it."

Everyone looked at her. She grinned, "Time to call in the big guns." She kneeled in the sand and started to pray. The others looked at her and joined her.

The wind screamed, the sand flew, and the praise soared. Jack heard straight from the Father. *"Jack, take your people to the east, the enemy of mankind will overstep their authority and I will gain esteem through the earthly enemy and all his army, his tanks, his fighting vehicles, and his troops. The enemy will know that I am God".*

Jack was excited enough to stand up and the wind was strong enough to blow him over again. Shaking the sand out of his ears he crawled over to the others. Yahveh says, "Head east and Yahveh will gain glory through our enemies."

The core of the Crossfire Team pulled their hoods up and headed east with the wind at their backs.

CHAPTER FORTY-TWO

Catching up with the last of the stragglers, the team ran on to the front of the crowd of people. Reaching the front they walked with Colonel Baldwin and explained the situation and what they had to do. Mark, Sarah, Su Li, along with Sensei Grady worked with the first group to form the people into a semblance of a marching troop with the two Humvees in the lead, lighting the way. The SOG troopers and the team members urged the people on through flying sand into the dark to the east.

Laura and Jack went back to the rear of the formation and took ten of the SOG warriors with them. Just as they arranged themselves as a delaying force, the first of the enemy troops appeared about a hundred yards away. These were just visible through the blowing sand and the darkness to the troops with night vision goggles. Jack whispered to wait until they were closer so as to not give away their strategy or positions.

But, the enemy also had NVG and started firing almost as Jack spoke. One of the rounds punched through Jack's liner and impacted on his trauma plate in a pocket of his Kevlar body armor. The force of the round knocked the wind out of him and dropped him to his knees. Two of the SOG troops returned the fire and saw that the enemy's body armor wasn't up to the 6.8 SPC rounds. Two of the enemy soldiers went down and the rest faded back into the sand and darkness beyond the range of the SOG's vision.

Jack got his wind back and struggled to the rocks looking west. Wheezing, he said, "Fall back, immediately!"

The twelve of them ran two hundred yards to the east and found new fighting positions. Less than two minutes later a tank came into view and its main gun pounded their original position into more sand.

Kevin looked at his brother, Craig, "That's no fair; they've got bigger guns than we do."

Craig looked at his brother as if he had become stupid, "That's what a tank is for dummy! Didn't they train you at all?"

Kevin laughed at his brother's seriousness, "Must have missed that class."

Jack said, "Knock it off. We're not going to be able to stop them at all. Let's fall back and help get the people through that canyon."

One of the SOG warriors said, "We won't be able to stop them but we can make them drag their feet a bit." He raised an anti-tank, shoulder mounted missile launcher with a HEAT (high explosive, anti-tank) round and fired it at the tank that had shot at them. The HEAT round struck the tank at the base of its turret. The first round burned it's way into the tank and the secondary round sent 5000 degree heat throughout the tank. The tank exploded violently enough to blow the turret off of the tank in huge fireball that lit up the desert and canyon walls on either side of the tank.

Kevin smiled, "That should really tick them off!"

The twelve of them quickly faded back into the mist of sand and darkness. The sun had apparently come up but it only changed the world from dark black to dark ocher and gray.

Jack called Charlie Wu. "Charlie, what can you tell me about their movements?"

Charlie's voice was still clear despite the sand storm. "I've only got an intermittent view of them or you for that matter. That sand storm is hard to penetrate."

Mark chimed in, "Oh yeah? You ought to try it from this end."

Jack said, "Okay Charlie, are there any assets being sent to help us?"

"The Mexican Army has mobilized a Battalion but they are grounded until the storm passes that area. From what I see it will be at least five hours before it is over."

Signing off, Jack was about to tell the others what he had heard when he got a call from Mark, Jack, you'd bettered come to the front of the line. We've got a serious problem."

Jack and Laura made their way to the front of the mass of people who were now just standing still and trying to protect themselves from the blowing sand. As he came up to Mark's position he saw the problem. The way was completely blocked by a wall of sand over a hundred feet tall and very steep.

In the darkness, the moaning wind and flying sand underscored the hopelessness of the situation. Jack looked at Mark, "What do we do?"

Mark shook his head, "There is a break in the rock wall here. It's supposed to be about fifty feet across and over a quarter mile long. Some of the people here went through it last week. But the storm has dumped tons of sand into it. We can't get through here and the walls of sand on either side are almost as tall. We've got to go back."

Jack shook his head. "That's not possible. That armored column is less than a thousand yards behind us and they are closing the gap quickly. If we stand and fight we will all be killed." Su Li quipped "At least they can't put any aircraft up either."

Laura had been praying and suddenly her eyes flew open. She put her hand on Jack's arm. Shouting to be heard over the wind, she said, "Seek the Father, Jack".

As Jack asked the Father what to do, He clearly heard, *"Raise the crucifixion nail and stretch out your hand over the blockage to divide the sand, so that the people can go through the gap free of sand. I will harden the hearts of the pursuers so that they will follow you."*

Jack took a big breath and handed his rifle to Mark. Then he walked to one side and faced the blockage. The wind picked up even more and so much sand was being added to the barrier it was running down the face of the dune in front of them like a river.

Reaching inside his jacket he took out the box with the crucifixion nail in it. He opened the box and took the nail out. Holding the nail as high as he could in front of him. Jack prayed, *"Father, I'm no Moses but I trust you and know that you are able..."*

CHAPTER FORTY-THREE

Confident that her plan would result in the destruction of the Crossfire Team, Cat's glee turned to triumph when she saw the crucifixion nail held up by Jack. This would be the crowning achievement of her career. She knew that she could step into their world and snatch the nail from the weak human man and transition back to the demonic world in less time than it would take to tell it.

Ecstatic with greed and desire she made the transition to the other world.

There was an audible "crack" behind Jack and he spun around to see a winged, black demon stepping into the human dimension and it was headed straight for him. Although it was not as ugly as most demons, it more than made up for it's sleekness by the sheer evil it generated. The fingers on both arms ended in long black talons that looked very sharp. Jack's spirit recoiled at the presence of Cat as she strode forth to take the crucifixion nail from him.

There was another flash but this time it was golden. Laura's armor and sword had appeared as Cat had stepped into the human dimension. Laura was reciting the last verses of Psalm 91 over and over again as a prayer. *"I will protect him, for he acknowledges my name. "He will call upon me, and I will answer him; I will be with him in trouble, I will deliver him and honor him. With long life will I satisfy him and show him my salvation."*

Sensing the threat, Cat turned towards Laura and raised her deadly claws to defend herself. Cat snarled as Laura stepped forward and swung the white-hot sword streaming with the Esteem of Yahveh. Cat jumped backwards nimbly and the sword passed in front of her.

Jumping back towards Laura, Cat slashed her right-hand claws across the front of the meddlesome female. Cat was taken aback when the claws slid across the golden armor without penetrating or even leaving a scratch. Cat had to quickly throw herself backwards to avoid the backhand thrust of the sword by Laura.

Cat jumped in the air and came down directly at Laura whose sword was not in position to engage her. Sensing Cat's move, Laura also threw herself forward and executed a forward roll which ended with her coming back to her feet with her back to Cat.

Cat saw her chance and pounced at the back of the woman in the golden armor. This time she would end this farce. Cat tensed her arms to drive her claws through the throat of her enemy.

A blinding glare and an excruciating pain in her chest stopped her completely. Cat looked down and saw the woman had anticipated her move. As she had come to her feet Laura had thrust the sword backward over her left shoulder in a technique Jack had shown her. Cat's leap had impaled her chest on the sword.

Laura quickly spun around and pulled the sword out of the demon. In her pain and strange weakness Cat suddenly realized that she had overstepped Yahveh's permission when she had personally gone into the human dimension after the nail. That had not been in the petition. She was intelligent enough to know that Yahveh's punishment would be swift for such an offense. Laura swung the sword from right to left and beheaded Cat, ending her existence.

Jack turned around again and held the nail in the air.

A tremendous wind, that seemed to suddenly spring directly from the ground started blowing all of the tons and tons of sand in front of them to the sides and up above the cleft in the rock. Jack stood in awe as he saw the sand blow upward and then stay suspended in the air rather than being blown away.

A loud explosion behind him told him that the enemy had started to use their cannons to destroy the hostages and the Crossfire Team.

Mark was nodding his head as he watched the way in front of the people being blown free of sand. Even though the passage wasn't clear all the way through, he started to walk forward followed by the Sensei and Su Li. Mark waved with his arm for the people to follow him. A few started and then more came. The trickle became a rushing river of people as more shells exploded around them. As the last of the two hundred and twenty-five ex-hostages and the thirty-three SOG and Crossfire Team straggled through the cleft, Jack and Laura ran behind them with Jack holding the nail above his head. As they ran through the quarter mile long opening in the sand they looked back to see how close the enemy had come. To their horror they saw a cannon shell from one of the tanks heading directly for them.

A flash of white and gold flickered for a second and the tank shell caromed upward and exploded high above the sand floating above them. Jack and Laura yelled at the same time, "Rose!"

As they hurried out of the far end of the cleft, Jack heard the words of the Father again. *"Hold your hand up until I tell you to drop it."*

As Jack stood there, the hundreds of tons of sand continued to hover above the small canyon or cleft. The air in front of him was clearer now and he could see the suspended sand swirling around in circles.

Jack heard the enemy troops charging through the cleft screaming their anger at the escape. The clank and roar of the tanks was a heavy backdrop to the screaming of the troops. Bullets started flying around Jack as the troops in the lead targeted him as he stood there. He had the peace of Yahshua covering him at that point. It didn't matter if he survived this or not. He was completely in Yahveh's hand and working for the esteem of God.

CHAPTER FORTY-FOUR

As Jack stood tall in the face of the on-rushing troops and the hundreds of rounds being fired at him he heard Yahveh say, "*Lower your hand.*"

Jack lowered his hand and the hundreds of tons of suspended sand crashed down on the troops and the tanks with such a tremendous roar and the ground shook so violently that both Jack and Laura fell to the sand. The clouds of sand blown outward concealed the death and destruction it caused.

Several minutes later Jack stood there with Laura and looked at the solid wall of sand that towered over a hundred feet above them. The new wall had cut off the wind from the west and the only sand that hit them was falling from a long way above them.

As Jack and Laura were filled with gratitude they dropped to their knees in humble thanks to a loving Yahveh. The rest of the team and most of the people that had been rescued followed suit. As they stood again, Jack smiled at Laura in the sand that fell like gritty snowflakes. He grabbed her and hugged her. "That was a fantastic battle! You saved my life again and I really don't know how to thank you."

Looking at the wall of sand covering the enemy troops she shuddered slightly and said, "I think you more than made up for my one little effort."

Jack put the crucifixion nail back into its protective box and replaced it under his armor. He shook his head, "I didn't do anything but follow orders."

Mark came up and put his arm around Jack's shoulders. "Remind me to stick close to you at times like this, okay?"

Jack smiled, "Sure". He looked at the hundreds of people and had pity on their condition. "But let's see what we can do to make these people more comfortable until this storm passes."

Staying in the lee of the wall of sand and rock, the team and the SOG built shelters out of their ponchos and some tarps from the two Humvees. The ex-hostages huddled under these makeshift shelters as the sand storm continued.

Jack was concerned about what might have happened to Tim Carson and Captain Morales and the fact that he wasn't able to raise Charlie Wu on the radio. Talking to Mark, Jack decided to move straight east away from the escarpment that was sheltering them. Mark thought that the iron or magnetism in the rocks was blocking the communications.

Five of the SOG personnel tied themselves together with their rappelling ropes and the last man was tied to Jack. Altogether they walked east until the first man stopped at a hundred feet. Each man had another hundred feet of rope and then he would stop. You couldn't see for more than fifty feet even with goggles. Jack left the last man and continued to walk east as his electronic compass indicated.

When Jack reached the end of the rope he was six hundred feet away from the rocks. He keyed his radio. "Charlie, are you there?"

Charlie's elated tones came back clearly. "Jack! You're alive! We were really worried up here. What's happened?"

Jack could hear cheering in the background while he brought Charlie up to date and then asked about Tim and Captain Morales.

Charlie didn't have any good information. "I saw the attack and the blast that stopped your communications with Tim. Then I saw the enemy overrun the headquarters base. I haven't been able to raise anyone there since then."

Jack asked, "Did you see where the enemy troops went?"

Charlie said quietly, "Yeah, they joined up with the troops from the north. I think they were part of the group that Yahveh just made a part of the desert."

Jack inquired as to how much longer the sand storm would last and how quickly the Mexican government could get some relief for the hostages. Charlie told him that the storm was abating just to the west of them and should stop completely in the next hour or so. The Mexican authorities would reach them within an hour after that with heavy transport helicopters to airlift the team and the ex-hostages back to their village. They would also be sending troops to the headquarters base to see if they could find any survivors.

Jack thanked him, signed off and started walking into the sand and wind following the rope. Slowly they collected each of the other five men and got back to the shelters. Jack shook each of the five men's hands and congratulated them. Jack could see a lightening to the sky to the west and both the sand and the wind were slacking off.

Less than two hours later, the weary people and the team disembarked at El Barreal. There were a lot of happy reunions for the people and flowers for the warriors.

Jack was in communication with Charlie when the news from the southern army base was relayed. Both Tim and Captain Morales were found alive. They had been buried by the explosion that destroyed the headquarters tent. They had spent nearly five hours buried under several hundred pounds of debris and sand. But they were examined and released. Tim was already on his way to El Barreal. The Captain was returning to Mexico City to start an investigation into the group that attacked them.

CHAPTER FORTY-FIVE

Thirty minutes later, a small helicopter landed and Tim Carson jumped out and walked over to the rest of the team. Coming up to Mark he said, "Next time, I implore you, take me with you, please. I didn't get to see the miracle and I got blown up and spent a lot of time under the sand. The only good thing was that I also got to lead the Captain to God. He was a captive audience considering that we were buried together in a space the size of a double-decker coffin, you know, very friendly, very close. If we didn't have my combat light, water, and rations to help pass the time I think we would of both gone crazy." It was obvious that Tim was still unwinding after his near death experience.

Mark asked him how they had ended up in a hole in the ground with everything else on top of them. Tim shook his head, "I'll tell you but I don't know if I really understand it. One of the shells from either a tank or artillery hit the back of the tent and blew a giant hole in the sand. Then a second one hit just outside the front of the tent and blew the two of us out of the tent and into the first shell's hole. Then everything else followed us into the hole. After that, all we could do was wait until someone found us. Thank Yahveh it was friendly Mexican army troops that heard us and dug us out."

Mark asked him, "Do you have any idea who attacked you or anything that would help us identify them?"

Tim smiled ruefully, "This was my first combat and to be honest, I was scared because I didn't understand anything until the Captain explained what had happened before we got buried. He said that an unidentified force apparently wiped out the company of men he had stationed to the north of the hostage site. Then the shelling and shooting started where we were. The Captain was trying to raise his command for reinforcements when the shells hit." Tim looked a little thoughtful for a second. "On the other hand, I might be able to give you a clue. After we were buried a while my hearing was coming back. The shooting stopped and I could faintly hear people moving around above our position. We stayed quiet because we thought it would be the people that attacked us. We hoped they would think everyone was dead and not search for us. But, I did hear some voices talking. I couldn't make out what they were saying but they were speaking Spanish for sure."

Mark looked at Jack, "Possibly a home-grown assault group that the Mexicans don't know about. What do you want to do?"

Jack thought about that and all the other happenings. "I think I want Charlie to give me some information."

Sarah was sitting on the tailgate of a truck and nodded. She keyed her microphone and told Charlie what Jack wanted. She nodded and looked over to Jack. "He said that he'd have an identification and source on that crew by sundown our time."

Su Li looked to the west. "Well, that gives him about an hour."

A delegation of the local inhabitants came over to the troops and sought out Jack. The leader was an older Mexican with some papers in his hand. Coming up to Jack he said, "Senor, the people of this town want to thank you and your men." He stopped and looked at the weary troops. "And women, who rescued our people from those maniacs. We have a large assembly building and would be grateful if you and your men, and women, would stay there tonight." He looked hopefully at Jack.

Jack looked at the tired troops still knocking the sand out of everything they had. A night out of the sand would be a morale boost. He mentally asked the Father if that was the right thing to do and felt it was in his spirit. "It would be an honor for us to stay with you tonight. We will also keep a guard over your village tonight to make sure no more of the "maniacs" bother you."

The villagers smiled and led the way to the biggest building in their town. Mark made the assignments and set the troops up as a bivouac in the building. He assigned himself, Sarah, Sensei Grady, and Jack as the first watch. Tim offered to help but Mark was a lot more experienced in how combat affects a person and told him to get as much rest as he could tonight.

Mark found Jack eating an MRE and made a face. "Ugh! How can you stand those?"

Jack smiled tiredly back at his best friend. "Right now it tastes great."

Mark shook his head. Meals Ready to Eat, or MREs were actually sufficient caloric intake for troops to survive on but they lacked when compared to cuisine. "It's a good thing you took the villagers up on their offer. The wind is picking up again and we may have blowing sand again tonight." Mark studied Jack's face for a few seconds. "I take it that you want to stay here until we can determine our new enemy's strength and home base?"

Jack nodded his head as Laura and Sarah came over to their husbands and dropped to the floor exhausted. Laura looked at Jack's MRE and tried some of the meat. It tasted just like chicken. She dug two more of the MREs out of the supply bag and gave one to Sarah. Sarah opened her meal and started eating without comment. She was obviously familiar with MREs.

Jack continued his comments to Mark. "I wanted to do a lot of things but when I prayed about this on the helicopter ride here God told me that I would be given an offer and to accept it. I'm waiting for His direction for all of us."

Laura finished her meal and set the container down. "It looks like sundown is in about 45 minutes. I'm going to take a nap. Wake me when it's time for my turn at sentry." She got up and threw her meal container in a trash sack and crawled into her sleeping bag. She was asleep before her head hit the pillow. Su Li had already gone to bed and was sound asleep.

Sarah got up and snuggled up next to Mark. Mark looked around knowing that it wouldn't be appropriate for the SOG troopers to see this kind of action in the field. But he should have known that Sarah was field-smart. The three of them were the only ones awake at the moment. He hugged his wife and told her that she didn't have to pull guard duty right then. He, Sensei Grady and Jack could cover the small village by themselves.

Sarah looked at her empty sleeping bag and smiled at Mark. "What do you think you're doing? I've probably pulled longer shifts than you have in the last five years.

You've been a strategist and planner. Rear echelon stuff. I'll do my duty husband dear; you just try to stay awake for the next four hours."

Mark affected a hurt look. "Rear echelon? Me? You've got to be kidding. I spent more time in combat than half your group in the Mossad over their entire lifetimes!"

Somewhere out of the sea of sleeping troops came a tired voice. "Can it, will you? Sirs?"

The three of them chuckled and fell quiet. Jim Grady walked over to them and sat down on the floor. "I've been talking to the villagers. They think the whole thing was a trap for us and they weren't really important except as bait."

Jack's combat communications tone sounded in his ear. "Go ahead", he said.

Charlie Wu spoke confidently. "I have a bunch of information on your attackers. First, the man ultimately behind that group is a Mexican drug Lord named Pablo Mollina who goes by the name Pablo the Cruel. It is his money that put together the small army. I understand that he is fielding this force without Mexico's approval. By the way, he lost over thirty percent of his little army and all of his expensive tanks fighting against you. Rumor has it that he personally shot five of his officers for incompetence over this affair."

Jack had indicated that Mark and Sarah listen in on this call. Mark asked, "Charlie, where is the rest of his army and the man himself? We want to ask him some questions."

Charlie chuckled, "Even though the man was born in Tamaulipas, Mexico he has up scaled his environment. He has the rest of his army protecting him outside of Nuevo Leon. His hacienda is located near the Huasteca national park in Santa Catarina. I'll send you maps and photos in a few minutes. One thing my CIA pal told me is that this Pablo guy is a real tough nut to crack. He rules his people with fear and has bribed the entire country around where he lives with so much drug money that it is like his own little country. Mexico City leaves him alone because he has a lot of high level friends in the federal government. You can read "paid for" as in bribes for those high level friends. Not only that, but he is well liked by everyone because of his generosity. And, he can afford to be generous, his drug cartel adds over a billion dollars to his personal wealth every two years and he doesn't pay any taxes. The U.S. has considered taking him out themselves but haven't been able to prove the cocaine connection in the world's eyes. The man is apparently untouchable."

Jack's eyes had turned that dangerous color of icy-blue. "How good is his protection other than the military assets?"

Charlie flipped through the information he had on Pablo Mollina. "According to the NSA file on him, he has the latest in detection gear and automated security systems; it might even be a NovaStar system. You should check your factory shipping lists. The man only goes out of his hacienda once a week to make an appearance at a Catholic Church. The security for these trips is massive. You'd have a better chance at the President of the U.S. when he is on the road."

Jack simply said, "Just send us the information Charlie. I'll let you know what we plan to do as soon as I know." Jack broke the connection. Looking at Mark and Sarah he said, "I don't just want to kill him, I want to dissect him until we know why he gave up a third of his troops to kill us and how he knew where we'd be. I assume he is the one that set up the phony nuke deal to get us here, but who put him up to it? Drug Lords are not easily convinced to squander their hard-earned resources or to take up other people's causes." Jack looked pensive and uncertain.

Sarah studied his face, "What's wrong Jack?"

Jack looked at the Israeli woman sitting there in desert camos and realized she'd be beautiful no matter what she wore. "I have to pray about this because I am so mad at the man for attempting to kill us and incidentally a couple of hundred of his own people. But, I know that anger isn't of the Lord. I need to know if Yahveh wants us to go after Pablo Mollina before we make a move."

CHAPTER FORTY-SIX

Pablo Mollina sat in his high-tech office and stared listlessly at the myriad of television screens showing his property and the building he sat in at the moment. He looked at the sensor screens and found nothing to alarm him. He could see the hundred or so military guards at their posts and being very alert for any type of attack or incursion. He checked the echo screens for the radar and found no aircraft anywhere near his hacienda.

Then why was he so scared? What was frightening him? The fear was formless and menacing and terrible. He broke out in a sweat which was hard to do in the icy air-conditioned room. There was nothing to threaten him but he was in fear!

As usual he turned the fear into anger and needed a satisfactory target for that anger. Definitely someone else than himself. Who?

There was a knock on the door. Pablo considered the door for a few seconds and then said, "Come!"

Juan Cardenas opened the door and stepped into the elaborate room. Juan was tall for a Mexican. He stood over six feet tall and was built like a football player from the United States. His skills in hand-to-hand combat, weapons, stealth, and wet work were excellent and he could be very lethal. But the look on his face was downcast and worried. Just what Pablo didn't want right then. "What do you want, Juan?"

Juan strode over to Pablo's desk and sat in the visitor's chair. He looked nervous; actually, he looked absolutely spooked. This sent Pablo's fears into high gear. Which he showed as anger. Slapping his hand on the desk he demanded, "Explain yourself! You're acting like a sniveling coward!"

Normally Juan would explode with his own anger and yell back at Pablo. He was the only one who could. Anybody else raises his voice at Pablo and he was dead. Right then. This time Juan looked at his boss and searched his eyes for sanity and craftiness. "Pablo, I have bad news.

I have checked this over several times before bringing it to you. But, believe me; we don't want to fight against this Crossfire Team."

Pablo knew the thoroughness of Juan Cardenas. If he said something he had the facts to back it up. "Why not?"

Juan took a deep breath, "Because God is fighting for them." There! It was said.

Pablo tried to compute what Juan had just told him. "God! God was fighting for this American combat team? How could that be?" The thought rattled him.

Pablo got up and paced back and forth behind his desk. The anger built into a head of steam. Then he stopped and stared at Juan. "Who built this empire? Me. Who built this army? Me. Who controls it with an iron fist?' Me! I did it all. Don't forget that the people worship ME! I am God! Forget that nonsense about God fighting for them. I didn't fight for them, but against them. I am God! And your Catholic or Christian God is not allowed here! I will decide who lives and who dies. It is by my will everything happens. Do you understand? I am more powerful than any God! Now, get back to work and find out where they are and how I can destroy them!"

Juan's soul shuddered as he listened to Pablo. He thought to himself "The man is insane. He actually believes he is mightier than God! He is blaspheming and will bring down the wrath of God on himself and all of us." Outwardly he hardened his face and nodded acquiescence to Pablo's orders. To do otherwise was foolish and would only result in his immediate death. He rose to his feet and left the room. As he walked down the corridor he made up his mind to be as far away from this place as possible. Under his breath he prayed. "Oh God, I tremble at your anger and have read of your wrath. This man is crazy and I ask your forgiveness for having ever known him. I am leaving as quickly as I can and will never return, Oh God. His blasphemy is like a rotten stench and I want nothing to do with it. Spare me God."

Juan walked out and called the Colonel in charge of the military group. "I am going to personally check out these rumors of God's involvement in the destruction of our men. Protect the hacienda and Pablo from all harm in my absence. Do you understand your orders?"

The Colonel saluted Juan and called his personal helicopter to be readied.

As the helicopter left the ground, Juan Cardenas wished all association with the place would break off and stay there. He had an idea how long the arm of the Lord was and he didn't want to suffer with what he was sure to befall Pablo Mollina in the near future. When he got to where he was going he was going to disappear from human sight and seek God's forgiveness. If the Lord of the universe would give him a second chance, he was going to change his stripes and become a good man.

CHAPTER FORTY-SEVEN

Over the last four years, Pablo the Cruel had become a violent force in the lives of everyone in a fifty mile radius of his hacienda. The majority of the people recognized the power represented by the man and bowed to his wishes. They were rewarded with a good life, money, opportunities, and all the things that weren't available to them before. But they had to agree to Pablo's view on everything. Drugs were good because they brought money into the community. The fact that drugs were a deadly blight on their own people as well as the "customers" was ignored. That was their problem; it didn't seem to bother anyone that they were manufacturing death.

If Pablo or his men liked a pretty girl, she became their property and no one complained. In fact it had become a status symbol to have one of the family's girls at the hacienda. The girls themselves behaved as told or frightful things happened to both them and their family. They quickly learned it was a privilege to "serve" Pablo Mollina and his men regardless how degrading it was.

Pablo's debauchery, murders, and iron control of everything from the Catholic Church in the town to the smallest operation in "his" country was not only accepted but enforced by the people themselves. They renounced any moral or ethical standards they had before his arrival. Pablo himself dictated what morals were and only his ethics counted. The people knew that they were better off, so nobody should complain. Complainers disappeared, never to be heard from again. The "good people" of the area near Santa Catarina became a thing of the past. It was not good to think about those people if you wanted in on the gravy train that Pablo offered.

As the years went by and the past disappeared, people begin to see Pablo as their provision and source of everything including justice. Many people admired him, wanted to be like him. It wasn't too long before people begin to adore him and look to him for everything. It wasn't really a big jump for people to start to worship

Pablo. Once he saw their worship he decided he was worthy of it. Another small leap of imagination and he begin to demand their worship and their prayers. By now Pablo felt like God and it took his vanity to heights he'd never known before. Things begin to happen that were definitely supernatural and impossible for humans to do. Pablo performed some minor miracles, some staged and some just happened.

Once the miracles occurred Pablo was assured of his divinity and so were the people. The old religions were thrown away in light of the new "god". Pablo wasn't in the least worried when he came up with the idea of destroying the Crossfire Team. He even had thought of a plan to do it.

There was still a remnant that had silently anguished over the depravations and the detestable things done in the name of "progress" under Pablo the Cruel. They prayed and asked God for relief. This latest thing, Pablo's deity. Truly detestable and hated by God. They wouldn't bow their knee or worship anyone except Jesus Christ, the true King of Kings and His Father, the creator of the universe. They did their best to keep their opinions to themselves and unless they were forced they would stay out of the public eye. It was suicide otherwise. Like one older woman said, "I don't feel led of the Lord to thumb my nose at a killer like Pablo the Cruel."

CHAPTER FORTY-EIGHT

Jack went to an empty area of the large building and sat down to pray. The wind had picked up and he could hear bursts of sand as they stuck the windward side of the building. He could also hear the moan of the wind and it made a sound that was lonely and forlorn. Centering his mind he started praising Yahveh for all of his mercy and his love for humanity. He thanked the Father for saving the hostages and his people and destroying the enemy that pursued them through the desert. As his prayer deepened the surrounding sounds disappeared and there were no distractions. He felt the love in his heart for Yahshua and it knew no limits. Jack had fallen in love with the Father and pursued that relationship with everything he had. He felt the Father's love in return and reveled in it.

He had forgotten why he had started to pray. It really didn't matter to him anymore. But God hadn't forgotten and in his mind's eye he saw a large, middle-aged, muscular Mexican man with a cruel look on his face and an outrageously loud sport jacket in bight chartreuse. Without knowing how he knew, Jack knew the man he saw was Pablo Mollina. He also knew that God had arranged things so that the Crossfire Team would be enemies with the warlord drug kingpin. That settled, Jack returned to the communion he had with the Father.

Twenty minutes later he had informed Mark and Sarah of Yahveh's leading and the three of them went out on patrol. As he patrolled, Jack looked out over a deserted landscape. Nothing moved by natural sight or by NVG. As he patrolled, Jack talked to Charlie three times and once to Linda Wu, arranging their next move and getting the CRAY computers to determine an approach to Mollina that had a chance of working.

At midnight, Mark woke three of the SOG troopers and sent them out to patrol while Sarah, Jack, and Mark himself got a chance to sleep.

The next morning, Colonel Baldwin led the SOG troopers through a series of exercises and self-defense drills. The command structure of the Crossfire Team attempted to work out an approach to Pablo Mollina that wouldn't get them all killed.

By early afternoon they were frustrated with the lack of possibilities and Laura suggested they have a light lunch and then ask the Father what to do.

When they started praying, several of the SOG warriors, including Craig and Kevin Steele joined them in their worship and prayer time. Sometime after they started seriously seeking the Father's direction Jack noticed the "heavy" feeling his spirit experienced whenever Yahveh's Spirit brought them into a deep communion with the Father. Everyone fell silent as the heaviness grew. It wasn't uncomfortable but rather it was awe-inspiring and each person felt their smallness and unworthiness when Yahveh was so close.

Jack was aware of Laura, Sarah, and Mark's spirits and many others. They were all bowing down to Yahveh's spirit. Jack suddenly saw the mighty angel that had carried Laura to heaven. He was impressive, especially his eyes. They were bluer than blue and seemed to look right through a person. Jack wanted to ask the angel his name but found he couldn't speak.

The angel's voice was like the sound of a bass viola but still understandable. *"Men and women of the Crossfire Team. The Most High Yahveh has heard your prayers. He has judged Pablo Mollina for his pride and arrogance against Yahveh Himself. He will serve that judgment against Mollina by His own hand."*

The angel disappeared from Jack's mind and the heaviness lifted. He got up and walked out of the building to find Laura. As he exited the building he looked up and was stunned. Everyone in sight, troopers and civilians alike were scattered around on the street and yards. All of them were on their knees, laying on the ground, or sitting with their heads bowed. Many of them were weeping deeply. He looked at Laura and she smiled. "When Yahveh shows up, everyone sees how miserable they are when they are held up against perfection. Repentance or denials are the normal reactions. The Father's Spirit fell on everyone in this village and I doubt that they will forget it for a long time."

The SOG troopers were mostly up and helping the Mexican people that were looking for an explanation. Since there were only so many troopers that spoke Spanish and only a few locals that spoke English, it was group meetings for many of them.

The mayor of the town came to where the team sat. He looked at each of them out of big eyes in his old face. "I have never felt the Father like that before. I doubt that any of my people have either. Before you and your people leave, would you pray for us that the Father would visit us like that again?"

Jack knew that he had to handle this rather than submit it to Laura. But before he could say anything a new voice joined the group.

Tim Carson stepped forward. "Senor, we would be proud to pray for you and your people, but if you want Yahveh to visit you again, you will have to do the work necessary. It is not us or our group that is important; we are but servants of the Most High Yahveh. We are the same as you and the people of this village. What is required is sincere repentance and a seeking after Yahshua in love. He isn't fooled by a heart that just wants Yahveh's help to escape going to hell, which only wants His touch or one that has a sinful nature. He wants people that love Him for who he is and are willing to pursue Him with all their heart. Once you have people that are like that, then He will visit you. But make sure that is what you want. It says in His word that **when** suffering comes, not, **if** suffering comes. You have to take on His pains and sorrows before you can know Him. That means going through the fire with Him."

The mayor took all of this in and translated it to the men with him who had come up while Tim was speaking. There was a look of deep determination on most of their faces. Tim was evaluating the group and nodding his head.

Tim held up his hand and pointed. "Why don't we go inside and talk about this?" The men nodded when the translation was made. They trooped into the building behind Tim. As he entered the building he looked back at the four of them and winked.

Laura smiled at that. "I think I like Tim more now than I did when we met him." Looking around she asked, "Where is Jim Grady?"

The four of them spread out looking for the Sensei. Sarah found him sitting on the floor of the building across from where Tim was speaking to the village elders. He looked up at her with tears in his eyes. It was a pleading look and no words were spoken. Sarah felt his anguish in her heart. She keyed her combat microphone. "I found him. He's okay and we're going to talk for a while, give us some space please."

Sarah held out her hand and helped the older man up from the floor. She pulled him toward her and held him while he sobbed. She didn't try to fix anything or explain anything. She just comforted him in his distress. After a bit, he stopped crying and held her out at arm's length. He looked deeply into her eyes and saw the love of Yahshua looking back at him. He took her hand and they walked over to a table with some chairs. He held her seat for her as a gentleman would and then seated himself in the other chair, facing her. He still looked into her eyes and he said, "Dear Yahshua, I am nothing but a worthless bag of bones. I am sorry that I am in such a sad shape and that I am in your presence. I am not worthy that you should . . ."

Sarah put her fingers over his mouth and shook her head. "Don't presume to tell the Father of the universe who he should attend or not attend. He chooses and if he has chosen you, who are you to deny Him? We are wretched next to His perfection but we are washed in the blood of the lamb and the Father sees His Son when he looks at you. Remember, it is He who is coming near to you and that is His right and His choice. Praise Him but don't deny Him. He knows exactly what you are and He loves you as you are. He wants you to pursue Him and become like Him but he loves you as you are and He loves you on each step of the journey as you are. Sensei, you are very intelligent. That is both a blessing and it is a curse. Stop trying to analyze your relationship or determine the correctness of Yahveh's actions. We can't, no one can. Just love Him back and know that He will never leave you or abandon you. He just wants you to love Him and reach out for Him."

Jim sat there for several minutes and digested what he had just heard. His countenance lightened and he looked up to heaven and praised the Father with gratitude and determination to never judge the Father's actions again. He jumped up and picked Sarah up in a bear hug that lifted her out of her chair and high into the air. She was startled by his strength but was laughing anyway.

The Sensei put her feet down on the floor and kissed her on the forehead. "I thank you Sarah Connelly, I had it backwards and you led me to the truth!"

She smiled back and took his hands and started to dance the Hora, the Jewish dance of celebration. They swung across the floor, startling the elders of the village with their laughter.

Realizing their intrusive behavior they calmed down and waved to the men and then walked out of the building.

CHAPTER FORTY-NINE

In heaven a voice called out loudly, "Bring the guards for this city here, each with a weapon in his hand."

Six men came from the direction of the upper gate, which faces north, each with a deadly weapon in his hand. With them was a man clothed in linen, who had a writing kit at his side. They came in and stood beside the bronze altar.

Now the glory of Yahveh went up from above the cherubim, where it had been, and moved to the threshold of the temple. Then the voice called to the man clothed in linen who had the writing kit at his side, and said to him, "Go throughout the polluted area near Santa Catarina that has been corrupted by this man, and put a mark on the foreheads of those who grieve and lament over all the detestable things that are being done by this man, those who will not worship him as god."

Then the voice said to the armed men, "Follow him through the area and kill, without showing pity or compassion, Slaughter old men, young men and maidens, women and children, but do not touch anyone who has the mark. Begin at the periphery of the area and go inward until it is finished."

The voice continued, "The sin of these people is exceeding great; the land is full of bloodshed and the land is full of injustice. They do not believe in me anymore so they say I don't see their abominations. I will not look on them with pity or spare them, but I will bring down on their own heads what they have done."

The area controlled by Pablo Mollina and his army was roughly a circle with a radius of 25 miles. Within this, approximately, 1960 square miles, the people had done evil in the eyes of God. The angels started at the outer reaches of his control and moved inward towards his hacienda. There were over three hundred and seventy thousand souls in this area. By the time the angels reached the first units of the army surrounding the hacienda there were only twenty-two thousand, four hundred, and sixty-one people still alive.

Increasing silence from the outlying areas of his control alerted Pablo that something was happening. He did not know what it was but it pumped the fear in his mind to new heights. His screaming and demanding for answers went unanswered. He sent his best men out to find out what was happening. None of them reported in again. It was like a black cloud of silence that was everywhere but at the same time it was drawing ever nearer to him. He put the army on the highest alert and armed himself with three pistols and a military rifle.

In rapid secession each of the army units failed to report. It was like a switch was thrown and a whole company died. He did hear screams but they were cut off in mid-scream. There was ragged and scattered gunfire but that too stopped quickly. He watched his television screens but he couldn't detect the enemy. He did see many of his soldiers drop suddenly to the ground and stop moving. Whole squads would suddenly collapse. Pablo thought "I am God aren't I?" He demanded that this stop. Then all his guards in the hacienda itself stopped reporting. Suddenly, Pablo knew he wasn't alone. He spun around in his chair and sprayed his high-tech room with his full automatic rifle in all directions because he couldn't see the enemy. Then the bolt locked back when he ran out of bullets. He wanted to grab his pistols but what he did see caused his muscles to freeze. He couldn't make a sound.

The powerful angel appeared before him with righteous anger in his eyes and his sword raised. The sight drove terror through Pablo's brain just before the angel swung the shining sword down. All the human fear ended as abruptly as Pablo's short run as a would-be god.

Then Pablo came to judgment before a righteous and just Yahshua. It is truly a terrible thing to stand before an angry God.

In Nuevo Leon the Mexican army responded to hundreds of panic calls from the region. The units of the army rolled into the small towns outside of Santa Catarina and were met with an eerie silence. There were dead people everywhere, sitting in chairs, lying on the ground. They looked to have been doing normal, everyday chores.

Men, women, children, all dead, but none of them showed any wounds or signs of disease. The army called their national disease control center and asked for emergency help Five hours later, the U.S. CDC in Atlanta, Georgia got an emergency request for assistance in the region from the Mexican government.

It took less than eight hours for the CDC to rule out any type of communicable disease or trauma. The deaths were labeled, correctly so, "an act of God".

A week later the great columns of smoke begin to wane as the hundreds of thousands of bodies were finally consumed by fire to prevent the spread of disease. Pablo Mollina's body was just one of several hundred to be burned in a pyre near the hacienda.

Because the area was fairly remote and most of the people were local, the Mexican government thought it best not to make it a world issue, but to keep the news blocked. So, there was no international cry for information or investigation. The government officials involved and the locals that had survived the purge knew why most of the people in the region had died. The survivors knew why they had not, they thanked God for their survival, but they still mourned for many that did die.

Another reason that no one in the Mexican government wanted to announce to the world what had happened was because twenty of their own officials had mysteriously died at the same time as the disaster in Nuevo Leon. All twenty of these men had been associated with Pablo Mollina. Yahveh had avenged the wrongs of Pablo Mollina and those that worked for him, and no one wanted to incur further wrath. The matter was closed and buried except for some small leaks, mainly in the underworld where it struck fear in all who realized who Yahveh was.

In a shabby motel room in New Mexico that sat by a little-used highway near the Mexican border, Juan Cardenas hung up the phone and sat and cried for the few people he had liked and known in Pablo's world. He kept his word to Yahveh and knelt next to the bed and asked God to use him. His education was just beginning. Yahveh would use his obedience to the glory of the Kingdom. It would never be easy for Juan, but it would be fulfilling.

CHAPTER FIFTY

The Crossfire Team and the SOG troopers were present when the complete CIA report concerning the death of Pablo Mollina and approximately three hundred thousand others was given by Mark. The drug cartel's elimination along with the local population was shown in some extremely graphic and clear satellite videos.

The effect of Yahveh's wrath on so many seemingly innocent people was a major shock for many of the men and women there. Surprisingly, Tim Carson stood up and calmed the dozens of contentious conversations by asking to speak. When things were silent he said, "I have been in prayer for much of the last two days and one thing I will tell you, with no uncertainty, is that no one died who had not offended Yahveh by worshiping Pablo Mollina as a god."

One of the SOG troopers held up his hand and Tim acknowledged him. "Sir, I understand that Yahveh is never wrong about anyone but I have a hard time understanding why the young children died. They could not of known that they were supposed to worship the true Yahveh and not this drug lord. Why did Yahveh kill them?"

Tim understood the man's quandary because he had once felt the same way, years ago. "I can tell you why, as I understand it, that Yahveh kills women and children. Yahveh is just, He cannot change his nature. Women and children are part of Yahveh's judgment in order to completely destroy the worldly and spiritual influence and Idolatry caused by the family's worship of any idol or false Yahveh."

Tim gestured to make his point. "It matters not how or when a person dies. It matters what a person's relationship to Yahveh is. If children are "innocent" they will be judged by Yahveh as such even if they die as part of Yahveh's judgment against the group in which they live. Remember that this earth is merely a testing ground for each of us. We have to make the correct choices as we struggle through this life. The children, even babes, were exposed to the demonic spirits when the spiritual head of the family, the father, choose to worship someone other than the true Yahveh. You can think of it as being infected. In a sense, the children are spared having to make the right choices and struggle throughout a tainted life because they were destroyed at such an early age."

Tim sighed, "We tend to think that Yahveh is robbing them of their future. Actually he is guaranteeing their future in heaven because they are judged while still "innocent". They get to skip the trials, training, and tests here on earth and instead go straight to heaven. The same applies to women in a family who may have no knowledge or involvement in the wrong-doing. The only difference is that since they are beyond the age of accountability their relationship with Yahshua will be the deciding factor in their judgment."

Looking out over the sea of brave faces, Tim finished by saying, "Yahveh doesn't make mistakes. He knows the end from the beginning. And, he is fair, just, and loving. This life seems like all there is to most people. That's not the truth. This life is but a flickering moment in each person's life. It is a chance to choose Yahveh, walk with God and learn His ways, and to do His will as He directs. Like I said, it is only a test, but it is one each person must pass. The "innocent" men, women, and children who were washed away today in the hills of Mexico will receive the crown of life and live with the King. They don't have to face any more temptations or choices. They are already where we want to be." At that Tim sat down.

Tim's talk had given everyone a better understanding of Yahveh and his judgment on the people of Pablo Mollina. When the group broke up to attend to packing for departure, a dozen or so men and women of the SOG came up to shake Tim's hand or to hug him and thank him.

Mark and Jack allowed the village leaders to hear a censored version of the CIA report and some of the videos and explained how Yahveh had judged their enemy for his abominations. Tim was needed to explain about the women and children again. This time through a translator. But they had the same reaction to the end of the drug issue as the SOG troopers had.

The C5A had returned and would drop the Crossfire Team off in Denver before taking the SOG back to their base camp in California. Mike White would arrange to have the Team's jet returned to Denver and Su Li got to ride in the third seat in the cockpit of the C5A. Their gear was stowed on the giant aircraft and they had policed up the building they had been given. The team and the SOG attended a brief prayer service with the entire town it seemed like. They asked Yahveh to be merciful on the people of the village and to reward them for their faithfulness in the face of the suffering that they had gone through with the hostage situation. As they finished praying there was a disturbance in the crowd. Two of the elders escorted an elderly woman up to the team.

Eli smiled at the woman and then at the Americans. In fairly good English he told them. "Yahveh is with us. Antonia has been blind since birth, some eighty-three years ago. Yahveh just gave her sight!"

Laura walked over to the woman and looked at her. Hugging her she said something so quietly no one else heard what it was. Antonia looked at the younger, taller woman and said in Spanish, "May Yahveh always bless you my child. I have never seen before but I can tell you are a beautiful woman in the spirit. I bless Yahveh for giving me a chance to see the world before I see Him."

The woman slowly turned around and smiled at the sea of happy faces she saw in front of her. She looked at the old white and red cane she had used all her life and threw it away into the air. The crowd cheered wildly and you could tell that there was an all-night party about to begin.

Jack signaled the SOG and the team to board the C5A. He turned and presented a gift to Eli, who it turned out was the mayor. "My troops and I want you to have this. It is a solar-powered cell phone that sends its signal through satellites. It is a communication device that you can use for many things but if you push the number one, three times, you will be able to talk to us. Call us if you need us."

Eli had tears in his eyes as he hugged Jack. "Remember Senor, you and any of your people are always welcome in this village or in my home. I expect we will meet again."

They shook hands and Jack trotted up to the ladder and climbed into the plane. The C5A accelerated and quickly climbed into the air. Many of the villagers waved until the plane was out of sight.

CHAPTER FIFTY-ONE

As the C5A taxied away from them at DIA, the six members of the Crossfire Team lifted their gear and weapons bags into the Cadillac Escalade. Linda Wu made sure they were all in and smoothly guided the big SUV away from the hanger at the private field section of Denver's International Airport. Tim rode up front with Linda while Jack, Laura and Su Li rode in the second row of seats. Mark and Sarah sat in the rear seats. Sensei Grady had his own car parked at the airport and had bid them goodbye as he headed home.

As they rode along in the quiet comfort of the Escalade, Jack asked Linda if there were any new developments in their personal war with the forces of darkness.

Linda nodded as she negotiated a right hand turn. "There have been two incidents since you left for your Mexican vacation." Her sense of humor was more pronounced than that of her husband.

Mark dryly commented, "Remind me to invite you along on our next "vacation".

Linda laughed, a delightful sound in itself. "I'd be glad to do some field work again. Anyway, there was a transdimensional attack on a Colorado Highway Department crew working on Upper Beaver Creek Road near Brookdale. Three demons came into our dimension and scared the stuffings out of the road crew. The crew fled and the demons took some equipment from their truck and disappeared."

Mark asked, "What equipment did they take?"

Linda thought for a few seconds, "Two power meters and about three hundred feet of power line."

Jack asked what the other incident was. Linda shook her head, "It's weird, a demon apparently stole a medieval costume from a stage company. I would have disregarded this one except it was caught by the security cameras. Nothing recorded walks in from the right, grabs the outfit and exits back to the right."

She hung a sharp left and accelerated on the road that led to the fortress. "Everything else is just the normal terrorist and mayhem stuff."

Jack turned around and looked at Mark. "What do you make of the two incidents?" Mark shook his head, "Insufficient data. Not enough details to make a reasonable conclusion at this time."

Jack was about to suggest a line of reasoning when Linda slammed on the brakes and threw the SUV into a lurid swerve to the left.

A gaping hole that looked like the entrance to a cave had suddenly appeared above the road leading to the fortress. Her evasive tactics almost worked but the hole was moving towards them. The SUV was swallowed up as they came to a halt sideward in the road. The light quickly faded until there was only darkness about the vehicle. Linda turned on the lights but they illuminated nothing.

As they started to lose light Mark and Sarah both reached for their weapons bags behind the third row of seats. Pulling out the night vision goggles they handed them out to the people in front of them. The inside of the space they were in was visible in shades of gray and green. Laura asked a general question to anyone who might know. "Can they have transported us into the demonic realm?"

Mark's new information let him answer. "No. To do that they would have to had Yahveh's approval. This is an illusion, a trick to make us think they are in control and that we are at their mercy. Linda, do we have any communications?"

Linda unsuccessfully tried to reach her husband who was physically less than a mile away. "No. Whatever they've done, we're cut off from all forms of communication with the fortress."

Jack had listened to them talk. "Linda, power up the local map and put it on the screen."

She punched the buttons and the screen lit up to show them their position on the road leading to the first gate to the fortress. The detail was good enough to show the vehicle at right angles to the road.

Jack said, "Okay, now back us down the road using the map."

Linda figured out what he was doing. She shifted the SUV into reverse and started backing them down the road they had just come up. She kept backing for two hundred feet. The chamber they were in moved with them. She braked to a stop, shifted and floored the accelerator. The SUV surged ahead quickly. Still the chamber didn't change. Stopping again she looked over her shoulder at Jack. "What now?"

Tim asked, "If we're getting a map doesn't that mean we have data communications with the world?"

Jack shook his head, "No. The map is from a DVD here in the car. Inertial guidance keeps it accurate." He looked at Mark. "Any ideas? Obviously they aren't attacking us because Laura's armor hasn't appeared, yet."

Mark sat in his seat and prayed out loud. "Dear Yahshua, the enemy has come against us again. *We who dwell in the shelter of the Most High will rest in the shadow of the Almighty. We will say of the Father, "He is our refuge and our fortress, Our Yahveh in who we trust. Surely He will save us from the fowler's snare and cover us with His feathers, and under His wings we will find refuge."* As Mark quoted the first part of Psalm 91, the people in the car felt the familiar heaviness on their spirits at the nearness of Yahveh's Spirit. Mark heard, *"Stand firm in your faith."*

Mark mentioned what he had heard. Laura suggested they combine their faith with action and start trusting the Father and praising him for their rescue. She started singing, "I see the Father, high and lifted up, . . ."and the others joined in praising the Father. There was no doubt, no fear, and no anxiety, only sweet worship.

As they sang it became brighter around the SUV and flames started rising against the darkness. It never crossed anybody's mind that the car could be on fire because the purity of the flames was obvious. They sang on and the flames grew in size and intensity, devouring the darkness until it seemed to sag and melt away. With the sound of a rushing wind the cavern, or whatever it was, was suddenly blown away and disappeared completely.

The people in the SUV thanked the Father for their salvation from this latest attempt against them by the enemy and Linda started forward, only to stop abruptly again.

Standing in the road was the biggest demon they had seen since Laura had faced the strong man in China. Vileness took a stride forward and with one hand smashed the front end of the SUV into the ground. His blow destroyed the grill, the hood, the engine and both front tires.

Laura's armor had appeared as she prayed but she couldn't get out of the car because the smashed front fenders had jammed the doors on her side of the car.

Jack opened his door and stepped out of the car. He turned and fired his .45 caliber handgun at the demon that ignored the attack completely. Raising his fist again to smash the passenger compartment, Vileness allowed small smile to show on his extremely ugly face. He was upset that he had to personally destroy these people but they had proved too much for everyone he had assigned the job to so far.

Laura was praying harder than she could every remember praying. Linda Wu and Tim Carson were trapped in the front seats and couldn't get out in time before the giant fist came down again and smashed them to pulp. Laura wanted her sword to appear so that she could intercede.

Mark and Sarah were trapped in the back seats and couldn't get to the one open door next to Laura. Jack remembered his training and knew that when you don't hear from the Father in a particular situation, do whatever the last thing He did tell you to do. He had pulled the box with the crucifixion nail out of his armor and opened it. He raised the nail above his head in the direction of the demon and opened his mouth. The words that came out weren't his words.

Vileness was alerted by some supernatural sense and he froze in position and looked at the one human who was out of the vehicle. What he saw wasn't a rusty-brown spike but a nexus for supernatural energy that went off the scale. Then he heard the words.

Jack's voice rang out clearly. "You have exceeded your authority. You are condemned to the pit, to remain until you are judged and then you will be thrown into the lake of burning sulfur, where you will be tormented day and night for ever and ever. Be Gone!"

Vileness didn't even have time to scream, he simply blinked out of sight. Jack lowered the nail as a fatigue greater than any he had ever known sapped his strength to remain standing. He sank to the ground with a prayer of thanksgiving to the Father on his lips.

The rest of the crew worked their way out of the SUV and picked Jack up. Laura took the nail from his open hand and replaced it in the box. Mark was able to reach Charlie with his combat comm gear and a rescue team was quickly dispatched to the scene.

CHAPTER FIFTY-TWO

Jack felt better after a short while. He ate and rested until nine p.m. and then joined the rest of the team in the war room. Mark got up and gave him a hug. As Jack sat down in his seat, Mark sat down on the console and stared at his best friend.

Jack was beginning to wonder what Mark was doing when Mark said, "We need to talk. This whole demon assault thing has changed the rules about the type of warfare we do. I'm not sure we need to carry guns anymore. This last mission was almost entirely prayer and God doing the battle for us. Should we to be sheep and not sheepdogs anymore?" Mark didn't look upset. "I really am concerned that we need to fight the battles that Yahveh gives us and the way he wants us to do them. This new information God gave me makes it obvious that the powers, rulers, and authorities, not to mention the wickedness in high places is pretty immune to our firepower but not our prayers. What do you think?"

Jack had been praying most of the time he had been resting. He had gotten some answers to this question which had been on his mind also. He looked at one of the most capable counter-terrorist experts in the world and smiled. "I believe that our season of direct demonic combat is over. We were doing our part to defeat the human element in the schemes that the dark side was spawning. For that reason they decided to jump on us themselves. They couldn't tempt us, lure us, or deceive us, so they tried to strongarm us themselves."

He looked around the table at the faces that reflected the seasoned veterans that the members of the team had become. God showed me that the demon that Laura defeated in the desert and the one Yahshua defeated on the road outside were the heavy hitters against us, so to speak. Apparently there is a demonic auditor somewhere and the costs incurred in direct action against our team have exceeded a preset limit. After the big guy outside, whose name was "Vileness", was sent to the pit, the auditor pulled the plug on the whole operation against us. I think it will be quite a while before they'll try direct action again. That's not to say they won't try to have their human agents attempt to take us out by any means possible."

Su Li, who had reviewed the events outside the fortress asked, "I don't understand why we can shoot the snot out of some demons and not others."

Jack looked at Mark. Mark smiled, "That's because the higher level the demon is, the better his protection against damage is. But that doesn't really matter. The demon you shot in China and Mr. Vileness had permission from Yahveh to enter our dimension. Bullets and bombs don't affect them because they retained their essence which protects them. Most demons don't have permission to enter our dimension as anything but disembodied spirits. If they enter physically they can be killed by gunfire or bombs as soon as they step into our dimension."

Su Li sighed, "Then I guess we'd bettered shoot all of them and see which ones die, right?"

Mark nodded, "If you run into one again, I'd say that is a good operating parameter."

The phone on Laura's desk rang. She picked it up and talked for a few minutes. She signed off and hung up. Swiveling around in her chair she looked the rest of the crew. "We have been "asked" to go to Washington to explain to the President what, as he said, "the heck", happened in Mexico. He would like us to explain it to him and the Mexican President who will be there at the same time."

Mark said, "Have fun kids, only this time try not to end up in the hospital." Mark was referring to a previous trip for Jack and Laura when Chinese agents had attempted to kill them both and almost succeeded.

Laura smiled at him. "This was an "all parties" invite. And the President especially wanted to hear how you destroyed that armored battalion, General Connelly."

Mark turned around and looked at Jack. "Just how did I do that?" Everyone laughed at that.

Tim's cell phone chirped and he answered it. A look of concern came over the happiness he had a moment before. After he talked for several minutes he hung up and contemplated the information he'd just received.

Sarah asked him, "Bad news, Pastor Tim?"

Tim looked up and said, "Yes, but I don't know what to do other than pray."

Laura asked him, "Is there anything we can do?"

Tim looked taken aback, "Oh, no. I wouldn't want to ask you to get involved in my problems."

Su Li laughed at that. "Forget it, Tim. You went to Mexico and got blown up and buried for us, so I think that we owe you one."

Tim smiled, "There is that. God is using our Senior Pastor and his wife to respond to cries of help for salvation and healing. They only go where the Father tells them to go. Normally a person or a church will be led by the Father to ask them for help, even though they probably don't have a clue as to whom Frank and Andrea Mullins are. They've been doing this for several years now with amazing success. There have been literally thousands of salivations and healings every year. Anyway, they have been to the Philippines on four missionary trips and they are on one right now. This time they are way back in the southern jungles, working with remote tribes some of which haven't seen white missionaries or heard the gospel before".

Tim paused and looked at the assembled team. "The Philippine Government faces threats from armed communist insurgencies and from Zultarian separatists in the south. The Philippines are also astride the typhoon belt, and are usually affected by fifteen and struck by five to six cyclonic storms per year. They've also got landslides; active volcanoes; destructive earthquakes and tsunamis. Our minister and his wife are highly regarded and sought after by the churches there because of the gifts of the spirit that work through them. Unfortunately their repeated successes have raised their profile in the country and there are several rebel groups that have targeted them in the past. They have survived because they have been protected by the Father so far." He stopped and thought for a few seconds.

He looked up again. "I just heard from one of the pastors that sponsor their ministry trips to the Philippines and this time it looks really bad. One of the strongest rebel groups among the Zultarians has announced that they have captured the Mullins. They have demanded a three million dollar ransom from the churches. The sad thing is that these rebels know that there is no way the poor churches can raise that kind of money. It is just a maneuver to justify them when they kill the Mullins." He shook his head and looked at the floor.

Mark looked at Jack, Sarah, and Laura and an understanding flowed between them. He looked at Tim. "Hang on to that thought for a little bit, will you?" Mark started to get up and then asked Tim, "How long did the rebels give the churches to raise the money?"

Tim looked at Mark with hope, "Three days, and that time started seven hours ago."

Mark, Jack, and Laura got up and went into the living area of the fortress. Sarah joined them after a minute. The four of them prayed and asked the Father for direction concerning the Mullins.

Sarah laughed after a few minutes. She said, "Yahveh just told me that He didn't bring us this problem so that we should ignore it. He wants us to help save the Pastor and his wife from the rebels. But, He said it will cost us to be obedient." She shook her head, "He didn't tell me what that meant."

Jack nodded, "Okay, with only two and a half days this will have to be a really quick thing. The Philippines are nine hours behind us and we need to get there, find them, and rescue them in the next sixty-two hours."

Mark got up and went into the war room. Tim looked up at him. Mark smiled and said, "I'll tell you what Pastor. Yahveh is willing, so, if you're not too tired from your "vacation" in Mexico, you might want to guide us on a short tour of the southern jungles of the Philippines to find the Mullins and help them to get home.

Tim looked up in surprise. "Can you do that?"

Jack walked in behind Mark and said, "Considering the urgency involved, we need to ask the President to reschedule our talk with him and the Mexican President but I think he will agree."

Tim shook his head, "I hope you know how much this could cost you."

Mark turned serious. "We are willing to pay the cost, Yahveh wants us to go."

The Crossfire Team returns soon in **_"Island Crossfire"_**.

If this story has awakened your spirit or moved you to seek the love of Christ and His power for your life, whether you've never accepted Jesus as your savior or you've fallen away, repeat the following prayer and begin a most wonderful journey into eternal life with Him today.

Father God in heaven, As You said in Your Holy Word, (Romans 10:9) that if we confess the Lord our God and believe in our hearts that God raised Jesus from the dead, we shall be saved.

(The prayer on the next page is a sample prayer when asking Jesus into your heart as your Savior. You can also pray this in your own words.)

Salvation Prayer

Dear God in heaven, I come to you in the name of Jesus. I confess to You that I am a sinner, and I am sorry for my sins and the life that I have lived; I need your forgiveness. I believe that your only begotten Son Jesus Christ shed His precious blood on the cross at Calvary and died for my sins, and I am now willing to turn from my sin.

Right now I confess Jesus as the Lord of my life and my soul. With all my heart, I truly believe that your Holy Spirit raised Jesus from the dead. Today I accept Jesus Christ as my personal Savior and according to Your Word, right now I am saved.

I thank you Jesus, for your unlimited grace which has saved me from my sins. I thank you Jesus that your grace that never leads to license, but rather it always leads to repentance. Therefore Lord Jesus, transform my life so that I may bring glory and honor to you alone and not to myself.

I thank you Lord Jesus, for dying for me at Calvary and giving me eternal life.

Amen.

If you just said this prayer and you meant it with all your heart, believe that you are now saved and have been born again.

You may ask, "Now that I am saved, what do I do next?" First of all you need to get into a spirit-filled, bible-based church that teaches the Scriptures, and you need to study God's Word.

Once you have found a church home, you will want to become water-baptized. By accepting Christ you are baptized in the spirit, but it is through water-baptism that you publically announce your obedience to the Lord Jesus. Water baptism is a symbol of your salvation from the dead. You were dead but now you live, for Jesus Christ has redeemed you for a price! The price was His atoning death on the cross. May God Bless You!